THE MEMOIRS OF A VOLUPTUARY

The Memoirs of a Voluptuary

Wordsworth Classic Erotica

This edition published 1996 by
Wordsworth Editions Limited
Cumberland House, Crib Street
Ware, Hertfordshire SG12 9ET

ISBN 1 85326 638 8

© Wordsworth Editions Limited 1996

Wordsworth® is a registered trade mark of
Wordsworth Editions Ltd

Typeset by Antony Gray
Printed and bound in Great Britain by
Mackays of Chatham plc, Chatham, Kent

CONTENTS

PREFACE

In penning these memoirs, it occurs to me that they may not prove an uninteresting contribution to the general body of amatory literature, as they deal with a subject not often touched upon therein – the secret life of an English boarding-school. That I have not drawn an unreal picture will, I am sure, be felt by all those who can bring the light of personal experience to bear on these pages. It would not be true to say that all scholastic institutions are exactly as I have depicted, as the governing principles of these establishments differ very considerably; but there is always a strong undercurrent of eroticism present, which only needs the existence of favourable circumstances to render itself prominent on the surface as well as below it.

These preceding remarks leave it unnecessary for me to say that the present volume deals principally with my school-time, and treats of the awakening in me of the germinal instincts of sensualism and of my preliminary initiation into the Mysteries of Eros. Crude and unregulated as my ideas were in the period which I have treated of, I cannot but have an affectionate regard for that embryonic stage, in which, indeed, I am satisfied that all the component parts of the system of passional philosophy I have since formed were present in a dormant state, and only awaited fructification in due season.

Whether I shall follow this work up by others dealing with my later life, depends upon the reception the one now under consideration will be accorded, and I shall therefore regard its career with corresponding solicitude.

I have nothing further to add in conclusion, beyond craving the reader's indulgence for the many errors and shortcomings which will doubtless be apparent to him.

CHAPTER ONE

The Gates of Dawn

Having overcome my diffidence by the few words which preface this volume, I can now plunge boldly into my tale.

My mother died in giving me birth, and by reason of this my father, Thomas Powerscourt, lord of the manor of Woodbury and deputy-lieutenant of the county of Warwickshire, imbibed a certain dislike for me, which showed itself, not indeed in harshness, but in a studied indifference to my existence. He had married my mother rather late in life, and the loss of her so soon after their union was so much of a blow to him that he seemed determined to vent his displeasure on me, whom he unjustly regarded as in a way the author of his misfortune; and, wrapping himself up in the literary and scientific studies to which he was addicted, seemed to forget altogether that he was a parent.

I was brought up under the care of a middle-aged and kindly but somewhat taciturn Scotch nurse. None of the other servants were permitted to converse familiarly with me, and I had scarcely any young friends of my own age – none indeed, to speak correctly; so that up to the time I was past thirteen years of age I was about as innocent of the mysteries of human life as a youngster could well be, and any curiosity that I had evinced upon such matters had always been severely checked, both by my nurse and by the governess who was afterwards engaged to instil the first principles of learning into my mind.

At the period I am speaking of, however, I was sent to a boarding-school in Devonshire, and in more ways than one the change was a very eventful one for me. The school had been selected on the advice of my father's greatest friend, Colonel Rutherford, whose own son was a pupil there.

It was arranged that a day or two before going to school I should proceed to Rutherford's home, so as to travel down with him; and accordingly, in due time, I was despatched with my luggage to Everton Grange in Wiltshire, where the Rutherfords lived.

I was greeted most kindly on my arrival, and found it a very different household from that which I had left behind, the only point of resemblance being the fact that Bob was an only child. Colonel Rutherford and his wife, Lady Florence, were both of them amiable and society-loving, and the dinner table, at which Bob and I were given seats, presented a great contrast, with the lively conversation which took place there, to the silent and gloomy meals I had been condemned to at home.

I found that it had been arranged for me to sleep with Bob for the sake of the company, and I was not altogether displeased at the prospect. He was a fairly big and well-built lad of sixteen, pleasant-mannered and good-looking, and I took a liking to him from the first.

At about ten o'clock we bade 'Good-night' to the Colonel and Lady Florence, and retired to our bedroom, which was a large and very comfortable apartment at the rear of the house.

Bob talked to me very kindly as we undressed, and at length we got into bed. The feeling of strangeness which is natural amid new surroundings kept me from feeling very sleepy, while Bob still continued his animated chat. At last there came a pause in the conversation, and I was beginning to wonder whether Bob would put out the light, or let it stay on all night, when I felt his hand wander down, pull up my nightshirt and rest on my thighs. He did not make any further movement for a time, apparently waiting to see whether I should say or do anything in response. However, finding I remained quite still and silent, Bob threw off the bedclothes, and next instant was kneeling over me.

'Don't get in a funk,' he said, smiling; 'I only want to have a look at you,' and getting hold of my nightshirt, he began to pull it off. I made a faint resistance with my hands, scarcely knowing what I was doing, so much was I taken by surprise, but he gently though firmly overcame my efforts, and, unbuttoning the garment at the neck and wrists, deftly drew it over my head, leaving me lying on the bed quite naked.

'I say! You are a fine little chap, Charlie,' he said, and, sitting down beside me, he let his eyes rove all over my body with very evident admiration, and passed his hands caressingly over my breast and legs and arms.

I said or did nothing, overcome by the strangeness of the situation, but let him do as he liked, and his examination of me seemed to give him great pleasure, for he persisted in it for quite a long time, making remarks about the smoothness of my skin, the soft fleshiness of my limbs, and so on, till I thought he would never stop.

At length he made me turn over, and ran his fingers all over my back, my neck and my calves. Presently, turning me on my back again, he lay down by my side, with his right arm round my neck, and we stayed so for a minute; then his left hand stole down, crept slowly over my belly, and came to a halt between my legs.

'What a jolly little cock you've got, Charlie,' said he, as his fingers took hold of the member in question and began to toy with it; 'and a fine little pair of balls, too,' he went on, feeling them.

I was still silent. I had never experienced anything of this sort before, and, though I did not feel sure whether it was wrong or not, a keen sensation of pleasure came over me, suggestive of some extraordinary enjoyment connected with the parts he touched.

Finding that I did not protest, he raised himself up, saying, 'I must have a better look at it,' and, kneeling down at the foot of the bed, he bent forward and gloated over me with eyes and fingers in an ecstasy of delight, while I lay with my head back on the pillow, full of this new joy that had taken possession of me.

How long we were so I do not know, but presently there was a downward motion on his part, and next moment I was conscious of a warm feeling between my thighs. Looking down, I saw to my intense astonishment that he had taken my cock into his mouth, and was sucking it with the greatest avidity. Then I found my voice.

'What are you doing?' I whispered.

He lifted his head.

'Don't make a row,' he replied; 'this is fine. I learned all about it from my big cousin, who got to know how to do all this sort of thing when he was staying in Paris.'

And, without waiting for my reply, he bent down again, and went on sucking, not only taking my cock into his mouth, but letting his tongue travel all round my balls, over my belly, and right in between my legs.

All this set up in me voluptuous sensations of a kind entirely new, and beneath the warm, moist influence of his tongue and lips my cock began to swell.

'It's getting quite stiff,' said he, presently, taking hold of it with his fingers, and pressing the skin back, so as to uncover the top. 'We'll have some fine times together, I hope, Charlie. You're a jolly little beggar, and I know we shall get on all right. I like you very much.'

All the while he kept fingering my cock, and moving the skin up and down, so that it got stiffer than ever. Of course, I remembered it being stiff before, but I had never thought anything of it, and had attached no interest to the circumstance; but now I felt that there was a meaning in this stiffening which I had never guessed at before, and as he pressed it down and let it fly back against my belly I could contain myself no longer, but raised my head up to speak to him.

'Is yours stiff like that? Let me have a look at it, will you?' I said; and without a word he pulled up his shirt and exhibited himself to me.

He had a very large cock, as it seemed to me, with big balls hanging below, and a quantity of dark curling hair all round. I had never seen such a sight before, and was full of interest, taking hold of his member, feeling his balls, and running my fingers through his hairs, with a delight new-born but strong; and while I did so he drew his nightshirt off, remaining in the same position, however, and not attempting to hinder my curiosity.

Holding his cock in one of my hands, I pressed down the skin, uncovering the top completely, then pulled the skin up again, repeating the operation with absorbed interest.

'You had better not do that,' said Bob; 'unless you want to make me come.'

'What do you mean?' I asked; 'I don't understand.'

'Don't you know?' he replied; 'that is the way to make spunk. What babies are made from, you know.'

I stared at him in great surprise. I was evidently on the brink of momentous discoveries, but scarcely knew whether to believe him or not; yet he seemed perfectly sincere as he met my look.

'You don't know anything about these things, I can tell,' he exclaimed with a low laugh. 'Would you like to see, then?'

I answered in the affirmative, so he sat close to my side, and told me to keep moving his cock up and down as I had been doing before. I did so, and he lay half back on the pillow, his legs slightly apart, and evidently full of enjoyment.

I kept on with my task, too absorbed with interest and excitement to say anything, and watching eagerly to see what the result would be.

'Don't stop,' he whispered hoarsely, as I relaxed for a minute. 'It won't be long now. Go a little faster.'

I complied, and after another interval he exclaimed, 'Go slowly now. It's coming!'

I rubbed very gently.

'Hold it tighter,' he continued; 'and don't let go until I tell you.'

I took a firmer grasp, as directed, and went on with a slow measured movement, uncovering the top of his cock fully each time I pressed downwards. Presently he straightened his legs out and pressed further back on the pillow; his belly heaved, I felt his cock increase in stiffness and give two or three big throbs, then out spurted some whitish liquid, shooting up into the air and falling back on to his body, while a quantity followed with less force and ran over my fingers and the back of my hand. I kept on rubbing, but in a few moments, Bob told me to stop, and I bent over to see the new and strange sight, while he leaned down and picked up a handkerchief. When he had got this he bade me let go, and I did so, when he proceeded to wipe himself, and then dried my hand.

'That's spunk,' he explained. 'You have never seen it before, have you?'

'No,' I replied. 'Do you think I could make any?'

'We'll try, if you like. Let me do you!' So saying, Bob arranged himself in a convenient position, and took my cock between his thumb and forefinger – it was, of course, not large enough for him to hold with his whole hand. It was not stiff now, the exertion of rubbing him having distracted my attention, but it soon swelled and stiffened under his nimble fingers, and in a few seconds was fully as erect as it had been before.

'You have never wanked yourself off before, have you?' Bob asked, as he proceeded.

'No,' I replied.

There was little more conversation. Bob seemed to find quite sufficient pleasure in what he was doing without anything else being needed, while I was too full of this new and delightful feeling of voluptuousness to talk. For a long time I felt nothing beyond a general sense of pleasure, and Bob changed hands several times as one got tired out. Gradually, however, the pleasure increased, something seemed to stir and thrill all through me, my muscles stiffened and I held my breath and closed my teeth on my lower lip with suppressed emotion.

'Do you feel anything yet?' Bob asked at length.

'Yes,' I replied; 'I seem to tickle all over.'

'Ah! I expect it is soon coming then,' and he went on faster than ever.

The sensations I was feeling began to increase, and gained in strength more and more. I stretched my legs out, with every toe distended, and then suddenly a great wave of intense delight seemed to rush through my whole body, and I shut my eyes tightly, gasping out 'Stop, Bob, stop!' while I sank on to the pillow, overcome with the extreme pleasure. At the same time Rutherford moved down lower on the bed and took my cock in his mouth, sucking it strongly. The extravagant joy seemed too great to bear, and I tried to push him away, saying feebly, 'Don't, Bob! I can't stand it!' but he seized my hands and went on sucking. It seemed as if he were drawing all the life out of me, and, prostrated altogether by the intolerable ecstasy, I think I must have almost fainted – I could do nothing but lie still, my mouth open, breathing heavily, my head thrown right back, and my eyes turned up, showing the whites, just as if I were in a fit of unconsciousness. After a time, however, my senses came back to me, and I raised my head.

Rutherford, who had not left off sucking all this time, now looked up, and said, 'How did you like it?' smiling as he spoke.

'It was lovely,' I returned. 'Will you do it again sometime?'

'I don't mind a bit,' he answered. 'We'll go to sleep now, I think, unless you wouldn't mind me doing one thing more?'

'What is that?' I asked.

'Will you let me put my cock in your bottom. Fuck you, you know! They call it fucking,' said Bob.

'Won't it hurt?' I interrogated.

'No! It won't hurt you. I used to do it with other chaps. It won't take long. My cock's awfully stiff. Look at it!'

Yielding to his persuasions, I lay on my side, and he placed himself by me.

'You are sure it won't hurt?' I said, half hesitating.

'Of course not. You don't suppose I want to hurt you, do you?' he replied.

Getting close to me, he felt for the position of the hole in my bottom with a finger, and, when he had found it, thrust himself forward, and brought the tip of his cock to the orifice.

'I won't hurt. I'm not going to push hard,' he said; and then I felt his body close up towards mine, and the end of his member very gradually entering my bottom. I was still afraid that he would hurt me, but he pushed very softly, and the knob of his cock after a little exertion sank in with a sort of jerk, my bottom-hole closing tightly around it; but so far I did not experience any pain, and became reassured.

'It's right in now! I'm going to fuck,' said Bob, and he threw one leg over mine while he began to thrust backwards and forwards, sending his member further in each time. It seemed to go right up inside my body, the feeling of tightness was considerable, and once or twice I was on the point of calling out, but little by little the strain wore off, and I commenced to like the sensation. Bob's hand crept over my hips and started to play with my cock, which now felt very loose and limp, but I did not stop him, and he kept his hold, feeling my genitals, while he continued to work his own cock in my bottom, pressing his belly close up against me as he did so. His warm flesh rubbing against my buttocks made me feel rather excited and my cock began to get stiff, though nothing like it had been before. As he felt it stiffen, he rubbed it up and down with his finger and thumb, but did not stop his pushing.

'This is splendid,' he said. 'My cousin told me they used to do it a lot at Eton. He says now he would rather do it than have a girl; and there are a lot he knows like that. I am not sure myself, as I have not tried anything else ever, but I like this all right.'

So talking, he went on toying with my cock and pushing. Then his thrusts got shorter and quicker, he breathed deeply, his hand stopped moving, though he still kept hold of my member. Presently he gave big heaves and shoves, making me wince as he drove his weapon into me right up to the hilt. Then he ceased and pressed tightly against me, while I felt his cock throb excitedly inside my bottom, and a warm glow as of some hot liquid being spurted into it.

'Have you let the spunk come inside?' I asked in some trepidation.

'Yes,' he replied.

'But won't it hurt?' I again asked.

'No, you silly! How can it hurt? Well, it's finished now, but it was fine. You must let me do it again another time, won't you?'

I replied that I would, and he pulled his member out of me, wiped it and wiped my bottom carefully also.

'There you are. It's all right. It won't hurt really,' he assured me, when he had finished doing this.

'We will put the light out and go to sleep now,' he went on.

We pulled on our nightshirts again, and Bob arranged the bedclothes comfortably, after which we settled down snugly, my companion putting one arm round me, and in this position I remained until sleep claimed me within a very short time.

So ended my first day away from home – a day during which so much had been added to my knowledge of life that part of it came into my dreams.

CHAPTER TWO

A New Acquaintance

When I opened my eyes next morning, I found Bob already awake, and he greeted me with a cheery, 'Good-morning!'

'Is it time to get up yet, Bob?' I asked, after returning his salutation.

'Very nearly,' he replied. 'How is your cock this morning?'

'It feels rather funny,' I said, as I pushed down the clothes and exposed it. 'Do you know, I was dreaming last night about you playing with it.'

Bob laughed. 'That accounts for things then. I woke up early this morning, and had a feel, and your cock was as stiff as a poker.'

A few minutes later a servant knocked at the door to call us, so we rose and dressed leisurely, getting downstairs just in time for breakfast.

It was Sunday, but the Rutherfords were not very strict Sabbatarians, and after we got back from church Bob gave me a lesson in billiards, while in the afternoon the colonel took us for a drive. As we were leaving the following day, we stayed up rather longer after dinner than on the previous evening, and it was eleven o'clock ere we reached the privacy of our bedroom.

'We had better go to sleep early tonight, Charlie,' said Bob, as he began to undress. 'We shall have to be up in good time tomorrow morning as there are a lot of things I want to do before leaving.'

I was in hopes of renewing the last night's experiences. However, I said nothing, but when we had got into bed I slyly slid my hand under Bob's nightshirt, and took hold of his cock, finding it quite stiff.

He was unable to resist the temptation, and, turning round, exclaimed, 'I say, Charlie! Will you suck it?'

'If you like,' I replied. 'But put the light on first; I want to be able to see.'

Bob got out and lighted the lamp, after which he returned to bed and lay down with his legs apart. I knelt between them, and took hold of his genital organ, pulling down the skin as far as it would go. The idea of what I was about to do overcame me for a moment with its strangeness, but my hesitancy did not last long, and, lowering my head, I took the purple top between my lips. As I touched it, its silky softness fascinated me, and I shut my mouth tighter on it, letting my tongue wander all round the knob.

'You are doing it a treat,' said Bob, as he wriggled his bottom under my luscious caresses; 'it feels ripping.'

I took his cock farther into my mouth, and sucked and tickled it with my tongue, carrying out the operation with a will, the pleasure I was giving to Bob seeming to pass by a sympathetic vibration into my own body.

'You are a good hand at this,' said Bob presently. 'I'm sure I shan't be long coming. I'm tickling all over already.'

'Will you let it come in my mouth?' I enquired in some doubt, pausing and raising my head.

'Yes. Why not? It won't hurt. But go on again; don't leave off,' Bob returned.

I continued thereupon, and soon Bob began to writhe and twist with voluptuousness. 'Oh! I say. It's too dee–licious,' he cried huskily, as I sucked with all my strength. 'Keep at it,' he went on, squeezing me between his knees.

The climax was evidently approaching; he gasped deeply two or three times, and then cried in a suppressed voice, 'Look out, Charlie. It's coming. Oh, oh!'

His cock sensibly swelled and stiffened, seeming to fill my mouth, and next moment it began to quiver and jump, knocking against my teeth, while at the same time out gushed the hot, thick sperm, shooting in jets on to my tongue and palate. I did not move, however, but continued sucking, as I did so swallowing the discharge, which was of a peculiar and indescribable flavour, but not disagreeable, as I thought; and all the time Bob lay limp and exhausted, his eyes shut and his mouth slightly open. I found him so when at last I lifted up my head, but as I looked at him his eyelids parted and our gaze met.

'That *was* a one,' he said. 'You know how to do it properly, Charlie, and no mistake. I felt as if I were going to pieces, and all the little atoms were whirling round and round in all kinds of beautiful sensations and trying to rush towards your mouth. Did you swallow the spunk when it came?'

'Yes,' I replied; 'it wasn't nasty. I rather like sucking you. You'll let me do it again, won't you?'

'You needn't ask that. I shall be ready anywhere,' Bob replied; adding, 'I think we had better get to sleep now.'

'There isn't time for you to do me, I suppose, is there?' I asked.

'I don't think we had better go in for any more tonight, Charlie. It's rather late, you know. We shall have plenty of chances when we get to school.'

'Do you do this sort of thing at school?' I asked, with some curiosity.

'Oh, rather! I've had lots of fun down there. I can do anything with Mrs Percival, and I will get you put into my room, so you can depend upon having a jolly good time. Now, let's settle down, after I've blown out the light.'

He extinguished the lamp, and came back to bed.

'Come close to me, Bob, and hold my cock, will you? Then I shall go to sleep all right,' I said. He obeyed my instructions, somewhat soothing the warmth of the emotions which had taken hold of me, and after a time I sank into a calm slumber.

Neither of us awoke until we were called next morning, and we then both got up at once, dressing ourselves as quickly as possible. We were busily occupied after breakfast in getting ready for our departure, and at last, after a very kindly farewell from Lady Florence, drove off to the railway station, whither Colonel Rutherford accompanied us. I felt some regret at so soon having to leave the pleasant household, but amid the excitement of the journey this was soon forgotten, while the arrival at the school soon supplied plenty to occupy my attention.

It was only a small private establishment, there being but a score or so of pupils, who were of varying ages from ten or eleven upwards, Bob being the eldest; it was, however, very select, having a reputation in this respect. The Revd John Percival was the principal, and there were two assistant masters, named Ferguson and Chadwick.

This being the opening day of term, there was no work in particular to be done, and I was mostly occupied in making acquaintance with my new comrades, who behaved very well to me, due no doubt in a great degree to my position as a friend of the senior boy. Bob busied himself in showing me over the school and playground, and introducing me all round, so I soon came to the conclusion that school would not prove at all a bad place, and felt sure that I should be happy there.

One thing, however, struck me, and that was the easy air with which some of the boys used words, many of which I did not know, but others I recognised as having heard from the menservants at home sometimes, and which I knew were bad, being what are called 'swear words'; I had once when very young repeated such a word in the presence of my father, who was extremely angry, asking me where I had heard it, and when I said that a groom had used the word in front of me he had the man in his study and severely reprimanded him, at the same time forbidding me to go to the stables any more.

When I was alone for a few minutes with Bob, I spoke to him about the language I had heard made use of, but he laughed and cut me short, saying, 'Look here, Charlie! Don't you be a muff. You'll hear plenty of that here, I dare say, but you'll soon get used to it. I don't swear much myself, as I think it's rather bad form, but don't you be such a fool as to cut up about it to anybody else.' This quite satisfied me, and I determined not to refer to the subject any more.

'Oh, look!' cried Bob, as a little later on we were strolling towards the house. 'Do you see that chap coming along?' and he nodded towards a lad of my own age, or perhaps a little more, who was approaching us. 'We shall see a good deal of him, as he will be in our dormitory; Mrs Percival has been talking to me about the arrangements, and we are going to have a room right away from the others with four beds in it. Of course, I said I wanted you to be with me, and she told me that would be all right. And then she mentioned this chap. He's a sort of relative of mine, and I believe he's an awfully decent little fellow, although I've only seen him once before. He's a duke, you know – the Duke of Surrey; my mother belongs to that family. My cousin, whom I was telling you about, Lord Henry Wilmot, is this kid's uncle, and he has often told me that he is a very nice youngster, which means, I think, that he is all right for a lark; anyhow, we shall soon know. Well, as he is related to me, Mrs Percival thought it would be a good idea to put him in our room. I don't quite know yet who the fourth is to be; Mrs Percival said something about it, but I didn't exactly catch.'

By this time the object of our conversation had neared us. He was a very good-looking boy, with chubby, fair cheeks, wavy chestnut hair, and a pair of fine dark-blue eyes, sparkling with merriment.

'Hallo, Jimmy!' shouted Bob, 'how are you getting on? This is Charlie Powerscourt – a new boy. He's going to be in our room, so I've been wanting to introduce you. He's an awfully decent sort, and I'm sure you will like him.'

I felt rather abashed at Bob's eulogy, and the colour rose into my cheeks, but the young duke soon put me at my ease by his warm greeting. 'I'm glad I am going to be put with some decent chaps,' he said. 'I know you are all right, Bob, although I didn't think you would remember much about me. And Powerscourt here looks game, so I am sure we are in for a good time.'

The three of us were soon talking together as if we had known each other all our lives, so that the time passed quickly, especially for me, and the day came to an end almost before I had time to realise it. After supper, Mr Percival read prayers and our youthful company was told off to the dormitories.

The room assigned to us was in the east wing, and situated right at the end of a corridor, being at some distance from the other sleeping-apartments. 'I was put here,' Bob explained, 'being the oldest boy in the school, and Mr Percival looks upon me as a sort of monitor. We are never disturbed here, as old Percival trusts me to see that everything goes on properly, and I have never given him any cause for interference by kicking up a shindy; so, as I am in charge, you will know how to conduct yourselves. There is one jolly thing about this room, which is that there are wooden shutters to the windows. Of course, we are not supposed to close them, but when we want to have some extra fun we can easily do so, and then we could keep the light on as long as we like. The windows face the stables too, so in any case there would be very little chance of the light being noticed.'

The duke had undressed and got between the sheets in a wonderfully short space of time, and before Bob and I had nearly got our clothes off. 'You chaps are as slow as tortoises,' he shouted at us from the depths of his bed. 'Why don't you buck up? Or do you want to stick about there all night?'

'Now then, Jimmy; you be civil,' laughed Bob. 'Remember, I am in charge here, and I shall have to show my authority if you give us any cheek.'

'Oh! I say. I like that,' returned the person addressed. 'Shut up; and don't start giving yourself airs,' and he put his fingers to his nose in the sauciest manner imaginable.

'That is gross disrespect, and deserves punishment. Doesn't it, Charlie?' said Bob, smiling mischievously. 'Just wait a minute.'

As soon as he had slipped off the remainder of his clothing and donned his night-shift, in which I followed his example, Bob strode across to the duke's bed, calling to me to join him.

'Now, Jimmy! What have you to say for yourself that you should not receive punishment?' asked Rutherford.

Jimmy looked up, his round, smooth cheeks wreathed in smiles, and for all answer put out his tongue mockingly.

'Worse and worse!' exclaimed Bob; 'I declare, he is incorrigible. What shall we do to him, Charlie? I know, let's have a look at his cock. I have never seen a duke's cock. Have you, Charlie? I wonder if it's a better one than other people's?'

'It's no go. I shan't let you,' said Jimmy, clutching the bedclothes.

'It doesn't matter whether you let us or not,' replied Bob, with much amusement; 'we're going to have a look all the same,' and he took hold of Jimmy's wrists. 'Uncover him, Charlie,' Rutherford continued; and, nothing loth, I quickly turned down the sheets and counterpane. The young duke wriggled himself on one side, and tried to disengage his wrists, but his captor held him fast. I was about to pull him over on his back, when Bob cried, 'I've got him fast! Unbutton his nightshirt and pull it off, while I hold him.' I did not find this a very difficult task, and when I had drawn the garment over his head, Bob forced Jimmy flat on his back, so that he was fully exposed to our observation. He was a splendidly made boy, with a very plump body, beautifully rounded arms and limbs, and a soft clear skin of extreme whiteness; but our gaze was principally directed to his private parts.

'Look, Charlie! The little beggar has got a cockstand,' cried Bob; and, releasing one of Jimmy's wrists, he took hold of his member, which stood up quite stiff and nodded its head in the most impertinent manner conceivable.

Jimmy laughed convulsively, and drew his legs up, at the same time pushing Bob away with his free hand. But Rutherford seized Jimmy's wrist again, and cried out to me, 'Keep his legs out straight, Charlie!' I did so, and leaned across his knees to keep them flat. He was now at our mercy, for although he struggled at first, he was unable to release himself; but he evidently took the whole proceedings as a joke, and only giggled when I laid hold of his cock and began to pull it about.

'He's got a bigger one than you, Charlie,' said Bob; and, though I did not say so, I felt bound to confess that this was true. It was certainly a shapely member, fairly fat and long, although not too much so for his age, and a pair of tolerably well-developed balls hung gracefully below. The milk-white thighs and belly, through the transparent surface of which the veins showed in a delicate blue tracery, were quite devoid of hair, however, as yet – a fact upon which Bob remarked, saying, 'He hasn't got any hairs yet. A good thing too; I like to see it ever so much better without. I wish I didn't have any; I think they are a nuisance, and I don't know what they grow for.'

I agreed with him, as I passed my left hand over Jimmy's middle, as though to satisfy myself by touch as well as by sight that there was no growth there, while with my right I was all the time handling his member, pressing it backwards and forwards, squeezing and stroking it, and pushing back the skin.

'Isn't he stiff, Bob?' I said, and to bear out my statement pulled Jimmy's cock down towards his legs and then, suddenly releasing it, let it fly back against his belly with quite a loud thump.

'Give him a little rub, Charlie. I think that will do him good,' Bob returned, smiling at me meaningly; and I immediately acted on the suggestion, moving the duke's member quickly up and down with my right hand, while with my left I held his balls.

'How do you like that, Jimmy?' asked Rutherford. 'I hope we have not offended your grace.'

'You wait,' replied Jimmy; 'I'll pay you out. But his face did not bear out the fierceness of his words, and it was plain that he did not mind the proceedings, for he lay quite still now and did not attempt even to draw his wrists away from Bob's grasp.

I went on with my task with much enjoyment, and I was, indeed, not a little pleased to find that our companion evinced no objection to our form of amusement, which promised well for the future.

'Oh!' cried Jimmy to me presently; 'you were pulling down the skin rather too hard then; it hurt a bit. Can we just wet the top? It will go much easier afterwards.'

In answer, I stooped and took his member between my lips, well lubricating it with saliva. When I had done so, Jimmy laughed at me, saying, 'You evidently know something. I thought you would wet it with your finger; I didn't expect you would take it in your mouth. Go on, now; I feel awfully randy.'

'I don't think I need trouble to hold his hands any longer,' said Bob, a few minutes later. 'I'm sure he'll keep quiet; I can see he's enjoying himself.' He accordingly released his hold, and contented himself with patting Jimmy's cheeks and tickling him under the chin, stroking his legs and chest, and smoothing and rubbing his face and body with his palms and the tips of his fingers, by these means vastly increasing the duke's excitement.

'Keep on,' cried Jimmy to me in a tone of deep appeal, as I slackened speed a little. 'Go as fast as you like. It won't be much longer;' and he wriggled and twisted about like an eel in the excess of his emotions, as I exerted myself to the utmost in compliance with his request.

'Tickle my balls, Powerscourt,' he called out presently, and, as I worked and kneaded them with all the skilfulness I could bring to bear for the occasion, his writhings increased.

'That's fine!' he exclaimed, his voice full of agitation. 'Oh, oh! my cock's bursting; I'm burning all over,' and he began to shiver and tremble with convulsions of voluptuousness. His belly sank and rose in quick heaves, his hands opened and shut, clutching at the sheet, his sweetly-curving, dimpled, rich scarlet lips were parted as he drew deep breaths, his brilliant white teeth ever and anon clenching firmly, and his eyes rolled under the stimulus of the sensations he was experiencing. He panted so deeply that it was almost a groan, immediately after crying in an agonised tone, 'Look out! It's coming! Stop, stop!' while his cock gave a succession of little jumps, and a drop of light-coloured fluid jetted on to my finger, a further flow oozing slowly out from the swollen knob.

'Quick, Charlie! Suck him,' said Bob; and I lost no time in applying my lips to Jimmy's member.

'Oh, oh!' he exclaimed, nearly in a scream. 'It's too much. You're killing me. I shall faint.'

He was nearly beside himself with inordinate delight, and contorted his body in a vain attempt to obtain release from the too great spasm of voluptuousness, but we kept him in position and he subsided into an enervated languor, disturbed only by the heavy sighs which he was unable to suppress.

In a few minutes, however, he had recovered, and when we had set him free he raised himself up.

'You did give me a doing,' he said, smiling at us, his normal self again. 'It was just heavenly, though it seemed as if I could hardly bear it at the time.'

'I thought your grace appeared to be in a bad way,' said Bob. 'Anyhow, you know, we had to give you something for your cheek, and if you are impudent again we shall have to repeat the dose, so you know what to expect.'

'Oh! I don't mind at all. I am only glad you chaps are all right. We'll have no end of fun when Blackie comes; he's the most out-and-out sort you ever came across.'

'Who is Blackie?' asked Bob. 'Is that the fellow who will be in this room with us? Mrs Percival did say something about him, but told me that he hadn't turned up today.'

'Yes. That's right,' replied the young duke; 'he won't be here till tomorrow. He's the son of a very great friend of my mother's; I've known him ever so long as he used to spend a lot of time with us. His name is Gaston de Beaupré – he's a Frenchman, you know. I nicknamed him Blackie because he's so dark. He is an awfully jolly sort, and always ready for some fun. My eye! he knows a thing or two; I tell you, he will surprise you. But he's not a bit cocky with it.'

'How old is he?' enquired Bob, after listening with interest to the foregoing word-portrait.

'He's about a month or two older than I,' replied Jimmy. 'He has never been to school before, as he had a tutor. He has always been about with his mother, and, I can give you my word, he has seen no end of sights. The tales he can tell you will make you open your eyes.'

'If he is anything like as good as you say, we shall have a ripping time, Jimmy,' said Bob. 'I'm dying to know your chum.'

'My cock *is* stiff,' I exclaimed, turning the conversation; and, to emphasise the words, I pulled up my nightshirt and thrust out my belly, to bring into greater prominence my genital organ, which was turning up its nose in the most aggressive way, as if bent upon calling attention to itself.

'Come on the bed,' cried the duke, taking pity on my condition, 'and I'll give it a shaking up for you.'

It did not take me many seconds to follow his direction, and, tucking up my nightshirt as high as possible, I stretched myself out at full length while Jimmy sat on one side of me and seized my cock.

'I want to give you as good a one as you gave me,' he said; and he seemed bent on carrying out his object, for he held my member and moved the skin rapidly up and down with a dexterousness that had apparently been well-trained, while with his other hand he tickled my balls, handling them in the most exciting manner, following this up later on by feeling the cheeks of my buttocks, persuasively tickling the furrow in between and thrusting one finger gently in and out of my bottom-hole, so that I was soon thrilling all over with lustful pleasure.

'I'm going to wet the top, just to make it go better,' he said presently. 'All right,' I replied. 'Do what you like.' And he gave my cock a good long sucking, which only served to increase its already overheated state.

When he had finished doing this, he went on rubbing, and also continued tickling my bottom, laughing from time to time at the way I squirmed under the intense excitation.

'You must let Blackie have a go with you. He'll make you sit up. He's a wonder, I can tell you. I don't believe anybody could do it better than he does. My uncle Henry says there is a sort of magnetism or something of that kind in his hands. There! I've let something out now. Well, you mustn't say anything about it, but Blackie and I go to stay with my uncle sometimes, and then there are some rare doings.'

'I know something about your uncle, or Cousin Harry, as I call him,' said Bob, with a grin that conveyed a great deal. 'He has often mentioned you, Jimmy; but of course he has never told me of the little games you have together.'

'Oh! He wouldn't, I know. But, look here! I'll see if I can't get him to invite us all to his place. I'm sure he will if I ask him; and if you fellows can only come, I can promise you some glorious fun. Uncle Harry is a rattling good sort, and no mistake; isn't he, Bob?'

'Rather!' agreed Bob. 'I should just think he is.'

Jimmy had not relaxed his occupation while talking, and I felt that the supreme moment would be upon me soon. My muscles stiffened and my legs closed tightly, imprisoning the duke's hand between my thighs. I pursed my lips closely, and knitted my brows, in a strong effort to keep calm under the stress of emotion. And then, with an almost violent suddenness, the finality came. A tremor passed through my body, my tongue seemed to cleave to the roof of my mouth. I strove to speak, but the words would not come; my interior economy felt as if it were bursting asunder, and I thrust forward my hand spasmodically as a great wave of raging fire consumed me.

'He's come!' cried Jimmy, as an effusion of my boyish essence wetted his fingers. I had screwed up my eyes tightly in the desperateness of my sensations, but, opening them the moment after he spoke, I saw that the top of my cock was running over with the liquid it had exuded, which glistened in the light; but the glimpse was only a brief one, for directly afterwards the duke had fastened his lips upon it, sucking with such effect that it seemed as if my entrails were being drawn forth, and I felt utterly benumbed by the potency of physical delight, so that I could only lie back incapable of movement, prostrated with the intensity of the pleasure.

After a time I regained control of myself and sat up.

'How did you like it?' said Jimmy. 'Did you find it all right?'

'First-rate,' I replied, with enthusiasm. 'If your friend Blackie can manage any better, he must be a good hand.'

'Ah! You wait and see. He'll astonish you.'

'I suppose we had better be settling down for the night, now, hadn't we?' I ventured.

'What about me?' put in Bob. 'It seems as if I am to be left out in the cold.'

'Look here!' rejoined Jimmy; 'let's wait now until tomorrow night. I'll put Blackie up to it; and I promise you a better bit of fun than you have ever had before in your life.'

'Well, I suppose I shall have to wait, then,' said Bob, rather glumly; 'but I shall keep you up to the mark. And you have been telling us such a lot about this chap Blackie; I hope we shan't be disappointed with him.'

'You needn't be afraid about that,' answered Jimmy airily. 'If he isn't all I have made him out to be, you can give me a good licking, so there!'

'All right,' said Bob, with a laugh. 'I shall remember that, so you had better look out. But just turn over for a moment, Jimmy, and let us have a look at your bottom. I've got rather a fancy for nice bottoms.'

'There you are, then,' replied the duke. 'I suppose you would like to fuck me, eh? Well, I'll promise you that, too, if you wait till tomorrow.' And he turned over on his face, exhibiting to view his fat, snow-white buttocks, smooth as satin, and voluptuous enough in their swelling rotundity to turn the head of a far more experienced connoisseur than Rutherford. The latter stroked and patted the soft surface and pinched the plump, velvety cheeks with a lingering abandon of pleasure, and a gleam of longing in his eyes; but he had finally to tear himself away from their deep attractions, and, with a last look at the delicious prospect, said, 'Very well, Jimmy. I'll let you off for tonight. But I am like the boy in the advertisement for Pears' Soap, I shan't be happy till I get it. So you mustn't forget your promise tomorrow night. I feel awfully hot now, and I don't know whether I shall be able to keep from wanking when I get into bed, but I mean to try to, so that I shall enjoy myself all the better tomorrow night. Are you chaps ready now, because I am going to put the light out?'

Jimmy and I got into our beds, and arranged ourselves comfortably, after which Bob extinguished the light and followed our example. 'Good-night,' he called out, when he had settled down. 'Good-night,' we replied; and as we were all now feeling a little tired, or at least, speaking for myself, I was, silence reigned, quickly followed in my case by sleep.

CHAPTER THREE

Doctissimus Puer

At seven o'clock next morning the school-bell rang to awaken us, but none of us felt any inclination to get up at once, and it was not until the second bell had sent forth its warning note that we finally turned out, and then all our efforts were required to dress in time, so that we had no opportunities for playing about, having to confine ourselves to an interchange of jocular remarks, more or less personal, the only diversion being caused by Jimmy hurling a wet sponge at me, which I avoided by ducking, and the missile catching Bob full in the face.

'All right, my boy,' said that aggrieved individual to the duke. 'It's lucky for you that we are in such a hurry, otherwise I wouldn't let you off.'

The sober routine of school started in earnest today, but I did not find it at all irksome, and was only too pleased with the vivacity I encountered on all sides.

In the afternoon, Gaston de Beaupré arrived, and naturally both Rutherford and I were eager to make his acquaintance. His appearance impressed us very favourably, and we felt that Jimmy's praises of him might not be unjustified by any means. He was a well-set-up boy, rather inclined to be slender, with a complexion of a clear, rich olive tint, straight, regular features, thick, glossy black hair, and dark lustrous eyes, gleaming with good humour and full of a reckless dare-devil fire. In fact, from the look of him, we judged that his friend's description of his character had not been at all overdrawn. He spoke English with a perfect accent and thorough command of the language, which was no doubt due to his having been so much in this country.

The duke introduced him to us, and we found his manner most agreeable, even charming, without a trace of 'side', which I, and I think Bob, too, had been rather afraid he would exhibit.

When bedtime came, and we went upstairs, he expressed himself delighted with the room. Nothing worthy of note passed until we had undressed, when Jimmy walked quietly up to de Beaupré, and, making a swift dive, slid his hand under Gaston's nightshirt, saying, as he did so, 'How's your cock, Blackie?'

De Beaupré retreated with a short laugh, and flashed a look of enquiry at Bob and myself.

'Oh! that's all right,' exclaimed Jimmy. 'You needn't be afraid of them. They are good sorts, and I've told them what kind of a chap you are, so, you see, it's no good you trying to look innocent. And I say, Blackie! I promised them that when you came we would have a proper bit of fun to celebrate the occasion; so you can't back out after that. Let's have a cock-show all round to start with.'

He beckoned to Rutherford and me to join them, and without more ado we pulled up our shirts to let each other see our private parts. Blackie had a good-sized genital instrument, with rather large balls, and a little fringe of short, silky, black hairs was just beginning to make its appearance around the parts. I had imagined at first sight that he was a slim lad, as he gave this appearance when dressed, but I found that his body was much better fleshed than I thought, his legs, posteriors and arms being particularly well developed, and the display of muscles seemed to point to his being rather strong, which, indeed, proved to be the case. While we were thus regarding him inquisitively, he surveyed us with equal curiosity, and appeared to be much attracted towards Bob, who was naturally considerably more advanced physically than any of us, being the only one whose generative organs showed signs of approaching maturity. De Beaupré's interest led him to the length of handling Bob's member, in order to examine it the better, and as he took hold of the cock, which was already half-erect, and drew back the skin, fully exposing the rapidly-hardening knob, he said, 'You're just a treat, Rutherford. Let me take you on to start with.'

But the duke interposed. Bob's my property, Blackie, to begin with. We arranged that last night. You go with Charlie here first; you'll find him game enough. And, I say! I want you to give him a go in your best style, just to let him see what you can do. He is new altogether to this sort of thing, so he will like it all the better.'

'I don't mind. It is all the same to me,' replied de Beaupré. 'Come on, Powerscourt – Charlie, I shall call you, and you can call me Blackie. Jimmy christened me, but it doesn't much matter – one name is as good as another, as long as it suits you. Pull off your nightshirt – that's right!' and he drew off his own at the same time. 'Now we are ready.'

He made me get flat on the bed, and lying over me with his arms round my body, began to kiss my cheeks and forehead, finally pressing his mouth against mine and thrusting his tongue between my lips and against my tongue with quick movements, his saliva joining with mine and running in a little stream down my throat. This action of his infected me with an intense feeling of lasciviousness, so that I began to experience a wonderful passion of sensuality throughout every part of my form. Then he made me turn over, and began to kiss and lick and tickle me with tongue and lips, travelling from the nape of my neck all over my shoulders and spine, and every square inch of my bottom, pressing open the cheeks, and titillating all round the base of the buttocks, and forcing his hot labial member into my bottom-hole, so that I fairly shivered with voluptuous excitement, and my inordinately stiff and bursting cock glowed so fiercely that it almost seemed as if it were on the point of discharging, as I pressed tightly against the sheets with lustful twistings. Leaving my bottom, he let his tongue wander down over my legs and calves and the soles of my feet, occasioning further tremors of extraordinary physical enjoyment; and when he desisted using his mouth, he began to rub and stroke and tickle me with his fingers and palms, going over the same ground again. Truly, what Jimmy had told us, that Lord Henry had said there was a kind of magnetism in de Beaupré's hands, appeared to me to be absolutely correct, for each touch sent deep thrills of animal electricity through me.

When he considered that he had paid sufficient attention to my back, he directed me to turn over again, and when I had done so he devoted himself to caressing the front part of my body with even more assiduity than he had bestowed on the opposite side. The skill and dexterity he displayed were something marvellous; he seemed to be a perfect master of the arts of lubricity and I throbbed and tingled through and through with sheer ecstasy, unutterable in its deliciousness. Beginning with my feet, sucking each toe separately, tickling with his tongue in between, and kissing my ankles and insteps with the tenderest warmth, he travelled slowly upwards, covering me with a shower of alluring osculations, and using his hands in all manner of the most captivating endearments at the same time, so that my flesh crept and shivered in a very transport of the most unbounded joy. Advancing higher, he overwhelmed my thighs and belly with similar embraces, till I felt on the verge of expiring from sheer lasciviousness. He appeared to make a point, however, of passing over my genital parts, and I could have cried at the omission, so thoroughly had he inspired me with eroticism. My cock positively flamed with lust, and shivered and palpitated with spasmodic pulsations, and I felt as if I would give anything to assuage the burning desire I experienced in this member; so much so that I clutched at it myself and began to rub it fiercely up and down. But de Beaupré gently though firmly removed my hold, and continued his operations in the same slow and unhurried way that he had been pursuing all along. Soon he had arrived at my navel, at which he made a little halt, and then he advanced over my bosom, stroking all the soft undulations, going over them with his mouth, and dwelling with seemingly affectionate emphasis on the little crimson nipples. My throat next came in for his attentions, and his touch thrilled me afresh; and when he had at length got beyond this, he lay over me again, twining his lithe limbs panther-like round my body, and gave himself up to the outpouring of a fresh ocean of kisses and caresses on my lips, chin, cheeks and brow. My excitement was so great that it seemed impossible I could contain myself any longer; the limit of endurance must surely be passed, I thought; and in an effort of despair I clasped him tightly to me, pressing his belly against mine, and writhing convulsively against him in a vain endeavour to soothe the raging lust of my cock. But relief was not to come yet. When at last he ceased from half-suffocating me, he turned his attentions to tickling me under the arms and rubbing the latter from shoulders to wrists, and stroking and squeezing my hands, which itched to get at my member. He seemed to be bent upon prolonging the affair as much as possible, while all the time I was smarting with eagerness to obtain an allaying of the fever that I burned with. At last, however, he took pity on me, and, sliding down my body, commenced to play with my cock and balls with a very light touch, which only added to my salacious frenzy.

I could bear the suspense no longer. 'Quick, Blackie!' I cried. But there was no hurrying him, and he went calmly on, just as before, moving my member from one side to the other, and slowly rubbing it up and down, sorely aggravating my impatience. Finally, he stopped and sucked my testicles, making me writhe again; and after a spell of this, he, at long last, took my member in his mouth, sucking it and tickling the top with his tongue, using all his powers of incitement in doing so, while with his hands he rubbed it briskly near the root, at the same time stroking and titillating my thighs and belly and balls.

If I had felt full of voluptuousness before, I did so now in a tenfold degree, and I clasped my legs tightly round his neck, squeezing him closely in the passion of the moment. The end came quickly, after all this wantonness of lubricity, as it was impossible for nature to hold out any longer. Every nerve and fibre thrilled and vibrated at fullest tension, so that they seemed on the point of snapping, wave after wave of the most delicious sensations surged through me, and then, just as I felt I could stand no more, my senses began to reel, and I was swallowed up in a flood of rapturous bliss, of such exquisite joy that it was almost painful. I put out my hands and seized de Beaupré's head to put a stop to the excruciating pleasure, but he caught my wrists and forced me to submit. The maddening force of the voluptuous sensations made my brain whirl in intoxication, and brought on a sort of delirium, which deprived me of all power of movement, so that I lay in a helpless stupor of ecstasy, ravished by the wondrous way in which de Beaupré had exerted his powers of touch upon me.

I think I lost consciousness for a time, as the next thing I remember was de Beaupré patting my cheek as he looked down into my face, and when I opened my eyes in response, he exclaimed, 'Why! I thought you had gone to sleep. How did you like it?'

'It was tremendous,' I replied. 'I feel as if all my breath had gone. Wherever did you learn to do it like that?'

'Oh! it's a trick I picked up, and it seems to come naturally to me. It takes it out of you a bit, doesn't it?'

'I should just think so,' I returned; 'but I feel pretty fit again now. I made a good lot come, didn't I? It felt like it, anyhow.'

'Pretty fair,' replied de Beaupré. 'There is generally more than usual, if you get worked up properly like that.'

'How are the others going on?' I asked.

'There they are. Just look at them,' he cried.

I got up and turned my gaze in the direction to which he pointed. Bob was sitting on the bed, with the duke lying across his knees, while he was working Jimmy's cock smartly up and down, toying with his balls with the other and.

'How is it going, Bob?' I called out.

'He's nearly coming, I believe,' he said, and both de Beaupré and I walked over to watch the denouement. It was very plain that Bob's surmise was correct, judging by the expression on Jimmy's face, and we had not been standing by more than a minute or two, when he called out, 'It's just coming, Bob,' and broke into low, hysterical laughter, twisting his feet together, as his juvenile sperm welled out.

The sight excited me again, and I turned to my companion, saying, 'Come on, Blackie, It's your turn now.'

'Very well,' he said at once. 'I'm ready.'

'How shall I do you?' I enquired, as we went back to my bed again.

'I am going to lie on my back,' he replied. 'You sit facing me. I'll put my legs over yours, and then you place yours each side of me, and come close up.'

I followed his instructions, bringing my belly against his bottom, my feet being under his arms, while he clasped me tightly round the loins with his thighs, crossing his feet behind my back. Putting his hands behind his head, he said, 'Now wank me, and keep as close to my bottom as you can. You can tickle my balls with your other hand.' I did as he told me, and he closed his eyes, resigning himself entirely to the pleasures of the moment. I rubbed his cock with an even and moderately rapid motion, squeezing and wriggling my belly against his posteriors, and gently tickling him with my fingers all over the belly as far as the navel. While I did this, I was much interested in surveying his body as it was presented before me. His skin was of a delightful, warm-looking brownish tint, not nearly so dark as his face, but offering a great contrast to the whiteness of my own. This gave him a decidedly unEnglish appearance, and particularly so when combined with his countenance, the oval features reminding me of some Italian portraits in the dining-room at home. Indeed, this was not strange, as I learned afterwards that his mother, the Princesse de Beaupré, came of Italian stock.

His cock, when fully erect, as now, was a good-sized one, as I have already remarked. It was as hard as possible, and so hot that it seemed almost to scorch my hand, denoting a very erotic temperament. He exhibited no signs of a want of self-control, so that I was quite taken by surprise when, after some little time, I felt something warm and wet trickling over my fingers, and I knew that he had come. There was quite a tolerable quantity, and it was much thicker and whiter than mine or Jimmy's, more resembling Bob's in this respect. After I had examined it to my satisfaction, I disengaged myself from the close contact with his body that I had hitherto maintained, and began to suck him. The straightening of his legs and the contraction of his muscles were the only signs of discomposure that he showed, although I felt sure that this calmness was an effort of will on his part, for a nature so licentious as he had shown his to be could not fail to be fully alive to sensual enjoyment, and his knitted brows and the firm way in which he kept his mouth shut, bore witness to my opinion being the correct one, especially as when he opened his eyes presently there was a misty, voluptuous, half-dazed look in them.

After a short pause we got up, and I proceeded to put on my nightshirt.

'You chaps have been having a good time, eh?' said Bob, smiling at us.

'Rather!' I replied; and 'Very good indeed!' said de Beaupré.

'We had some jolly good fun too, didn't we, Bob?' exclaimed the duke.

'Ripping!' Rutherford responded. 'Jimmy has got just about the finest and juciest bottom I have ever come across. I believe he has been broken in before, though, for with a little wetting I slipped in as easy as shelling peas, and he squeezed his fat arse about and fairly seemed to draw my cock in, so that I came in no time, and a tremendous lot, too. I am sure he's an old hand at it.'

Jimmy laughed. 'Perhaps I am, and perhaps I am not. Don't you ask questions, and you won't be told stories.'

As we had all now satisfied our desires, we quietly got into bed after this, and slept soundly until the next morning.

CHAPTER FOUR

Venus and Adonis

The next day was a half-holiday, and in the afternoon Bob, de Beaupré, the duke and I set out for a ramble, following the course of a little river which flowed through the woods and meadows in the neighbourhood of the school.

As we made our way slowly along, the duke revealed, 'Blackie has gone one better than most of us. He's had some adventures with girls.'

'Oh! do tell us,' exclaimed Bob and I eagerly, turning to de Beaupré.

He laughed. 'Jimmy is always piling on the agony about me. I believe his brain has turned after listening to one or two of my yarns.'

After a little more pressure, however, he gave in and said he would tell us of his first experience with the other sex.

'It was in Paris about six months ago,' he began. 'There was a great friend of my mother's named Cécile de Regnier, who used to visit us very frequently. Although she wasn't very old – only about twenty-two – she had been married, but her husband had died nearly two years before, and only a few months after the wedding. She lived in a big *appartement* by herself on the Avenue Hoche. She was always awfully jolly with me, used to bring me no end of sweets and that kind of thing, and gave me lots of presents. Once or twice she took me to the play, and you bet I liked her very much. One thing I noticed, however, and that was how she used to like to squeeze my hand and kiss me.

'Well, one day she called just as my mother was going to a garden-fête at the Austrian Embassy. She asked if I was going, too, and when my mother told her I was not, she said, "Poor boy! He will be awfully lonely. Do let me take him home this afternoon; he can stay to dinner, and I will send him back in the carriage afterwards." My mother saw no objection, so Cécile carried me off in triumph, and I was soon seated beside her in her victoria and being rattled along as fast as the horses could take us to the Avenue Hoche. When we got there, she took me upstairs to her boudoir – a ripping room, with stained-glass windows, and lots of flowers, and all that sort of thing. Cécile gave me some picture-books to look at, while she took off her hat and cloak, and then rang for the maid to bring up some fruit and wine.

'She made me drink two or three glasses, and then called to me to come and sit beside her on a big sofa that took up nearly all one side of the room. "You are a nice boy, Gaston," she said, putting her arms round me and kissing my cheek. The wine had got into my head a bit, and the heavy scent that the room was full of also affected me, so I kissed her back, and she seemed so pleased at this that she would not let me go, but kept hugging me. When at last she released her hold, she still let one arm remain round my neck, and pressed close against me. She had put on a sort of loose dressing-wrap or tea-gown after coming in, and I could see her neck and throat, while I could feel the heaving of her breasts as she leaned upon me. Then she began patting my cheeks and pulling my hair and so on, and telling me how fond she was of me. "I wish you were a little older, Gaston," she said, "and then we could get married. Wouldn't that be fun?" I don't remember what I said, and altogether, what with the wine and the perfume she had on her, I tell you I was beginning to feel rather funny. I had never been alone like this with a female before, and though I'm not exactly of a bashful nature, I can assure you I felt as shy as a kid. At the same time, I felt very hot, too, and my cock was sticking up as stiff as possible in my trousers. I was afraid she would see it, and was in a terrible funk in case she did, but I daren't put my hand down to shift it so that it couldn't be noticed, as she was looking at me all the time, and would be bound to observe what I was doing. I was in a nice pickle, and was wishing she would leave me, if only for a minute, when she put her hand in my lap right on my thing. It was no use trying to keep it still, as it was so stiff, and I couldn't help it jumping when her palm rested on it.

' "Good gracious!" she said, looking at the lump where it lifted my breeches up. "Whatever have you got in your pocket?" and before I could say or do anything to stop her, she was feeling for the cause. I went hot all over, and felt the blood rush up to my temples, only wishing that the floor would open, and let me through. "You silly boy! Let me see what it is," said Cécile; and I scarcely realised what she was doing before I felt her hands round my waist loosening my breeches. From the haste she showed, I think she was afraid I was going to stop her, and in the first shock of my consternation I jumped up and ran towards the door, only anxious to escape from the painfulness of my position. But Cécile caught me before I was half-way across the room, while at the same moment, in response to her call, the door leading into her bedroom opened and her maid, Marie, appeared.

' "This boy wants to be put to bed," said Cécile.

'The maid came across with a grin all over her face, and the two of them seized me by the arms and dragged me into the next room. I was more or less dazed with the wine I had drunk, and half-frightened and by no means pleased; but I was, of course, helpless in the hands of these two full-grown women, and in a very short time they had removed every stitch of clothing from me, and laid me on the bed as naked as when I was born. "Keep him there, Marie, for a minute," said Cécile, and the maid held me with her strong arms while her mistress rapidly threw of all her clothes till she was stark naked. I altogether forgot my humiliation as I saw a woman undressed for the first time, and at the sight my cock, which had had time to grow limp, rose up again – on seeing which the maid began to pull it about very freely.

'By this time I had collected myself somewhat, and the thought came upon me that I was in for a bit of luck after all, but I considered it best not to appear to give in too easily, and pretended to look rather sulky when Cécile came across to me. She only laughed, however, and stooped down to kiss me. I tried to turn away my head, but she held my cheeks between her hands, preventing me, and kissed and tongued me until I thought she would suck the breath right out of my body; and I had to laugh out loud as I tried to thrust her off. Then she got on the bed, which was a very big and soft one, and my curiosity soon got the better of all my other feelings. She signed to the maid to let go, and took me in her arms, but I insisted upon kneeling up and having a good look at her. She was an awfully pretty girl, with beautiful dark hair, and deep-blue eyes, almost black, and a very white, smooth skin. She had big round breasts like little mountains, and firm as anything, while the titties stood up almost as stiff as cocks – they do, you know, when women get excited. But, of course, what I was most anxious to see was the part lower down. I had often heard about girls' cunts, but I had never seen one before, and wondered what it was like. Cécile was giving me a grand opportunity, and you can stake your life that I took advantage of it. She let me do just as I liked, and didn't mind how I pulled her about.

'She had a lot of long, soft, dark hair on the lower part of her belly, and in the middle of this I could see the slit which I knew must be the opening of her cunt. I parted the hairs with my hands, so as to get a better view of it. It was much lower down than I had imagined it to be, and I had always thought of it more as a round hole. This seemed so close and narrow that I wondered how a man's cock could be got into it, but when I pressed the red lips apart and very gently inserted a finger, I began to understand better of what an elastic nature it was. There was also a sort of knob or button just above, which puzzled me. It was hard and stiff, and I was at a loss to give a name to it, but since then, I've found it is called the "clitoris". This knob interested me very much, and I let my fingers play with it, moving it about and rubbing it in different ways. While I was doing this, I had two fingers of my left hand inside Cécile's cunt, and was groping about in the interior regions, exploring all the secret corners of this new country, and rubbing the inner surface as I did so. I had only been engaged in this for a very little while when all of a sudden Cécile began to twist her legs and heave her belly, and before I could guess what was going to happen, she gave a little scream, her cunt seemed to close up, drawing my fingers right in, and next moment a regular stream of spunk poured out over my hand. I pulled my fingers out hastily, fearful at what I had done, but she sprang up and caught me in her arms, clasping me tightly, and saying. "Oh, you darling! What a little love you are!"

'Then she put her hand down and got hold of my cock, squeezing and fondling it until it seemed twice its usual size and was as stiff as a bar. Pushing me gently on to my back, she knelt up and commenced to toy with it with her fingers, pulling down the skin and pinching the top. "What a dear little thing! I must kiss it," she said, and ere I knew what she was going to do, she had straddled across me, and had taken my cock in her mouth, sucking it for all she was worth, while with her hands she started to play with my balls and tickle my bottom, pushing a finger right into the hole as far as she could get it, and working it in and out with a quick friction. She was lying over me in the opposite direction, and her hairy belly came right across my face. I didn't care for this much, as it pressed down over my mouth and nose until I was almost afraid I should be suffocated, and I tried to release my head from its position; but the maid, who had remained in the room all this time, and was narrowly watching me, said, "Kiss it," pointing to

Cécile's cunt, which rested against my mouth. The idea pleased me at once, and I put my lips to it. Cécile immediately responded by pressing her thighs tighter against my face, and some hidden instinct led me to push apart the lips of her slit and thrust in my tongue. Her bottom seemed to shiver as I did this, and in the excitement of the play I pushed in my tongue as far as possible, and curled it about in all directions inside. Her legs twitched nervously, and she wriggled her bottom and belly from side to side as I continued to tickle her cunt with my tongue, and squeezed her legs with my hands. This did not last long before she began to give a little tremble, I felt my tongue pinched, and then a quantity of thick, hot spunk gushed out and rained down into my mouth. Her legs closed tightly round my head, so that I was obliged to swallow the stuff, and I don't think it appeared to me to be nasty; and, as she kept me as I was before, I went on tongueing her again, until after another interval there was a further outpouring of warm cream, drenching my face, and it was not until I had had time to lick her cunt dry that Cécile removed herself from off me.

'I had not come myself yet, although I felt very near it. She did not suck me any more, however, but lay down by my side, and drew me up against her, bringing the point of my cock against her cunt. It easily slid inside, of course, but fortunately she had a very small orifice, otherwise there would not have been much fun for me. As soon as I had got fairly in, she threw her arms round me, holding me tightly against her. I had an idea, you know, of what you're supposed to do in fucking, although I had never done it before, and I began to push as hard as I could, while she assisted me by similar movements. After all that had gone before, you can fancy I was at fever-heat, and shoved with all my strength, panting in her face in my eagerness; but she did not mind this a bit, and only answered by kissing me, and pushing her tongue between my lips against mine, while with her hands she tickled my spine. As I felt myself coming, my pushes grew faster and quicker, while she responded with equal energy. She could not hold out against the strain herself, and presently she squeezed me still more tightly against her body, and her fingers dug into my back; she gave me one long, sucking kiss, ending in a deep sigh, and I felt her cunt contract again in a strong spasm; at the same moment, my cock seemed as if it were being drawn right up into her belly, and there was a delightful burning sensation in it, while a lovely glow spread all over me. I felt my thing throb and jump as it discharged into her what I was sure must be quite a lot of spunk for me, and at the exact instant this happened she spent again, drowning my member in the boiling shower, which ran all over my balls and down my legs.

'I was rather done up after this, but it was not until I begged her to let me go that Cécile disengaged herself from me. I lay on my back fairly fagged out, and the maid brought a sponge and towel, and very carefully wiped both Cécile and me. She was not at all a bad-looking girl, fair, and about the same age as her mistress, with well-developed bust and hips. As she moved softly about the room after having dried us, Cécile said, "Poor Marie! She must feel frightfully neglected." The maid turned towards us, and replied, "Not at all, madame. It afforded me much pleasure to watch you and monsieur; and it is not for me to have any wishes where madame is concerned." She looked very modest and fetching as she said this, and my blood began to rise again. I jumped off the bed, ran across to the maid, and pulled up her skirts. She stood quite still, without attempting to stop me, only crying, "Oh, monsieur!" Lifting her dress as high as I could, I knelt in front of her. She had no drawers on, her big thighs standing out white as ivory in contrast with the black stockings she wore. She had a tremendous growth of reddish hair all over the belly, very thick and long, and much coarser than Cécile's. I could read how excited she was, in spite of her quiet demeanour, by the inflamed appearance of her cunt, which seemed quite a large one, and her clitoris was stiff and swollen. Her legs were squeezed tightly together, so that I had some difficulty in forcing my hand between them. When I did so, I found the parts between her thighs all wet and slimy. My action in pushing in my hand affected her visibly; her knees trembled, she gave a smothered cry, and out streamed a river of spunk, over my fingers and down her legs, while little white drops bedewed the lowermost fringes of her hairs. I rose, drawing away my hand, but she seized and kissed it, all wet with her own spendings. Next moment, however, she had relapsed into the well-trained, demure maid again, and, having hastily wiped herself, dropped her skirts down and went on with her duties in arranging her mistress's toilet-table as if nothing had happened.

'We dressed ourselves after this, and Cécile and I returned to the boudoir, where she played and sang to me, doing everything she could think of for my amusement, but never referring in the slightest way to the scene in which we had just taken part. We had dinner together, and afterwards the carriage came to take me home, Cécile bidding me a

very tender farewell and promising to see me again soon. That was the
end of a very pleasant afternoon and evening.'

De Beaupré's clear and vivid narration had moved us greatly as we
listened to it, and my cock got so unruly that I had to keep my hand in
my pocket and hold it in an endeavour to calm its excitement. I could
tell also, from Bob's and Jimmy's movements, that they were similarly
troubled. We stopped for a moment as we came to a stile, and the duke
and de Beaupré climbed to the top rail and sat themselves astride it.
Taking advantage of the halt, I pulled out my cock, which was causing
me a good deal of discomfort by reason of its rubbing against my shirt
and breeches.

'I could just do with a rub now. It's so stiff, I can hardly walk,' I said.

They all looked down at my member, standing straight up like a
piece of stick, and smiled; but de Beaupré said, 'Not now, Charlie.
Keep cool, and wait till tonight. It's ever so much more fun then.'

'Oh, I say! I can't really,' I replied. 'If nobody else will help me, I
shall have to do it myself,' and I began to put the threat into operation.

Blackie jumped quickly off the stile, crying, 'Don't let him. Make
him wait till tonight.' My hands were seized and held, while Bob put
my cock inside and buttoned up my trousers, and they stood ready to
pounce on me in case I should make a further attempt upon myself.
'You will thank us tonight, Charlie, really,' exclaimed Bob apologeti-
cally, and I had to make the best of the situation.

'Do you see that paddock right over there?' presently said Rutherford,
pointing ahead; and on our signifying an affirmative answer he went on,
'I remember a very funny thing in connection with that. It belongs to a
farmer named Hopkins, an eccentric old chap and not over amiable; and
there are some very fine fruit trees in it. Well, one very hot day last
summer I was out for a stroll with a chap called Thompson – he has left
now; and we made a short cut across that paddock in coming back, as we
were a bit late. While we were running across, we heard a noise as if
someone were crying. We looked round, but couldn't see anyone, so
went on, but the noise still continued, seeming to get louder. "I believe
it's coming from among those trees over there," said Thompson; "let's
go and have a look. Perhaps somebody has been hurt." Well, we went
across, and when we got there we both had a fit at what we saw. There
was a chap about as big as Jimmy here, tied stark naked to a tree, and in
front of him was a young calf, not many weeks old, and, would you
believe it! the little brute had the fellow's cock in its mouth and was

sucking away for all the world as if it were at its mother's teat. The poor chap was in an awful funk, moaning and sobbing; and I dare say the animal was hurting him a bit, as it could give a pinch with its mouth, if it couldn't bite; but the sight was so absurdly funny that Thompson and I doubled up. However, as soon as we got our breath we came to the rescue, drove off the calf, and unfastened the captive, whose cock was all red where the calf had got hold of it, while the beast's sucking had made it come on the stand. As soon as we had set him free, the boy began to tumble into his clothes, which lay in a heap close by, and while he was doing this we asked him how he had got into such a pickle. As far as we could make out from his rambling yarn, it appeared that old Hopkins had caught him picking his fruit, and, instead of giving him a licking, had made him strip, and then tied him up to the tree and left him to repent his crime until he should return to release him. The calf was prowling about the paddock, and, coming along, advanced to examine the strange object attached to the tree; being in its sucking stage, it had fastened on the boy's cock, no doubt under the idea that it was a teat, while of course, the unfortunate chap, triced up as he was, couldn't do anything to stop it. As soon as he was dressed, he was off as fast as his legs could carry him, while Thompson and I made our way back to the school full of amusement. We often had a good laugh over the affair afterwards.'

This little anecdote diverted us all greatly, and also served to take my attention away from the little article inside my trousers which had been causing me so much trouble.

After a time, we turned our faces homewards, and I do not remember anything else worth recording until we retired to our room that night.

'What are the orders for this evening?' said Bob, after we had undressed.

'I vote we make Blackie master of ceremonies, and do whatever he tells us,' cried Jimmy.

Bob and I agreed, and de Beaupré gracefully signified his acceptance of the honour.

'I promised to give Bob a turn tonight,' he said; 'so you and Charlie can amuse yourselves together,' he added, turning to Jimmy.

'Very well,' replied the duke. 'We are quite ready to obey; aren't we, Charlie? How shall we begin?'

'Try a suck,' responded Blackie. 'You lie one way, and Charlie the other. That's what they call in France *soixante-neuf* – sixty-nine, you know, because a six and a nine are made exactly the same, only one is turned in the opposite direction.'

'We'll have a fuck, Blackie, eh?' said Bob. 'Will you kneel on the bed?'

'Yes. But don't put your cock in my bottom. I will show you a better way.'

'Very well,' replied Bob. 'I am ready to try anything you suggest.'

Before we started, Jimmy and I stood by to watch the operations of the others. Blackie lay flat on his back on the bed, and told Bob to lie on top of him, putting his cock between his (Blackie's) legs. Then Bob began to fuck, while Blackie's cock, squeezed between their two warm bellies, was submitted to a gentle and regular friction under Rutherford's movements. The natural result was not long in being brought about, and within a few moments after. Bob, following on some extra energetic pushes, sank down on Blackie in a state of happy quiescence, while his love-juice delivered itself between de Beaupré's thighs, Blackie's cock throbbed between their two bodies and gave out a discharge, wetting their bellies, which were almost glued together by the warm sticky stuff.

As soon as we had witnessed this consummation, Jimmy and I went over to my bed. I got on my back, and Jimmy placed himself over me in accordance with Blackie's instructions. The relative positions afforded excellent scope for mutual enjoyment, and spoke volumes for the genius of its inventor, whoever that unknown individual may have been. The feel of Jimmy's stiff and warm cock in my mouth excited me tremendously, and I used my tongue and lips on it with impatient eagerness, while at the same time I pulled and twisted his balls about, tickling the little pink hole with one finger, so as to do all I could to add to his pleasure. He returned the compliment with equal zest, sending me nearly wild with delight as he tongued my glowing member, working it up and down with his lips and rubbing the root with one finger and a thumb. Our bellies and thighs heaved and wriggled with the excess of our enjoyment, which only grew in strength as we continued. Bob and Blackie were now spectators in their turn, and watched us with great interest. Presently, Blackie commenced to tickle Jimmy's spine with his fingers; and Bob followed his example, as far as he was able, by stroking my thighs. This went on for some little time, until I felt a tingling sensation creeping over me, and knew that the end was not far off. I judged, too, by the way Jimmy quivered every now and then that he was in a very similar predicament; as he sank lower, thrusting his cock farther into my mouth, I heard him gasp, his hot breath pouring thickly out over my thighs. Then he almost fell on my face, his teeth closed tightly on my member, his own organ palpitated, and I felt something wet and warm trickling down my throat. Next minute the transport seized upon me, too; I gave a big heave upwards, and then all my muscles relaxed their tension, and I was conscious of nothing but the glorious, thrilling happiness that was setting my entire frame on fire as my cock jumped about excitedly in the act of throwing off its essence in Jimmy's mouth. The exquisite bliss prostrated us both, and we did not even move to change our position until the first effects had passed off, although we were causing each other the acutest physical sensations as our lips pressed upon one another's super-sensitive members; but at last Jimmy raised himself up, and we both proceeded to get into our nightshirts.

'Wasn't it just jolly?' exclaimed the duke, his eyes sparkling with enthusiasm at the vivid reminiscence.

'I should think it was – only more so!' I replied; adding, 'I propose that Blackie retain his office as master of ceremonies permanently. He reminds me of that chap you read about in the Roman histories – Petronius, was his name, wasn't it? – who used to plan out all the entertainments for Nero. Blackie would have done all right in that job, if he had lived then.'

They laughed, and after a little further talk we said good-night, the light was put out, and we prepared for sleep.

‐•§ ‰•‐

CHAPTER FIVE

A Masquerade and the Penalty

The following morning, a little before lunchtime, I went into one of the classrooms to get a Greek lexicon which I had left there. When I got to the room I found two of the boys standing there talking together. One was named Fred Davenport and the other Reggie Lawrence. They belonged to the ranks of the older pupils, both being about fifteen. I had scarcely more than a nodding acquaintance with them, as I had hardly had any occasion to speak to them up to the present, save in the most casual way, and indeed, I had not taken a strong liking to either. Davenport, who was the elder, was a rather tall and lanky lad, with a long nose and a decidedly vain air, though why he affected the latter I do not know, for I never discovered anything about him that he need be particularly conceited about. Lawrence was a short and thick-set boy, with sandy hair and a broad, freckled face, continually on the grin.

I said nothing to them, as they appeared to be engrossed in conversation, but walked straight across to the desk where my dictionary was lying, and picked it up, turning to go out again.

Then Davenport called out, 'What are you doing with that book, kid?'

'It's mine,' I replied shortly, not liking his tone.

'It isn't. It's mine. Put it down at once,' he said.

'I shan't do anything of the kind,' I retorted. 'This is my book. I left it here this morning, and I just came in to get it, as I want to use it this afternoon.'

'Look here, youngster! You just be careful how you talk to me. I say you're not to take that book away.'

'And I tell you it's mine, and I want it,' I returned, and retreated to the door, but Davenport placed himself between it and me.

'I don't want any cheek,' continued Davenport. 'I told you to put the book down, and you've got to do it. Just catch hold of him, Reggie, will you?'

Lawrence seized me by the arms, and in struggling to get away, I dropped the book. Still holding me with one hand, he stooped and picked it up. As he did so the cover fell open, and he caught sight of my name written on the first page.

'It's quite right, Fred. It is his book; his name is in it,' he said.

'Is it?' replied Davenport. 'Well, anyhow, it doesn't matter. He shouldn't have been so cheeky. These new kids give themselves no end of airs.'

'We had better let him go; hadn't we?' said Lawrence.

'I don't know,' replied Davenport. 'I think we ought to teach him manners. Suppose we freemason him, eh?'

'All right!' returned Lawrence. 'Lend a hand, then, Fred.'

Lawrence retained his hold of my arms, while Davenport seized me by the legs, and between them they lifted me bodily up and laid me on the desk.

'Shut up, you cads!' I cried, but they paid no attention, beyond Lawrence clapping a hand over my mouth. I struggled with all my might, but could do nothing against the two of them, and in spite of my efforts, they held me so firmly that I could not move a limb.

'You might as well keep quiet. We've got you safe,' said Davenport; and then, with a malicious grin all over his face, he calmly began to unbutton all the front of my breeches. I felt overcome with shame as he pushed up my shirt, baring my private parts to his and Lawrence's rude gaze.

'There it is! Look at it, Reggie,' he cried, taking my cock in his fingers, and both of them laughed hugely, while I was full of mortification at the outrage, and the blood reddened my cheeks and forehead.

Lawrence also had a feel, and when both had satisfied themselves with handling me, Davenport spat freely on my genitals, Lawrence following him by doing the same.

'Let him go now. He can take his book and be off,' exclaimed Davenport; and they released me, watching with mocking smiles as I sat up and set myself to the ignominious task of wiping off their spittle, which covered my cock and balls and overran my belly and thighs. As I did this and put my clothes in order again, I felt in anything but a pleasant frame of mind, and the taunting jeers which both hurled after me as I picked up my book and left the room made me thirst for an opportunity for revenge.

I communicated my wrongs to my chums, who sympathised with me greatly.

'That chap Davenport is a cocky ass,' said Bob; 'and Lawrence follows his lead in everything. Nobody likes them, and they both want taking down a peg. Davenport's rather in with old Percival, because he is well up in class, and he thinks he can do as he likes. I've interfered several times when he has been trying to bully some of the youngsters, and once he'd have got a good licking if Chadwick hadn't stopped us. They say he is very fond of playing rough jokes on new kids in his dormitory, but, of course, I don't know anything about that. If he tries any more nonsense on with you, Charlie, just let me know, and I'll see that he doesn't do it again.'

I was fated to meet with still further misfortune that day, for after tea I had occasion to go to a little room where we kept bats, tennis-rackets and articles of that kind. Who should be in there but Davenport and Lawrence, and two little chaps – one called Williams, and nicknamed Fatty, on account of his stodgy build, and the other Davenport Minor, who was only eleven, but was as insufferable in his way as his brother.

As soon as Davenport caught sight of me he smiled broadly, and said, 'Look, Reg! Here's that Powerscourt kid again. Hallo, youngster! have you kept your hair on since this morning?'

I did not condescend to reply, and hurried to get a box of games that I had come for, anxious to secure this and be off again. But Davenport, who had a great idea of always cutting a big figure in front of the juniors, so as to impress them, came up to me and caught hold of my wrist, giving it a little twist as he said, 'Why don't you answer when I speak to you?'

'Let go!' I cried, struggling in his grasp. 'I don't want to speak to you.'

'Oh!' he exclaimed, with a laugh. 'How particular some people are! Did you hear that, Reggie? He doesn't want to speak to us. I think we had better give him another lesson; don't you?'

'Shut up, Davenport!' I cried, firing up hotly, and trying to wrench my arm away. 'You had better not play about with me any more, or perhaps you will be sorry for it.'

'Really!' he replied, with a cold sneer. 'Things are coming to a pretty pass, aren't they, Reggie? when bits of kids talk to *us* like that,' with a grand emphasis on the word 'us'. ' I was going to let him go if he hadn't given us any slack; but I'm not going to stand that from him. He must learn to keep a civil tongue in his head. Come on, Reg!'

I was furious, and strove to tear myself away, hurling threats of dire consequences at them, but they paid no attention and, tripping me up, bore me to the ground. I began to shout at the top of my voice. 'Stop his row, or we shall have someone in here,' said Davenport; and Lawrence held his handkerchief over my mouth, almost stifling me. I was now reduced to complete helplessness, Davenport sitting on my legs and holding one wrist, while Lawrence held the other one, the two younger boys looking on at the scene with great relish. To my infinite disgust and humiliation, for the second time that day I was compelled to submit while they unbuttoned my breeches and uncovered my genital parts, and Davenport grinned in triumph as he felt them with lewd fingers and spat on them, then beckoned to the two youngsters to do the same; and when that wretched little shrimp, his brother, knelt over my middle and dropped his spittle, he smeared the slime all over my belly and balls with his hand. Davenport's tyranny was not yet satisfied, however. 'Fetch that pot of grease,' he said; and when his brother brought it to him, he dipped in his finger and proceeded to anoint my cock with the dirty fat.

'There you are! You can clear out now,' he exclaimed, when he had finished. 'You won't forget to behave properly another time, perhaps.'

I was smarting with vexation, and tears of impotent anger stood in my eyes as I got up and wiped the nasty substance off as well as I could; and all the time I was fastening my breeches I kept turning over in my mind plots for vengeance.

When I rejoined Bob and the others I gave them a recital of my woes, at which they were highly indignant.

'Davenport is going a bit too far,' cried Bob warmly. 'Never fear, Charlie! You shall have satisfaction for your wrongs, I promise you. I've always hated the fellow, but he has a sneaking way of avoiding me. I don't mean to let him, however, now. I'll show him he mustn't bully any friends of mine and I'm sure we won't have to wait long for an opportunity of bringing this home to him.'

During the course of the evening, I was able to recover my composure, and by bedtime was restored to good temper.

'What have you arranged for tonight, Blackie?' asked Bob.

'Well! Look here, you chaps; suppose we have a rest for tonight. It won't do any harm, and we can make up for it all the better tomorrow night.'

We were inclined to murmur, but at length agreed to the proposal as a good one. 'But on one condition, Blackie,' added Bob, 'and that is, that you give us another yarn.'

'All right! I'll do that,' replied the person addressed; 'but you must promise not to wank while I'm telling it. I warn you that if I see anyone start that, I shall chuck it.'

'You can depend upon me. You can tie my hands, if you like,' said Bob; and Jimmy and I also gave our word to keep control over ourselves.

'What shall I tell you about?' then asked Blackie, looking round at us.

'Let us hear some more about Cécile,' I said.

'Very well. Here goes!' he replied. 'A week or two after my first visit to her that I was telling you about, my mother had to go down into the country for a short trip to see someone she knew who was ill, and consequently she didn't like to take me. Cécile got wind of this, and at once offered to put me up at her place until my mother returned to Paris. The offer was immediately accepted, as it put a satisfactory end to the difficulty my mother had concerning me.

'The place where my mother was going to was in Touraine, and she left by train in the morning. After lunch, I went for a drive with Cécile in the Bois, and when we returned we repaired to her boudoir. You can imagine I didn't feel shy this time, and as she sat beside me I put my hand underneath her dress and felt her cunt. But she didn't seem the same as she was the time before, and I had hardly had my fingers between her warm thighs more than a minute, before she got up, kissing me tenderly with a peculiar look.

'I wondered what was the matter, and why she had changed, but I said nothing, guessing that she would explain herself presently. And I was not far out, for after an interval she took her place beside me again and, putting an arm round my neck, exclaimed, "I am very much troubled to know what to do tonight. Gaston. You know, I belong to a kind of club, which meets this evening, and as I am one of the principal members I ought to be present."

' "Well, couldn't you take me?" I asked.

' "Ah! no. That would be impossible. You see it is strictly limited to women."

' "I could dress up as a girl," I said jokingly, and without meaning the words; but she seized upon the idea at once, and clapped her hands with glee. But she grew more grave afterwards, saying, "I don't know whether it could be managed, and there would be a frightful fuss if it were found out. I must think. And if I take you, Gaston, you must be very careful how you speak and act. I must tell you that it is a club where we – well, amuse ourselves in different ways – so you mustn't betray surprise at anything you see. Can I trust you?"

' "Perfectly," I replied, foreseeing a rattling adventure; "I will be as sober as a judge, and as careful as an ambassador."

' "Oh, you jewel!" she cried, kissing me again. "I have not got all the plans in my mind yet, but I will think them out and let you know before it is time to start."

'Hereupon she rang for the maid, and when the latter appeared, she said, "I wish you to get some female clothes for Monsieur le Comte to wear tonight. I wish to take him with me." Marie never let the faintest gesture of surprise escape her, merely saying she would do her best. Well, the end of it was that by dinner-time I had been transformed altogether, and when I looked at myself in the long glass in Cécile's dressing-room I saw the reflection of what anyone would have taken for a smartly-dressed girl – and not such a bad-looking one either, I think, at least, so the two women said. I don't know how Marie had managed, but she had done marvels. She laced me up in a stiff satin corset, which was jolly uncomfortable at first, but this feeling wore of after a time. I had on petticoats with lots of beautiful lace frills all round, and long openwork silk stockings; and I just managed to squeeze into a pair of Cécile's high-heeled embroidered shoes. Over this was an evening dress of pink silk, cut rather high at the neck, and with loose sleeves reaching to the elbow. On my head they had placed a wig of dark hair, all frizzled and curled in the most fashionable way; and finally, to complete me, Cécile took out of her jewel-case some very handsome diamond and sapphire bracelets and rings, and put them on my wrists and fingers, also clasping a splendid necklace round my neck; as a finishing touch, Marie fastened a posy of pink roses on my breast, when she had done this stepping back to survey me better, and saying, "Mademoiselle looks indeed charming."

'We sat down to dinner, and while we partook of the meal Cécile instructed me in my part, making me repeat everything after her, to show that I thoroughly understood. She said that she would introduce me as a friend, which she was at perfect liberty to do, and it was also understood that no member's friend need take an active part in the proceedings, if not so inclined. Cécile took particular care to impress this upon me, warning me that I must resist all overtures that might be made, however pressing, while she on her part would plead my youth and inexperience as an exuse; and she assured me that if I kept proper watch over myself there would not be much risk of detection. "I shall say that you have lived all your life in the country, and have never been to Paris before; so that will be a sufficient reason for your appearing bashful."

'At last I convinced her that I was thoroughly up in my part, and eventually we left the house and drove off in the carriage, which took us some distance, stopping in front of a large house in a quiet by-street. The man in uniform at the entrance evidently knew my companion, for he gave her a deep salute, and we were at once admitted, passing through two doors, each presided over by several men, and finally reaching an elaborately decorated hall. Several lackeys came towards us, but Cécile lightly declined their officers of assistance, and tripped gaily up the broad and richly-carpeted staircase, I following as well as I could, and inwardly fearful that the awkwardness with which I managed my skirts would betray me; but I suppose this was not really as apparent as I thought, as no one seemed to take any special notice of me.

'On the second floor we arrived at a green-baize door, on which Cécile knocked, and presently a little panel was opened and a voice of enquiry came through. Cécile gave her name, which once again had a magic effect, and in a few seconds the door was unbolted, and we entered a small lobby or ante-room. Two women, dressed something like those who sell programmes and show you to your seats in the theatre, were in charge here, and we left our wraps with them. There was yet a further door to pass, but this was not locked, and on going through we found ourselves in a very large apartment, fitted up in the most lavish style, with great mirrors and painted panels on the walls, and rich heavy curtains drawn across the windows. The floor was covered with a carpet of velvet pile, so thick that the feet sank into it, and the furniture seemed to consist mainly of large, low divans and couches, plentifully supplied with cushions.

'There were present here a score or more of ladies, all young and good-looking and all beautifully dressed, and these came crowding up to greet Cécile, at the same time regarding me curiously, but as soon as my friend had introduced me as her cousin Elise, the whole of them in turn insisted upon embracing me and kissing my cheeks, while I was in a shocking fright, fearing every moment that my wig would come off. However, I survived the ordeal, and we all flocked together to the end of the room, where a table was spread with wines and cakes and other dainties. I sat between Cécile and a girl whom the others addressed as Isabelle, and the latter seemed a very lively sort, and kept talking at the top of her voice, and at a tremendous rate; but I was not altogether sorry for this, as it saved me from talking, so that there was no chance to give myself away.

'Presently Cécile asked, "Hasn't Hélène come yet?" but the words had scarcely left her mouth when the door opened and a tall, fine-looking woman with a lot of reddish hair came in, accompanied by another woman, slighter and younger. My neighbours immediately rose and advanced to the newcomer, Cécile whispering to me on the way that the tall woman was the president of the society. I felt a bit abashed as Cécile introduced me and Hélène's rather bold eyes fixed themselves on my face, but no suspicion as to my sex seemed to cross her mind.

'When the late arrivals had partaken of some refreshments, Hélène got up from her seat and said, "Come! Let us prepare for the business of the evening." I threw a quick glance at Cécile, who turned to the president, saying, "My little friend Elise does not feel equal to taking part in the ceremonies of this evening. She would prefer to remain only a spectator, and I am sure that you will not mind her doing so on this occasion. You see, she has led a life of such utter seclusion up to the present that it is hardly fair to impose too much upon her all at once. Dear Hélène! You will grant this small favour, won't you?" "Certainly," Hélène replied, "she shall do exactly as she likes. We must not expect too much of one so young; and I am sure that next time she pays us a visit she will not refuse to join in our pleasures."

'I felt very much relieved on hearing that this difficulty was overcome, and the remainder of the party retired through a door at the opposite end of the room to that by which we had entered, Cécile telling me that they would return shortly. I passed the time while they were away in munching bonbons, and in about a quarter of an hour they all came back. When I tell you that everyone was perfectly naked, you can fancy the state of my feelings. My heart suddenly started to beat like a hammer, and my legs were all of a tremble with excitement as I watched the procession of nude forms, and mentally compared the merits of the various big round bottoms, firm swelling breasts, and well-fringed cunts that were presented to my astonished but delighted gaze.

'Cécile came over and took her seat by my side, whispering, "Whatever you do, don't betray yourself." I gave her a meaning nod, to imply that I was sure she could depend upon me, but we had no opportunity for any further private conversation, as we were joined by Isabelle, who immediately started with her frivolous chatter. Here was I, wedged in between these two naked females, with an uninterrupted view of all their most secret charms, and the situation was a highly exciting one. Isabelle held me round the waist, and, taking my hand, placed it between her thighs, squeezing her legs together. "You are a silly not to join us," she said, wriggling her cunt against my fingers; "there is nothing to be frightened of, and there is no harm in one enjoying oneself." "You must not worry Elise," interposed Cécile; "you heard what Hélène said." "Oh! I don't want to interfere with the arrangement," replied Isabelle, with a saucy pout; "I was only saying what I thought."

'Just then Hélène called out, "Isabelle, you and Angèle are the first on the list. Are you ready?" Isabelle sprang forward eagerly, walking to the centre of the room where she joined the other girl, Angèle, who was a pretty brunette. They each placed themselves at full length on a low couch, while one of the company sat down and began to play a slow dreamy air on a grand pianoforte which stood at one side. Hélène turned to Cécile, saying, "Bring your little friend here, so that she may be able to see properly all that takes place, and she will then know what there is in store for her should she make up her mind to join our society another time." I was placed midway between the two couches, so that I had a good view of what took place on each, but as the proceedings were similar in either case I need only describe them as regards Isabelle. Cécile and another knelt down on either side of her, and took her teats in their mouths, sucking them, and tickling her neck and shoulders with their hands. Hélène placed herself at the foot of the divan, and began to titillate Isabelle's clitoris, parting the hairs with her hands, and at the same time thrusting her long, pointed tongue dart-like in between the lips of Isabelle's cunt. A most lascivious scene followed, Isabelle turning and twisting about something like a serpent, in the greatness of her excitement, while her breasts rose and fell with great spasms; and she kept up a running fire of little comments expressive of her feelings. This gradually ceased, however, and she relapsed into silence, only twining her body and drumming on the cushions in time to the languorous music. Her energy even in this began to fall off after a time, and she lay quite still for a few moments, then suddenly shook violently and started screaming and laughing, subsiding into long-drawn sighs as a thick volume of spunk poured out of her cunt. Angèle followed suit soon after, only with less palpable emotions, but the two who were tongueing them did not relax their labours and kept their patients on needle-points of unbearable voluptuousness, crying and tossing up and down in a perfect madness of lust, until their overwrought natures found relief in a further emission of creamy sperm.

'Then Hélène directed the four girls who had been sucking Angèle's and Isabelle's teats to take their places on the couches, a couple on each, in the position of sixty-nine that I told you about last night. Angèle and Isabelle took no further part yet, neither did the others, but Hélène, in company with the girl who had already been playing, performed a duet on the piano, and while they were doing this, Cécile sat on the floor between the two stools and, putting her hands between their thighs, tickled the clitoris of each at the same time. I walked across to watch them, and it was awfully funny to see the expression on their faces as they strove to fix their attention on the music in spite of the distracting effects of Cécile's fingers; although they did their best, they were unable to avoid a false note now and again, while, when at last the pangs of delight began to rack their bodies, they lost control of themselves altogether, and the tuneful bars of the duet ran off into a discord of loud jangling noise, as they rocked to and fro on their seats and their brimming cunts gave down a copious shower of warm liquid. After witnessing this finale, I returned to the couples on the couches, who had meanwhile been tongueing each other with great zest. They were in the deep throes of the keenest pleasure, wrestling with each other in a heated embrace, their faces buried between one another's thighs, and I could see that the engagement had already had its effects, for a white froth besprinkled their hairs, and the overflowing semen which had escaped their mouths was running in tiny rivulets down their legs.

'By this time, as you may think, I was so hot myself that I hardly knew how to bear up, and my cock, which was standing up as straight as a poker, had got entangled in the folds of my petticoats and made me feel so uncomfortable that I couldn't walk properly, but was forced to stoop a little forward in order to gain some slight ease. "This will never do," I thought, "I shall attract attention," and I steered my course to the nearest seat. Another source of trouble was that I didn't know how to alleviate the discomfort I was experiencing. If I had had my ordinary clothes on, I should have been all right, as it would have been the easiest thing in the world to dive my hand in my pocket and arrange myself to my content; but with those beastly skirts I was altogether at sea. The only possible way, that I could see, for me to manage, was to put my hand up underneath my skirt, but there were too many prying eyes about for me to venture upon this, as I didn't know how the action might be construed. They would probably think that I wanted to relieve the sensations in my cunt, and if they saw me appear to touch it they might insist upon my joining in their pastime, in spite of the arrangement that had already been come to in my regard.

'I was debating whether I couldn't screen myself behind a table or something of that kind, when Isabelle came to sit by my side, having apparently now recovered her usual form. After a few casual remarks, she leaned towards me and whispered, "Do just let me give you a little tickle – only one, Élise!" and attempted to slip her hand under my clothes; but I quietly stopped her action, and with a ready promptness with which I surprised myself, replied, "Not now, Isabelle. Two days ago I couldn't stop from doing it myself when I was hearing vespers at Saint Eustache, and I was so horrified afterwards at my conduct that I vowed to the Virgin that I would not do it again for a whole fortnight. I am sure you wouldn't like to make me break a promise of that kind." "Oh! my dear; of course not," she returned piously, and withdrew her hand, while I blessed my readiness in again escaping from an awkward position.

'After what was considered a sufficient pause, Hélène cried, "It is now the turn of Yvonne. You all know that she has come here tonight for the purpose of sacrificing her virginity. To you, Cécile, I assign the task. You can prepare at once."

'While I was wondering what the new item was to be, the girl addressed as Yvonne, a delicate-looking, golden-haired creature, who appeared to be rather younger than the others, came forward and placed herself on one of the divans, while the others gathered round her; and I took advantage of the confusion to make myself comfortable by smoothing my cock beneath my petticoats. The next thing I noticed was that Cécile had fetched a leather case, which she opened and from which she took an instrument covered in cream-coloured velvet and shaped like a man's member, with two balls hanging underneath, and the whole attached to a stout belt. I went up to her in order to examine this better, and she told me, with a smile, "This is what we call a *godmiché* or dildo with which we can manufacture an artificial man, almost like the real thing, and not nearly so troublesome, eh, Hélène? Poor Elise looks surprised, doesn't she? I am sure she has never seen anything of the kind before," and she looked archly at me as she spoke. Some warm milk was brought and poured into the balls, which were of india-rubber, and when this was done Cécile arrayed herself in the belt, which, when it was on, gave her the appearance of what is called a hermaphrodite – that is, you know, a creature half-man and half-woman. As soon as she was ready, she advanced on Yvonne and placed herself on top of her, Hélène guiding the end of the dildo towards the glowing entrance of Yvonne's cunt. As it glided in, Yvonne laughed nervously, and appeared to be in great suspense. Cécile waited for an instant, and then sank down with all her weight on the girl below. The latter rolled her eyes in her head and gave a shriek of pain as the instrument penetrated right into her, but after this first shock she made no further sign of distress, and Cécile commenced to thrust quickly backwards and forwards just as a man might do. I got as close as possible, in order to watch the novel operation, and I could see by Yvonne's face that all her thoughts had now given way to pleasure, and she twined her legs round Cécile as the last-named continued her pushes. The end soon came, and as Yvonne cried out that she was spending, Cécile quickly seized the balls and squeezed them, sending the hot milk they contained into the younger woman's belly. Yvonne seemed as if she were almost dying with the tremendous delight, but she held Cécile so tightly that the latter could not disengage herself. When she did eventually, she drew out the dildo, dripping with mingled spunk and milk, and as Hélène saw me looking on open-eyed, she said, "This is quite new to you, Elise, isn't it? You see how we can dispense with men. No man can give such a big and strong discharge as can this little instrument. I hope you will give us a chance of proving that to you someday." I smiled, inwardly amused at the unlikeliness of the probability.

'Hélène did not stay to embarrass me with further conversation, but turned to Cécile, saying, "Come, my dear! I cannot wait any longer. You must let me ride you *à la* St George." Cécile offered no protest, and as soon as the dildo had been cleansed and charged again with milk, she lay on her back, looking rather funny with the big white thing sticking up from her thighs, and Hélène quickly mounted on the divan, facing the other and squatting down over her so as to bring her quivering, bushy cunt immediately above the dildo. When she had got into the requisite posture, she sank lower, letting the dildo enter the lips of her grotto, and gradually pressed down until it was engulfed to the root. Then she began to rise and fall, to obtain the necessary amount of friction, and while she was doing this, Isabelle inserted a finger into Cécile's cunt and proceeded to rub the inner surface with a quick motion. Hélène looked a full-blooded woman, abounding with lustfulness, and I was not surprised when in a very few minutes she gave a quick signal to Isabelle, who at once squeezed one of the balls with all her force, and Hélène quivered as the stuff shot up into her with the force of a jet from a hand-pump, while her own hot liquor poured down in a torrent over the dildo and spread in streams on Cécile's belly. She did not cease her movements, however, but on the contrary, they became more rapid, and it was not until she had discharged twice more, and all the milk had been squirted into her, that she at length made up her mind to get off. Cécile, too, had come plentifully, and, as soon as Hélène gave her the opportunity, Isabelle bent down and licked up with much enjoyment the thick abundance of spunk that coated her thighs and still welled out of her palpitating cunt.

'Several of the others had now accoutred themselves with dildos. These found ready partners, so that when I turned to observe what they were doing, I found them dispersed in couples in various parts of the room, abandoning themselves to a regular debauch of sensuality, writhing and panting as they wrestled with one another, and subsiding into a chorus of hysterical screams and sighs as one after another the well-springs of their sperm gave way and they deluged each other with their spendings, until the hot exhalations from their bodies and the smell of the spilt semen seemed to combat and overpower the scents and the perfume of the flowers with which the room abounded. It was a scene of abandon such as I had never imagined, and it did not cease until all had become utterly worn-out and exhausted.

'Hélène at last notified the closing of the proceedings, and the members went into the adjoining room to dress, leaving me once more alone. Glad of the momentary escape from being observed, I quickly slid my hand under my petticoats and took hold of my throbbing cock in order to soothe it somewhat by a little rub, but I was too fearful of being surprised to be able to do it properly, and the only result was that it felt more inflamed when the ladies returned and I was compelled hastily to desist.

'On reaching the entrance-hall, we made our adieux, as all were going their several ways, but before we left Cécile begged me to wait for her a few minutes, as she was desirous of paying a visit to the lavatory. I had been standing about for a little while when a distinguished looking man in faultless evening-dress descended the stairs in company with another gentleman. They both looked hard at me, and the first individual, who bore himself very haughtily, went up to one of the lackeys and spoke to him in low tones. From the way they threw glances at me, I judged that I was the subject of their conversation, and I was not therefore altogether taken by surprise when the unknown individual, who seemed to be treated with an extraordinary amount of deference, advanced to me and bowed saying, "Will you do me the honour of accompanying me, mademoiselle. Madame la Duchesse will follow later." The request somewhat astonished me at first, but on reflecting for a moment, I concluded that Cécile must have made some further arrangements of which she had not notified me, so I permitted the stranger to lead me out, his companion following us.

'I was conducted to a well-appointed carriage, in which we all three took our seats. I noticed that the second man invariably addressed the other as "monseigneur", a title only used when speaking to personages of the highest rank, and I was not a little perturbed as I kept wondering who he could be. He was quite evidently, however, labouring under the impression that I was a female, as he continued to talk to me about Cécile, and asked me various questions relative to my history that put me at my wit's end to reply to without contradicting myself, but the devilment of the idea possessed me, and the whole adventure seemed so humorous that I determined to do my best to keep up the farce as long as possible.

'We were driving for perhaps a quarter of an hour, and I had a very remote notion of where we were, although I fancied it to be somewhere in the neighbourhood of the Boulevard Haussmann, but at last we alighted at an imposing mansion, and I was ushered into a spacious and magnificent vestibule, where an obsequious footman in a livery of blue and silver and a powdered wig relieved me of my opera-cloak.

'Monseigneur, whose grand air seemed to sit upon him like a well-fitting garment, conducted me up the marble staircase to an elegant *salon* above, where a table, set out with a fine display of plate and hothouse flowers and softly-tinted lamps, was laid for three. I thought at first that the third place might be for Cécile, but when our companion, who was addressed by monseigneur as François, took the seat, I began to feel much disturbed at my friend's desertion, and enquired when she would make her appearance. Monseigneur's manner was not altogether reassuring, although he answered and said, "Madame la Duchesse will be here later on, but she was unavoidably detained. In the meantime, mademoiselle, let us make the best of the occasion during her unfortunate absence, and enjoy what pleasure the present moment can give us." There was nothing more to be said, so I concealed the vexation I felt as well as I was able, and set myself to do as much justice as I could to the dainty supper which the deft and attentive servants placed before us. In the middle of the meal, monseigneur filled my glass with champagne and, raising his own, stood up, exclaiming with all the bearing of a *grand seigneur*, "Mademoiselle, will you permit me? I drink your health!" I bowed low, hiding my face for a moment lest it should express my feelings at the ludicrousness of the situation, but as I looked up again nothing in monseigneur's grave smile betrayed that he had any suspicion of me.

'A considerable amount of wine was consumed, although I took care not to allow too much to be pressed upon me, and my neighbours' faces were rather flushed before we had finished supper. Then monseigneur rose and held out his arm to me, saying, "May I have the honour, mademoiselle, of conducting you into the next room?" I could find no excuse for refusing, although I think I would have done so had I noticed that François did not come with us, but I was not aware that he had not followed us until the door of the adjoining apartment had been closed, leaving me alone with monseigneur. I found that I was in a luxurious bedroom, which had apparently been prepared for our reception, for all the crimson-shaded lamps were alight, and a fire burned brightly on the hearth. It began to dawn upon me that I had fallen into some sort of a trap, and I can tell you that I felt considerably alarmed as monseigneur, throwing off his majestic reserve, caught me to his breast and kissed my mouth. What was I to do? I hesitated to declare myself, fearing his anger, and glanced wildly on either side, seeking an opportunity for escape. But I could find none, and in the meantime monseigneur appeared to be working himself up to a high pitch of amorous passion, regarding me fixedly with ardent eyes as he continued to lavish embraces on my lips and cheeks, while his hot breath, reeking of champagne, fanned my face like the Arabian simoon. "At last we are alone! Come to my arms, mademoiselle," he cried. "Ah! monseigneur," I exclaimed in desperation, "you overwhelm me. Have pity, and let me go, I implore you." "Mademoiselle," he cried, "your wishes are commands to me. But before you deprive me of your society, will you not allow me the privilege of tasting those charms which I am sure are yours in the highest degree?" "Oh! monseigneur; I cannot," I said, looking at him as piteously as I knew how; "and what will Cécile say if she discovers me here?" "You can rest assured," he responded, "that Madame la Duchesse will be lenient with you. One so fond of pleasantry as she is, would not be hard on another."

'I entreated and besought him to let me go, but he turned a deaf ear to my earnest request, and sought to stop my words with caresses, while my apparent unwillingness infected him with increased fervour. His growing impatience added to my fright, and my eyes glistened with genuine tears as I endeavoured to tear myself away. Finding my efforts useless, I adopted an angry tone and threatened to complain to Cécile of his importunity as soon as she arrived. "That reminds me," he responded, speaking slowly and with some effort; "it is possible that Madame la Duchesse may not come. In fact, I do not think that she will." He paused in order to let the effect of this speech sink in, and in a moment the truth came upon me that he had brought me hither for his own purposes, unbeknown to Cécile, and I upbraided him with his treachery. "It was cruel of you, monseigneur; why have you done this? Cécile will be in terror thinking that I am lost." "Fear not," he replied; "I left word that you were safe, and in good company. Come, mademoiselle, you cannot escape me. Surrender yourself to my embraces. See! I kneel and kiss your hand," and he chose his actions in accordance with his words. I was silent and irresolute, pondering over this new turn in the situation, and before I had made up my mind what course to pursue, he rose and attempted to drag me to a sofa. I struggled and cried out, but was helpless in his strong hold, and in a moment he had forced me down on the cushions, supporting me with one arm and pressing his lips to mine again in a wine-soaked caress. I grew hot and cold by turns, and a numbness seized my limbs. Before I could summon up strength for further resistance, or even recover my voice, he had with a lightning movement got his free hand underneath my petticoats, and next instant it was resting between my thighs. The shock at what he felt there must have been great. He drew a long breath and did not move for a moment, then exclaimed hoarsely, "*Mon Dieu!* It is a boy."

'He gathered himself up and looked down at me with an amazed expression, while I averted my eyes, anticipating an outburst of wrath. But when at length he spoke, he was quite calm, although the deep tone of his voice betokened inward emotion. "Is this a ruse to fool me?" he demanded, "or what is the explanation? Does Madame la Duchesse de Régnier know of your masquerading?" Thinking it best to be entirely frank. I told him everything, and when I had finished he laughed aloud. "You scapegrace!" he cried. "Yet I have nothing to blame you for. If I was tricked, it was entirely my own fault. Meeting you where I did, and finding on enquiry that you were a friend of Madame la Duchesse, whom I know well, and being besides struck by your appearance – for you indeed make up wonderfully well as a girl – I conceived the idea of bringing you here in order to spend an enjoyable hour or two in your company, thinking that the message which I left for the duchess would be a satisfactory explanation of your departure."

'I smiled in turn, greatly relieved at this agreeable breaking of my suspense. "But you will now let me return, will you not?" I said, "for I am sure Cécile will be worrying herself to death about me." "You shall go, certainly," he replied; "but I think you owe me something for the deception. Before leaving, you shall gamahuche me." I did not understand the term, and he explained that he meant I was to suck him. I demurred, objecting to the further delay this would mean, but he insisted and would take no refusal. Sitting himself down, and bidding me kneel on the floor before him, he unbuttoned his trousers and directed me to take his cock out, which I did. I had ever seen such a weapon before. It was at full stand, and must have been at least six inches or more in length, and thick in proportion, with a great bulging head at the top of the long pinky-white column, on which the veins were swollen into a deep blue prominence. He would not permit me much time for examination, however, but pressed my head down towards it. It was the first time I had touched the member of a full-grown man, and I felt rather chary, while it seemed impossible that I could get the huge thing into my mouth. But he intended that I should adhere to his proposal, and as he appeared to be obdurate, I determined to get the task over as soon as possible, and, overcoming my hesitancy, applied my lips to the rounded knob. When he found that I had conceded his desire, he lay back, giving himself up to the pleasure I was affording him as I sucked and licked the burning head of his member; and he made no further movement beyond giving a gentle push now and then in order to force it a little farther into my mouth, continuing this until it was quite half-way within my lips, and seemed to fill all the space inside, causing me to breathe heavily through my nostrils. After a time he placed his hands on my head, holding it with a light pressure. Soon after doing this he leaned forward, forcing me back and raising himself up a little. His cock swelled still more and got stiffer, then suddenly became endowed with life, leaping and rattling against my teeth, and he held me firmly while such a torrent of boiling spunk poured forth into my mouth, with so much force and volume, that I doubt very greatly whether the opinion which had been expressed by Hélène of the superiority of the dildo in this respect could be vindicated. The superabundant flow nearly choked me, but as he did not release his hold, and my face being inclined slightly upwards, I could not prevent it from rolling down my throat. I closed my teeth on his member, in an endeavour to stop the discharge, but released my grip on his uttering a sharp ejaculation, not wishing to hurt him; and, being compelled to retain my position, I perforce swallowed the liquid, through sheer inability to do anything else, and it was not till he felt that I had drawn off the last drop that he suffered himself to withdraw. When he did so, he patted my cheek approvingly and, without adjusting his clothes, went to a table and poured out two glasses of a strong liqueur, handing one to me. I did not want to drink it particularly, but finally yielded to his persuasions, finding the cordial very warming and invigorating.

' "Really!" he said, presently; "you showed yourself so apt that I think I might have fared worse after all. I feel I cannot let you go without making a total conquest and invading your bottom." "But, monseigneur!" I cried in affright; "it would be quite impossible for you to get your enormous thing into me." "Not at all, as I will show you," he replied. "And I claim the trial as complete recompense for the very ridiculous position you placed me in during the first part of our meeting." "I cannot, really!" I answered; "the very idea frightens me. And think of Cécile waiting for me all this time!" "The sooner you grant my request," said he, "the sooner will you rejoin her. Come! I will not be denied. And I would like you to remove your clothing also." "You ask now what I cannot do," I said; "I could never get the things on again. It is my first acquaintance with female attire, and I'm sure I couldn't re-dress without proper assistance." "Set your mind at rest on that," he continued. "I will give you my help; and even should there be anything not quite right it would not matter, as you will go straight home afterwards, and the necessity for any extreme precaution no longer exists."

'He would listen to no further argument, and was already busying himself in loosening my bodice at the back. He displayed himself such an adept in the intricacies of feminine apparel, that in a very short time he had removed everything except my shoes and my long black silk stockings with their pink satin garters, and I could not help surveying myself curiously as I appeared thus in a great mirror opposite, the jewels on my neck and arms and fingers making a brave show as they flashed and glittered beneath the lamplight. Monseigneur looked me over critically, and caressingly touched my cock, which hung down limp, the agitation I was suffering preventing me from thinking of anything else but the coming ordeal. He appeared to be satisfied with his inspection, and, after making me give his member a little suck in order to bring it up to the ready again, he told me to get on all fours on the bed. When I had taken up this posture he well greased my bottom-hole and the top of his weapon with some pomade, and then mounted the bed behind me. I began to tremble as he closed up against my posteriors, where-upon he spoke soothingly to me. This did not overcome my apprehen-sion, however, and it was with great misgivings that I felt his organ beating at my stern for admittance. I am sure he could never have affected an entrance had it not been for the pomade, and as it was I felt as if I were being split open. I cried out to him to stop, but he paid no heed, and it seemed as if a bar of hot iron were being forced into me. Once the head of his cock had gained the interior of my orifice, however, the enormous strain eased a little, and as he commenced to thrust, I became more accustomed to the sensation. More than once, nevertheless, I had to bite my lip in order to repress a cry under the stress of his pushes, but when he put his hands round my loins and held my privates this helped to soften my emotions, and I forced myself to bear up. Fortunately, his operations were not very long in bringing him to a finish, and after three or four minutes he gave a few final quick shoves and then sank down motionless upon me, while I experienced a new but decidedly pleasant sensation as he discharged violently inside my bottom, sending a warm glow all over me, while the flow of the hot liquid acted as an effectual emollient and immediately relieved the previous wellnigh intolerable tightness. Shortly after this, he drew out his member, making a sound something like the pulling of a cork as he did so; and when he had wiped both me and himself carefully, he bestowed a kiss on each cheek of my bottom, and said with a smile, as I rose up, "You have fulfilled your part well; so admirably, indeed, that I feel it is I who am now indebted to you. Let me assist you to dress now." He performed this duty so expertly that I was fain to confess, when he had finished, that my appearance had not changed for the worse – I looked almost as well as when Marie had superintended my toilet.

'Monseigneur rang for his carriage to come for me, and while we waited he conversed most affably. "I have no need to feel disappointment at the mistake I made in the beginning," he said. "You have afforded me much enjoyment. Really! It is a fortunate thing for the sex that you are not a girl. As it is, you are quite charming; had you been a woman you would have been irresistible – and I fear, also, that in such a case you would have made many enemies among your kind, for women are jealous creatures, so I think you are much happier as you are."

'Going to his dressing-table, he took up a magnificent gold watch, and, returning to me, said, "Remember, if ever I can be of service to you, I shall always be at your disposition. Keep this trifling souvenir in memory of —", but I have given my word of honour not to disclose his name, which at that moment I heard for the first time; I can only tell you that he who addressed me was none other than one of the princes of the royal house of France.

'At length a footman appeared to announce that the carriage was at the door. Monseigneur led me downstairs, and himself accompanied me to the Avenue Hoche, on the way exacting from me a sacred promise that no one except Cécile should ever know the exact circumstances of the evening. As I bade farewell to him on alighting, he say, "Pray pay my respects to Madame la Duchesse, and tell her that I will personally offer my apologies at the earliest opportunity for any inconvenience I may have caused her." And then, in a louder voice, that the servants might hear, but with just a suspicion of a twinkle in his eyes, "Mademoiselle, I am your humble servant. Until our next meeting, adieu." "Au revoir, monseigneur," I murmured softly, and, with a low bow, he turned and re-entered the vehicle, while I passed on into the house and made my way to Cécile's rooms.

'On entering her boudoir, I found her lying on a couch, weeping in great distress, while Marie chafed her hands and held a bottle of smelling-salts to her nose. The maid was the first to notice my entrance, and on seeing me she immediately cried, "Oh! madame! Look and be comforted! Monsieur le Comte has returned." Cécile raised her head, dashing away with a fierce gesture the stray locks of hair which had come undone and hung over her eyes, and, as soon as she caught sight of me, ran forward with a scream and fell to hugging and kissing me, while the tears rained down over my face, "Oh, my darling!" she exclaimed, laughing and weeping at the same time, "where have you been? What has happened to you? I thought I should die, not knowing what had become of you – and how could I ever have faced your mother again?" I comforted her as well as I could, and, when I had reduced her to comparative calm, told her the history of my adventures. She listened attentively, only now and then making a gesture of indignation, but she could not help being amused at the way in which I had inveigled monseigneur into believing I was a girl right up to the last possible moment, and by the time I had finished my narrative she had regained her composure. "Monseigneur certainly did not behave so badly at the conclusion," she said, when I had done; "but I am not at all sure that I shall forgive him quite so easily as he imagines. He certainly did leave word that he had taken you with him, but that did not greatly relieve my anxiety, as I was quite at a loss to know where you had gone to, or what was happening to you. Of course, with him being who he is, one cannot speak too freely; but I shall certainly tell him what I think of his conduct when I see him. However, no harm has befallen you, and that is the principal thing, after all."

'It was well on in the early hours of the morning now, so after a brief interval we retired to rest, at which I was not altogether sorry, for I was beginning to feel very tired. When we got into bed, Cécile insisted upon having a look at my bottom, to make sure that monseigneur had not done it any injury, although I assured her that it was all right, beyond feeling a little sore. She would not be satisfied even after this, and, in spite of my protest, knelt down by my legs and took my cock in her mouth, saying that I need do nothing myself but lie still. I took her at her word, for, indeed, I was too weary to do anything else, and how long she kept on I cannot say, for I do not think it was very many minutes before I fell asleep, but I know that she was still sucking me up to the time I lost consciousness.'

◆◇◆

CHAPTER SIX

A Lesson in Physiology

As de Beaupré delivered himself of the last words mentioned in the preceding chapter, he looked around at us, and said, 'There, that is enough! I think we had better shut up for tonight.'

'Oh, I say!' cried Bob, 'I don't feel a bit sleepy. Tell us what happened next day, Blackie, there's a good sort,' and Jimmy and I chimed in to the same effect.

'It's rather late, you know,' demurred Blackie; 'we shall all feel beastly fagged tomorrow morning.'

'Nonsense!' Bob cried. 'What does that matter? Don't be a pig, Blackie.'

'Very well,' he replied; 'but don't blame me if you don't feel like getting up tomorrow. And Jimmy, I distinctly saw the bedclothes move just now. You know what I told you before I began.'

'It's all right!' the duke answered. 'I was only just keeping it quiet. How could anybody help it when listening to you?'

Bob and I laughed, and, indeed, we were in no better plight ourselves. My cock was fully erect, and I could tell by the way Bob kept putting his hand down towards his legs underneath the clothes, that his was in the same state.

'What did you do with the watch?' I asked.

'I gave it to Cécile to keep for me until I grew up. She said it was a much too valuable one for a chap like me to carry about. Well, I will go on for a bit longer,' he added, 'as you want me to.

'We didn't wake up very early on the following day, and Marie brought us breakfast in bed. We both felt very lazy, but about midday we got up and had a bath, which refreshed us a good deal. Cécile bathed at the same time as I did, and it was awfully jolly being in the bath with her. We splashed about famously, dashing handfuls of the warm water at each other, and she insisted on lathering me all over with a big soap-brush and rubbing me with her hands. It tickled frightfully when she daubed the brush all round my cock and balls and bottom; I couldn't speak for laughing and tried to stop her, but this only made her do it all the more; and it was just the same when she put the brush down and commenced to use her hands. However, I had my revenge when it came to my turn, and I made her nearly go into hysterics as I scoured her with the brush all over the thighs and belly, and, pressing open her cunt, pushed it inside, filling up the interior with the scented soap-froth. She shrieked out to me to desist, catching my wrists and forcing me away frantically, shouting that I had made her spend, which I have no doubt was the case, but I had no opportunity for seeing if it were so, for she overbalanced herself at the same moment and fell down in the water, scattering it all over the sides; but in any event the spunk would have been indistinguishable amid the thick coating of soap I had covered her with. When at last we had had enough of this sport, we stepped out and proceeded to dry each other with the warm towels placed in readiness for us, and as I wiped her down she caught hold of my cock, and squeezed and pulled it. This served to excite her a good deal again, and she would have me lie down on the long, cushioned bench at one side of the room, while she sucked me, which she seemed never tired of doing. I was in good condition for this, as in spite of all the lascivious events which I had witnessed or taken part in on the previous evening, I had never had an opportunity of satisfying my own desires. As I lay, I was dwelling upon these varied scenes in my mind, and the recollection considerably increased my sensual feelings. I would have liked to have Cécile let me fuck her, and proposed this, but she begged me to let her continue as she was doing, averring that nothing gave her so much pleasure as using her mouth on a pretty little cock, as she assured me mine was, so I gave her her own way, and lazily resigned myself to the enjoyment. She had a great art in sucking, moving me with pleasure to such an extent that I was consumed with delight, and my head swam; and within a period of very short duration, the interior machinery of my body responded to the strong calls made upon it, and I exclaimed that I was coming. She removed her lips, and watched with a rapturous smile the result of her efforts, as my young essence bubbled out and rolled slowly over the dome-shaped head of my member, which appeared very insignificant when I remembered the colossal article owned by monseigneur, and at

THE MEMOIRS OF A VOLUPTUARY

that moment I fell to wondering whether mine would ever attain such considerable proportions. "How adorable!" she cried, joyfully; and, after a minute's further admiring contemplation, she again took my immature organ, shining with moisture, between her lips, sucking it with a zealous passion, as though she would like to swallow it altogether and make it entirely her own, exhibiting such fondness that it was only with the greatest reluctance that she at last desisted.

'I would have followed by paying similar attentions to her, but she bade me wait, saying that there would be ample opportunity for doing so later on, but that we had better get ready for luncheon, which must by this time be ready. Accordingly we dressed, and I was glad to get into my own clothes again, having had enough of skirts for a time.

'On emerging from the bathroom, we found our meal ready, as Cécile had expected, and on finishing, we went into the boudoir, where my friend, at my request, gave me some music. When we had been there about half an hour, Marie came in to say that a young person giving the name of Julie Melnotte was waiting to see Cécile. "Show her in," said the latter; "it is the girl that the Ursuline sisters promised to send me. I told them that I wanted someone to assist as a maid under your superintendence, Marie, as now that Pauline has gone, I am sure you are in need of a little help. I said I should like one as young as possible, so that she would be easier to teach her duties to, and they replied that they felt certain they could entirely suit me. I hope that is so, but I have no doubt that under your tuition, Marie, she will quickly accustom herself to our ways. Let us see her now!"

'Marie left the room, and presently returned, bringing with her a girl of about fourteen or fifteen, quietly but respectably dressed, after the manner of the children who are reared in conventional establishments. She was rather pretty, with a clear-skinned, infantile face and brown hair, and wore a very shy and innocent expression. She appeared to be greatly impressed by the situation in which she found herself, and kept her eyes fixed on the ground. "Make your respects to Madame la Duchesse!" said Marie, placing her hand on the girl's shoulder. She reddened at her forgetfulness, and dropped a somewhat trembling curtsey, "You wish to enter my service?" interrogated Cécile. "Yes, if madame will be good enough to take me," the girl replied nervously and in a low voice, as if repeating a lesson. "Very well!" Cécile answered; "I have had a very good recommendation of you from the sisters, and I hope you will prove worthy of it. Marie will assure you, I know, that I am not a bad mistress, and I have the interests of all my servants at heart so long as they try to give me satisfaction." "I shall do my very best to please you, madame," responded the girl in the same low voice. "That is right!" said Cécile; "let that be your motto, and you will never regret having entered my household. I shall engage you, and you may stay with me as long as you like. You will have very light work to do, as I shall only need you to assist Marie in attending upon me. She will let you know all that will be required of you, and I hope that you will endeavour to prove a diligent pupil. I shall expect you always to look clean and nest, and Marie will supply you with all the clothes that you will want."

'Cécile paused, leaving the girl standing there motionless, not knowing whether to remain where she was or go. Marie advanced, looking at her mistress questioningly, to see what her orders might be. As she approached, Julie took it as a sign of dismissal, and, with another curtsey, was preparing to turn away, when Cécile exclaimed, "Wait one moment! I like to know that my maids are well made as well as good-featured. You will therefore oblige me by undressing, and giving me an opportunity to satisfy myself on this point." The girl blushed up to the roots of her hair, and said almost in a whisper. "Oh please, madame! I cannot!" "Good gracious, child! Why not?" cried Cécile, with much affected amazement; "you make me apprehensive. Surely, you have nothing the matter with you, have you? I could not have anyone about me who was not perfect." "Oh, madame! It is not that at all! But the shame, to uncover myself before people," and she threw a furtive glance at me. "Shame!" echoed Cécile; "I do not like you to use such a term before me. There is no one here that you need be afraid of. You cannot object to myself or Marie seeing you; and as for Monsieur le Comte here, he is present with my permission, and as he is my very dear and infinite friend there is no occasion for you to be ashamed. If I do not deny him the privacy of my chamber, you need not be alarmed at his being here. Besides, what does a boy like him matter; it is not as if it were a man. But, dear me! why should I stop to argue with you thus? Come now, and obey me! Marie, help her if she wants any assistance."

"Marie began to loosen Julie's dress, and the girl was too frightened to resist, but burst in to tears, covering her face with her hands. Cécile said nothing, watching her calmly, and Marie quickly carried out her task, until Julie stood before us in only a cotton shift reaching midway to the knees. Marie's next work was to remove the girl's boots and stockings, lifting up one foot at a time in order to do so. There now remained only the shift, and Marie caught hold of this next to remove it, but as Julie felt that the last vestige of her attire was about to be dragged from off her, she broke down altogether and fell on her knees, weeping bitterly. This had no effect, however, on Marie, and she rapidly stripped off the shift. No sooner had she done this than Julie fell forward on the floor, her body rocking with violent sobs. "How very ridiculous she is!" exclaimed Cécile in a hard voice; "Marie, pick her up and bring her here." Julie seemed to have no strength left whatever, and remained in a state of collapse, limp and still crying, while Marie lifted her in her arms and laid her on the couch between Cécile and me. She stayed motionless, with hands pressed to her eyes, and damp cheeks, while we overlooked her. She had a well-made body, soft and clear-skinned, but was evidently far from maturity. Her breasts were small and undeveloped, and she looked altogether a child. Her despair was so great that she remained quite passive as Cécile subjected her to a critical examination, pulling her about and turning her over unceremoniously, and as she lay on her face I noticed that she had a very respectable-sized bottom. "Why should you have made such a fuss?" said Cécile, when she had done overhauling her; "there is nothing at all wrong with you. I am very glad, I am sure, and you ought to be, also, as it only confirms me in my intention to engage you. Come, calm yourself! or I shall be vexed."

'Cécile placed Julie on her back again, but she did not appear to be able to recover from her distress, and continued to give vent to deep sobs. I took advantage of her supine condition to make a more close inspection of her form. She had a fat, hairless cunt, and the clitoris was small and had not yet arrived at its proper condition. I touched her with my hands, pleased at this opportunity of investigating a female member free from any concealment through natural growth around it. As she felt my fingers between her thighs, she broke into still more profuse crying, and I looked at Cécile, but she signed to me that I might proceed. Julie's slit was so small and tight that I had some trouble to force my fingers inside, but I at length managed to do so, and began to work quickly in and out, at the same time scratching lightly at her little button. The latter began to stiffen after a time, and her cunt relaxed and closed up now and then as I went on rubbing between the portals. Apparently, in spite of her terror, she could not help experiencing the natural instincts of her sex. She had not ceased weeping, nor removed her hands from her face, but as the final moment arrived, she gave a shrill scream, and raised herself up with a sudden bound, almost falling off the couch. Simultaneously with this, her cunt tightened, and I felt my fingers running over with moisture. She had spent. As I looked down I saw a thin trickle running down and dripping on to my hand. Cécile motioned me to make way for her, and, bending over Julie, she pressed her legs apart and opened her cunt as widely as possible, sucking the wet lips and burying her tongue in the hot aperture. Julie uncovered her tear-stained face and glanced down to ascertain the cause of the new sensation. When she saw what was taking place, she cried with a gasp, "Oh, madame! What are you doing?" "Keep still, child!" replied Cécile, pausing for a moment to speak, and then resuming her occupation, while the girl, forgetting even to cry, tossed and sighed with painful emphasis as she was brought to cognisance of sensual emotion for the first time. "Oh, madame! please do not. I shall faint! I shall die!" she cried at last, as her virgin orifice gave down its dew for a second time. "There, my dear child!" said Cécile, as she acceded to the girl's wishes and rose; "why did you permit yourself to become so agitated? You ought to thank us for showing you the hidden secrets of your nature. Come, tell me! was it not pleasant?" "Do not ask me, madame," Julie answered, having now recovered a little from her discomposure; "it was delightful, and yet it was dreadful. I feel as if I had done something terrible; the kind sisters never taught me anything about this." "You have now entered the world, Julie, and it is right that you should know what things are in it, and the capabilities which you have in yourself," replied Cécile. "The sisters willingly renounce the pleasures of human life as an act of sacrifice, but, as you are not going to take the veil, you are not called upon to do so, and I do not choose that you should remain in ignorance of the most wonderful works of the Bon Dieu. I would wager that you could not tell me what the difference is in reality between the male and the female. Well, I intend that you shall have a practical demonstration at this moment. How fortunate that we have an example close at our hand! Gaston, you will not I am sure refuse to oblige us by exhibiting your body to us?"

' "Madame, you frighten me again!" exclaimed the girl; "the sisters always warned us to be careful not to have anything to do with the male sex. Oh! I feel so troubled and perplexed, I do not know what to do. And, madame, you would not surely have me do anything wrong?" "I am glad to see you are so prudent, Julie, and have taken to heart so much of all that the good sisters have told you," responded Cécile; "but, as I explained, their rules are rules which are primarily made for those who intend to pass their lives in the cloister. You are not going to do so, therefore there is no sin in your being made acquainted with the governing principles existing in the outside world. In fact, it is only right that you should know, otherwise how can you expect to combat the evils which you will have to face at sometime or other? Besides, you must allow me to know what is best; and remember that I have your good at heart."

'Julie gave in to Cécile's reasoning, and meanwhile I was rapidly throwing off my clothes. I soon reduced myself to nudity, and when I was ready Cécile beckoned to me to come to her. Julie still seemed concerned, but a degree of interest began to appear in her face as she looked for the first occasion on the naked body of an individual of the opposite sex to herself, and her eyes wandered shyly from herself to me as if noting the differences in our relative physical construction. In particular, her gaze rested with a kind of astonished wonder on my private parts, as though she had never as yet conceived of the possibility of any other organs than those which a bountiful Providence has gifted womankind with. "You are now in a position to observe the principal points of distinction between the bodily characteristics of the male and the female," said Cécile, adopting the manner of a university professor. "You will notice that the full breasts of the female are absent in the male, and the nipples, although they exist in a certain way, are very minute, and are only mere imitations of the real thing, and, there being no duct or passage in them, they serve no useful purpose. The waist is also a little less slender, although with us the slenderness is often a more or less artificial effect, produced by an unnatural training. Going down lower, there is no special feature worthy of remark about the abdomen, but when we get beyond this we arrive at the most important instances of dissimilarity. Come closer, Gaston, so that I can indicate my meaning better. You see this projecting member here, Julie," and she touched my cock as she spoke; 'that is the organ by which a husband has union with his wife, and by this means they raise up children to themselves. It is known by various names, the principal ones being either *penis*, to use the Latin, or *phallus*, the Greek form. The way in which a man uses this to have connection with a woman is for him to place it in the receptacle which nature has provided for it, and which you have here," placing her hand on Julie's cunt. "This receptacle which woman has been provided with is also known by a variety of apellations, as for instance the Latin *vagina* or the Greek *cteis*. When the two have arrived in contact in the fashion which I have described, the man and woman set up a combined pushing movement. The object of so doing is in the first place to exercise a friction on the male organ. You will notice," and she proceeded to demonstrate her words on me, "that the skin of the masculine member is attached to it in such a manner that it moves easily up and down on the interior column, and with an elasticity and freedom that permits of the top being covered or uncovered at will. You will observe that this top is of a different colour and texture to the other portion of this wonderful instrument, and swells out very much like a knob at the end of a walking-cane, to use a very simple metaphor. The skin on it is tightly drawn, so as to give this part a more delicate sensibility. Before continuing, I think I ought to tell you that in its normal condition the organ hangs down quite soft and loose, but when it is required to be used for the chief purpose it was created for, it grows larger and raises itself up, becoming quite stiff – in fact, just as you see it now, for Gaston is a naughty boy, I am afraid, and his is liable to get erect under the influence of excitement, even although there may be no necessity for it to do so. Now, underneath this you can see a kind of bag of skin. Give me your hand!" and, as Julie obeyed, Cécile placed it on my balls. "There, you see! inside this bag are two oval or oblong-shaped articles. These are known as *testicles*. They act as a supply-store for the member above, and, just as water may be drawn from a well by working a pump, so a corresponding friction exercised on the penis draws forth a certain amount of the fluid with which the testicles are charged. But as a well is fed by springs, which keep it from becoming dried-up and exhausted, so the testicles are continually being re-charged as a result of natural causes ever at work in the body. I think I have made this all clear to you! Now for the part which the female enacts. The friction sustained by the male instrument naturally extends itself to that of the female, and this eventually results in the production from it of a fluid similar in nature to that emitted by the man. It is the mingling of these two within the woman that causes the gradual growth within her of a child, and the latter is in due time brought forth by her. This is the whole course of the process, which is so simple in itself, but yet has such marvellous results. But in addition to all this, the organs which I am speaking of were intended to be used in order that we might obtain pleasure from them. That the pleasure is by no means small, you have just had experience of; and it was principally to let you more fully understand all that I wished to tell you, that I desired you to experience in your own person some of the natural results consequent upon the use of your attributes. Tell me, Julie! have you followed me carefully?'

' "Quite, madame!" she replied, "I begin to see that there was much that the sisters left me to learn."

' "That is right, Julie!" Cécile went on; "I am very pleased that you have understood me, and also that you are beginning to comprehend these matters in the proper light, as I wish you to. Now, I propose to give you another demonstration further to my lecture. You shall see how the male member works in performing its offices, by experimenting on Monsieur le Comte here." "But how, madame?" cried Julie, shrinking back again; "I thought it was only for married people to take part in such things. Did I not understand you so, madame?" "That is so to some extent in theory," replied Cécile; "but these properties and instincts are given to all alike, whether married or single, and it is not wrong to use them with discretion. For the simple attainment of pleasure there are many methods of employing them, and it is not at all necessary that the penis should be introduced into the vagina in order to satisfy natural desires. Of course, it is very wrong for any persons not joined together by the holy church to unite in creating offspring; but even where the union that I have mentioned takes place, it is not necessary that it should result in producing children, as we are in a position to prevent this by taking proper precautions. However, were you and monsieur to conjoin together in such a fashion, there would not be any fear of unfortunate after-consequences, as you are both too young yet to be capable of fruitfulness. But I do not purpose that you should adopt such means at all; and, for another reason, were you to do so you would not be able to follow with your own eyes the event which I wish to be shown to you. What you must do is to take monsieur's organ in your hand, and with the latter bestow upon it the friction which would otherwise be given to it by your vagina. Gaston, come and sit beside Julie, so that she can do as I have said."

'I was not at all backward in doing this, as you can suppose, and I leaned back on the cushions in the most convenient position that I could think of, with my legs a little apart. My cock stood up splendidly, but Julie did not display any special eagerness to touch it, a sudden access of bashfulness having come upon her. Cécile urged her to begin, however, and at length Julie nerved herself to place her fingers lightly on my member – so lightly that I could hardly feel them. Gentle as the touch was, nevertheless my cock responded with a bound, and as it moved she withdrew her hand with a little scream. "Do not be stupid, Julie!" exclaimed Cécile; "I expected you to show a better spirit after all the trouble I have gone to on your behalf. Continue now! Gaston will show you how, if you wish it." Julie put out her hand again and timidly took hold of my organ. I arranged her fingers properly, and moved them up and down with the required motion once or twice, leaving her then to continue by herself, which she did with quick nervousness, a tint of crimson flushing her cheeks. Her unskilful methods promised to make the proceeding rather a long one, although I was only too ready to respond to a right appeal; and Cécile had to admonish her several times to bestow more care and attention on what she was doing. At last I felt myself coming, and stretched out my legs. In another minute my spunk leaped out, but as soon as the first drop appeared Julie let go her hold with a startled exclamation, causing the remainder of the emission to drop partly on my belly and partly on my thighs. Cécile frowned slightly at Julie's action, making the girl blush still deeper as she saw the look. "I am disappointed in you, Julie," said her mistress; "why do you betray such nervousness? Do you not see that you have scattered the discharged essence in a most unmannerly way over monsieur's body? Get down at once and remove it with your mouth." "Oh, madame!" Julie pleaded, "you cannot surely mean what you say! Is it possible that you can wish me to do such a thing?" "And why not?" replied Cécile; "did I not touch you yourself with my own lips? If I do not disdain to do a similar action to you, why should you wish to decline to do likewise to Monsieur le Comte?" Poor Julie had no reply to make to these crushing arguments, and though with much visible reluctance, complied by slowly bending over me and licking away the spots of semen with which I was sprinkled. This did not satisfy Cécile, however, for she said, "But you have not cleaned monsieur's member, Julie! Take it in your mouth and do so immediately." Julie gave a little involuntary shudder, but did as she was bid, and then hastily removed her lips and set about drying me with her long hair. Cécile apparently did not like the sight of anyone but herself enjoying me, and, exclaiming, "You do not do it at all well!" she knelt down and relieved her feelings by sucking me herself with a warmth in which was concentrated all her hitherto carefully controlled sensibilities.

'When she had desisted, she turned to Marie and said, "Julie is a virgin, as I have had occasion to ascertain. I do not think it advisable to let her remain so, as the thought would continually prey upon me. Besides, it is a deprivation from pleasure which she would be well to be rid of. There could be no fitter time than the present for her to undergo the ordeal. Kindly conduct her into my sleeping-chamber and place her on the bed. I will get ready at once, and shall be there in a few minutes. Gaston, come with me!' I followed her to her dressing-room, where she begged me to assist her in unclothing herself. When she had undressed completely, she opened a drawer and took out from amongst its contents a dildo similar to those I had already seen, but of much smaller dimensions. This she fixed on, and when she had adjusted it, directed me to follow her into the bedroom. Julie turned her face towards us as we entered, and stared with big-eyed amazement at my companion's appearance, as the latter approached. I doubt whether Julie had any idea of what she was intended to undergo, but possibly some dim perception entered her mind as her eyes rested on the protruding instrument attached to Cécile's front. "What are you going to do, madame?" she asked, tremblingly. "I am about to admit you into the freedom of a new life and a larger existence," replied Cécile; "do not be frightened. You may perhaps feel a little pain at first, but that will very shortly be altogether forgotten and swallowed up in such joy as you have never known before. Now! you need do nothing but remain as you are; I shall do all else that is required." Cécile mounted the bed as she spoke, and placed herself across Julie's body. The girl appeared very ill at ease, and gave a start of terror as Cécile lowered herself until she had brought the dildo against the shivering lips of Julie's cunt. "Oh, madame!" she cried, "you must not. Indeed, I could not bear your putting that thing into me. Oh, please let me alone!" and she began to whimper again, and attempted to push her mistress away from her. "Be silent, child!" cried Cécile; "Marie, hold her hands!" The maid did as directed, keeping the upper part of Julie's body still, while Cécile, as she lay over her, effectually prevented her from moving her legs. Feeling herself thus helpless, her presence of mind again deserted Julie, and she cried and moaned as she was conscious of the dildo touching and pressing against her outer orifice. But this did not deter Cécile in the slightest, and she made a slow but irresistible forward push. Julie gave a loud cry as the instrument entered into her, followed by a yet more piercing shriek as Cécile bore downwards, tearing open with the dildo, as she did so, the last defences of the girl's maiden citadel. The shriek dropped directly afterwards into a babble of sighs, and Julie's body was convulsed for a minute or two as she seemed to be endeavouring to break away from the cruel thing that pinned her down. She became a little quieter then, although her head moved slowly from side to side, with a sort of bewildered look in her eyes. This gradually deepened, but presently there came a sudden change, and they lighted up with a fixed and wondering glance, as she felt the strings of her being touched. Cécile noticed the expression, and increased the force and quickness of her movements. Julie raised her face slightly, no longer rocking it, but staring straight in front of her with a rapt and expectant look. Her brow and eyelids contracted, and she seemed full of an intense impatience of anticipation; she placed her hands flat on the bed and heaved upwards in an effort to cooperate with Cécile's actions. This rapidly brought the affair to a climax, and presently she almost leaped aloft, then fell inert and listless on her back with a long-protracted groan. Seeing that matters had come to a head, Cécile quickly got hold of the balls of the dildo, and syringed the whole contents in one powerful jet into Julie. This acted as the last straw on the girl's already overstrung frame. She gave a muffled scream, and vainly attempted to raise herself, threw up her arms in spontaneous wildness, and then subsided into immovability. Cécile at once took herself away from the prostrate form beneath her, and as she drew out the weapon with which she had accomplished Julie's ravishment, I noticed that the moisture which covered it was streaked with crimson, while a further glance showed me that thin streams of blood mingled with the other liquor that oozed out of the part where she had been invaded. I began to think that Cécile must have seriously hurt her, and pointed out the phenomenon with some emotion in my voice. But Cécile's smile tended to reassure me; and then it passed into my mind that a similar thing had happened when Cécile had, as she said, taken Yvonne's virginity the previous night. However, I did not quite understand why it should be, and accordingly begged for an explanation. Cécile, replying to my question, said, "Woman has been furnished with a remarkable peculiarity in this respect. Indeed, Nature seems to have worked in a most marvellous way in order to safeguard the interests of the male individual. Woman contains within herself a barrier to the full use of her physical constitution, which only succumbs to the attacks of violence; so that a man may always be able to find an incontrovertible proof when on the search for a vessel of chastity to take to his nuptial couch. Providence truly seems to be rather hard upon us; but perhaps the hardship is more apparent than real – and I am afraid the wife often makes up tenfold after marriage for any privations she may have been caused to endure before. But what is the matter, Marie? Can you not rouse Julie?" "She has fainted, madame. But it is nothing; I will quickly restore her." "Please do so," replied her mistress; "and look after her as well as you can. She might sleep here for an hour or two, until she feels herself again. Come and let me know presently how she progresses."

'I accompanied Cécile into the dressing-room, but she did not seem to be in a great hurry to garb herself again. On the contrary, she caught hold of me and, throwing herself down on a sofa, drew me over her lap, covering my face with warm, luscious kisses, while at the same time she sported in the most wanton manner with my genitals. I could feel her cunt throbbing and palpitating in the greatest excitement as one cheek of my bottom rested against it, and she appeared to be in a perfect turmoil of sensual agitation all over. I squeezed my buttock against her belly, pressing it inwards as much as I could, and she responded by twisting her thighs against me with an equal amount of force. Disengaging my face from hers, I turned and took one of her big, firm, crimson nipples between my lips, and bestowed on it all the suction I could bring to bear. Cécile gave a great gasp – the sensation was too much for her. She hugged me closer, straining me to her breast with such a passionate clasp that all my breath seemed to be forced out of me. Bending forward, she compressed my side against her thighs, and simultaneously I was conscious of a sudden access of warmth as her essence poured forth with the strength of a dammed-up river which has succeeded in bursting from its confinement. During the moments of ecstasy that succeeded this discharge, I seized the opportunity, as she lay back supinely amid the silken depths of the cushions, to slide from her lap, get between her legs, pushing them apart to suit my purpose, and put my cock, which had already, as I considered, endured sufficient irritation, in her saturated aperture. She had not seemed to notice me when I altered the position of her legs, but as soon as my member touched her she became electrified as with a magnetic shock. "Ah, you dear boy!" she cried; "it was for this that I would not have you touch that low-born girl in there. I want you for myself. Come to my arms! sink upon my breast! All that I have is yours; take and enjoy! Drink the cup to the full; I will not stop you!" She drew me towards her, at the same time thrusting out her middle, in order to meet me the better, while her legs closed tightly round me, her locked feet resting on my posteriors; and as my stiff and inflamed member entered into her gateway, swimming through a moat of thick sperm in order to do so, she gripped me strongly, sending my organ as far up into her interior regions as its somewhat limited length would allow it to penetrate. Small as it was, however, it was able to produce a powerful effect on her. I had only given half a dozen lunges, when again the torrents of her spunk gushed out, laving my thighs and genital parts in a hot shower-bath. She had no thought of releasing me, nevertheless, but only crushed me to her more tightly; and I had a good experience of how far a lustful woman can outvie a man in her achievements, for it was not until I had been the cause of making her discharge freely for the fourth time that I arrived at the same terminus of voluptuousness myself. However, I doubt whether her pleasure was as great as mine, when I did at length come to the crucial point, I cannot give you any idea of my sensations – they were too lovely altogether to be within the power of language to describe. I was transported out of myself entirely, and could only lie in Cécile's arms quiet and still, my cock yet soaking in her throbbing sheath, and my senses all merged in an exquisite dream of happiness.

'We stayed thus in each other's embrace for several minutes; then I got off, and Cécile, after hastily wiping herself, would clean my member with her mouth, spending quite an unnecessarily long period over the operation. She had not finished when Marie came in to say that Julie had fallen peacefully to sleep. On the appearance of the maid, Cécile rose and dressed. With her assistance, I also put on my clothes, and when we were both quite ready we went for an hour's drive.

'On getting back again, we sat in the boudoir for a time, and discussed some refreshments. Later on, Marie came to say that Julie was now awake, and asked whether she should remove her now to her own room. "We will go and see her first," replied Cécile; "come, Gaston!" We went into the sleeping-apartment, where Julie was still on the bed, but she rose as we entered. "How are you now?" asked Cécile. "I feel well at present, thank you, madame," she replied, but in a constrained voice. "She looks very dull!" exclaimed Cécile, regarding her intently; "I think she needs livening a little – what do you say, Marie? It would be a good idea to try just the mildest dose of the birch." "Oh, no, madame! You will kill me! And I feel quite all right, indeed I do," cried Julie in alarm. But Cécile signed to Marie, who produced from a cupboard a slender bunch of birch twigs tied with a narrow ribbon of blue velvet. "This will do you good, Julie," said Cécile; "it won't hurt you and you will be much better afterwards. It is only to restore the circulation of the blood." Julie's face blanched, and she began to tremble, but Cécile bade her stand upright, and placing two of the girl's fingers inside her recently violated orifice, gave her the strictest injunction to keep them in that position. As soon as these preliminaries had been arranged, Cécile signalled to Marie, and the latter brought down the birch with a smart but not too heavy swish on Julie's buttocks. She uttered a loud exclamation at the stinging stroke, and as it was followed up by others in regular succession, she writhed and twisted her body under the tingling blows, while every motion caused her cunt to be agitated by the two fingers inserted in it. This, added to the rousing effects of Marie's weapon, soon began to tell upon her, and before many minutes had passed the exercise had succeeded in bringing about a most lascivious scene. Each application of the rod made the girl squirm beneath it, and the intense bodily excitement, acting upon her nerves, led her to work her fingers in her now-no-longer-virgin slit with a fast and furious motion, while her face twitched nervously and her eyes were half-closed, and each expiration of her breath came with almost a hiss. I could not have imagined that the birch was capable of inducing such licentiousness had I not seen it with my own eyes. This extreme agitation certainly could not last long, and I was therefore not unprepared for the result when Julie's groans suddenly deepened, her knees quivered beneath her, and she wellnigh fell forward as, with a sort of gurgling scream, she clapped her other hand tightly over the first in an effort to stop the pulsations of her cunt, and next moment withdrew both, the fingers which she had kept up to now inside her portals wet with sperm, while drops of thick moisture dripped from the outer lips of the orifice. "There, that will do!" said Cécile presently; "you can dress now, and go with Marie."

'Cécile and I returned to the boudoir, where we remained until it was time to wash and dress for dinner. After we had bathed, Cécile proposed that we should not dress again properly, as we should be quite alone, but simply put on dressing-gowns. We did so, and when we again sat down in the boudoir I quickly found that Cécile had planned the arrangement to suit herself, for she immediately proceeded to open the front of my garment, so that she might have an unhindered view of and access to my body, which was of course fully exposed to her, as, beyond the dressing-gown, the only articles of attire I had on were my slippers. The attractions which I apparently had for her were unbounded, and she could not drag herself away from me for a moment, but persisted in a constant caressing and fondling of my legs and thighs and bosom, ever and anon bending over to impress kisses on my warm, naked flesh. After bearing with this for rather an inordinate time, I began to get restless, but to quiet me Cécile thrust an illustrated book into my hands, and I amused myself by glancing through this while my companion still went on with her own form of enjoyment.

'The announcement of dinner finally brought me relief. When we had finished and were sipping our cups of black coffee in the drawing-room, I questioned Cécile in regard to the use of the birch, as I had seen it brought into play in the afternoon. I had never connected the rod with any other idea but that of punishment. Cécile, however, enlightened me on the subject, explaining that the instrument played a much higher role, and was a great means towards the production of increased sensual excitement. I had already had evidence of this, and Cécile went on to give me further illustrations from her own experience. "There is a friend of mine, a Russian, Princess Gourkasoff, who is a very great advocate of flagellation, and is never weary of putting her theories into practice. She has several maids and pages whose sole duties are to attend personally on her, and she seizes every opportunity for exercising the discipline of the rod upon them. It cannot be said that she is cruel, as her castigation is never excessive or violent, but she seems to derive an extraordinary pleasure from making her attendants submit to her caprice, and the whole proceedings are carried out in such a ceremonious manner, and with such an extravagance of ostenta-tion, that it is quite a revelation to witness them. Perhaps I can manage to take you to visit her, and you will then be able to see her methods for yourself."

'Just as she had concluded, there was a sound of commotion outside, and Marie's voice was heard, couched in high-pitched tones. Cécile rang the bell violently and, as Marie entered, enquired what was the matter. "It is that Pierre!" explained Marie, in a vexed way; "he was bringing up a bottle of scent for madame, and the little dolt dropped it just outside, breaking the bottle, so that all the beautiful perfume is wasted." "How careless!" replied Cécile, looking at me with a half-smile, "bring him

into me, Marie;" and as the maid departed, my companion said, "Pierre
is one of the boys engaged by the concierge to run errands. The poor
fellow is always getting into trouble, but we will extract some amusement out of him this time, and you shall have an opportunity of
witnessing another experiment with the birch."

'Marie came back almost directly, bringing the culprit with her. He
was a little fellow of about twelve, dressed in a neat livery, and was a
typical *gamin* with a sharp and not ill-looking face, which at present
wore a very disconsolate expression, consequent upon his recent
misfortune. He kept his eyes on the carpet and shifted uneasily as he
faced Cécile. "You are very careless, Pierre!" said she; "what have you
to say for yourself?" He began to murmur some sort of apology, and
expressed his sorrow; but Cécile interposed – "It is all very well for you
to be sorry, Pierre, but that will not mend matters. The perfume is lost,
and it was very valuable. You cannot replace it, and if I tell the
concièrge he will dismiss you." He begged her to overlook his fault, and
promised not to offend again. Cécile paused, affecting to relent,
and then said, "Well, Pierre! I will not do as I said. But I must not
forgive you too easily, or you will soon forget. I shall punish you by
giving you a whipping. Will you take that, or shall I speak to the
concierge?" The boy did not make any reply, and Cécile treated his
silence as a sign of consent. "Fetch me the birch, Marie! Now, will you
please remove your clothes," she added, turning to Pierre. He slowly
and unwillingly commenced to fumble with his buttons, but had barely
got his tunic unfastened when Marie returned. She, however, soon
made him display more alacrity, and almost dragged off his clothes, not
desisting until he stood before us entirely unclad, and looking the
picture of dejection, his little cock hanging down with a forlorn and
bedraggled appearance. Cécile directed Marie to place him in a
kneeling posture on a prie-dieu, and when he was thus arranged, she
picked up the birch and, cutting the air with it as a preliminary,
brought it down with a flourish on Pierre's undefended posterior. He
writhed and uttered an exclamation, but Cécile warned him not to
move, or the punishment would be more severe, and, bracing herself to
the task, she wielded the rod on him until his buttocks blushed rosy-
red, and with consummate art so regulated the strokes that the lithe
and slender ends of the weapon curled in between his thighs and
lighted on the most sensitive parts of his body, making him twist and
emit suppressed cries incessantly. At last, Cécile tired herself out and

flung down the rod, on seeing which Marie raised Pierre up. I surveyed him with much interest to see what effect the chastisement had produced, and was scarcely able to repress an exclamation of wonder at the change in the appearance of his genital organ: instead of it being the tiny bit of flabby flesh that I had first gazed upon, it had swelled up abnormally, was now quite stiff, and glowed with a pink tinge from the rush of blood into its spongy tissues. Its condition seemed to embarrass him much, and he strove to conceal it with his hands as he fronted us, but Marie ordered him to keep his arms straight down by his side, so that he was deprived of even this consolation. "What are we to do with such a brazen young imp, madame?" exclaimed Marie, taking hold of the offending member with a view to drawing our attention to it, while Pierre looked hot and flushed at this further liberty which was being taken with him. Cécile regarded him with affected indifference, saying, "It is hard to instil good manners into such minds. A little application of cold water would no doubt be a good remedy." Marie took the hint and, going into the next room, returned shortly with a basin of water and a sponge, with which she bathed Pierre's private parts profusely. He winced and shuddered at the chilly operation, and it certainly had a very quick effect in reducing his member to its normal state, it appearing even smaller than at first when Marie had finished. He was then allowed to put on his clothes again, and Cécile gave him a whole franc afterwards, promising to say nothing further about the broken bottle, so that his spirits had risen considerably by the time of his departure.

'After the previous late night, we decided to go to bed early this evening, and it was not more than eleven when we retired. I had almost added "to sleep", but this would hardly be correct, for Cécile did not evince any ardent desire for immediate slumber. She was one of those women whose bodily cravings it is impossible to satisfy, and though I would fain have gone to rest at once, she betrayed no inclination to follow my example. As soon as we had got into bed, she prepared to suck me again, but I had imposed too much upon my body earlier in the day, and with all her efforts she could not excite me to stiffness. I pleaded my incapability, and she no doubt saw that it was futile to exact too much from me, so she eventually gave up her endeavours, saying, "I will not weary you any more, Gaston. But just give me a kiss or two before we go to sleep." She lay back on the pillows and opened her legs, so that I might crouch between them, and she pressed my head down towards her thighs. The "kiss or two" which she had spoken of meant that I had to give her a proper tongueing, and she kept me at it until I caused her insatiate orifice to swim and bubble over with a thick and redolent emission, which burst out over my face like a miniature waterspout. Even then, she would have had me still go on, and it was only at my earnest request that she would finally permit me to lie down by her side at rest. Once I had arranged myself comfortably, I felt sleep drawing on apace rapidly, but before losing myself to my surroundings I have a faint recollection of her getting close to me, and abandoning herself to the delights of fingering my cock and bottom – and I have no doubt she continued at this long after I had lapsed into slumber.

'There! I have kept my word, and given you another dose. But I decline to open my mouth any more, so you can all go to sleep as soon as you like.'

'I suppose it is time now,' commented Bob regretfully. 'Anyhow, we all agree that you are a trump, Blackie. Well, here goes! I'll be brave, and lead the way by settling down at once.'

We all felt the wisdom of the course, and after mutual good-nights, prepared for sleep as quickly as possible, although, speaking for myself, de Beaupré's exciting narrative had given me so much to think of that it was some time before I finally went off.

When I awoke, I found the others still asleep, and on looking at my watch I saw that it was not yet six o'clock. However, I did not feel inclined to close my eyes again, and cast about for something to occupy me until it was time to get up.

As my glance fell on the next bed, I noticed that Bob had kicked off the greater part of the clothes during the night, and lay with one leg outside, while his nightshirt had rucked up till he was almost bare. A sudden fancy seized me as I looked upon him, and, quietly stepping across the intervening space, I took my seat by his side. He slept heavily and, without disturbing him, I managed, by dint of soft and careful handling, to arrange him at full length on his back, with his sleeping-garment pushed right up on his breast. His body was thus exposed to me, and I could not help thinking what a finely made fellow he was. I have since learned that it is the opinion among the best critics that the male form is essentially more beautiful than the female. The ancient Greeks, who were in every sense a nation filled with the highest instincts of art, undoubtedly thought so, as their sculpture and poetry bear witness in their never-tiring adulations of Adonis and Narcissus,

Hyacinthus, Ganymede and Hylas, to mention only a few examples. I do not wish to lead the reader to suppose that such a thought as this came upon me at the time, but it is certainly true that the contemplation of Bob's form infected me with a distinct perception of the inherent symmetry of the masculine frame. Such idle thoughts did not hold me for long, however, and my attention was claimed more particularly by my friend's member, which hung down in the hollow of his thighs with a picturesque elegance of languor. In its erect state, the genital organ is more impressive and obtrusive, but I always think that it is more fascinating to the sight when lying in calm peacefulness. As it lay at rest, I stroked it gently, luxuriating in its wonderful softness, and with equal delight buried the tips of my fingers in the patch of curling hair that grew around the root where it joined the smoothly-swelling belly. My actions did not arouse him and, growing bolder, I took his cock in my hand, and very carefully and tenderly squeezed it. Even this had no effect on his slumbers, nor yet, when I uncovered the top as far as possible, did he do any more than move his body spasmodically. This was certainly enough at first to startle me into believing that I had awakened him, and I sat very still, watching him carefully for a minute or so, but when I saw that he gave no sign of being conscious I became reassured and went on with my amusement. Under the coaxing effect of my clasp, I was aware that Bob's member was swelling, and in response to every squeeze I gave it there came an answering throb. As soon as I became cognisant of the result I was producing, I devoted my whole attention to fostering it, and in a fairly short space of time had the satisfaction of finding the organ in complete erection. I was very much interested also in the discovery that I had achieved this without awakening him. My fears of so doing rapidly vanished, and I became correspondingly careless, allowing myself to carry on my play with the greatest freedom, feeling and tickling his balls, and rubbing his cock, at first slowly, and then at quite a fast rate. But I found presently that I was not now exercising sufficient precaution, and under the influence of my movements Bob started to murmur inarticulately and turned his body and limbs in a sudden restlessness. I immediately stopped, and did not go on again until his quietude and heavy breathing satisfied me that he was resting calmly once more; and I took greater care this time not to run too much risk of awakening him by my rashness. In the course of the proceedings, I found that it had comparatively little disturbing effect to touch his penis or his testicles, unless I exerted a rather hard pressure on the skin in uncovering the head; but his posterior portion was much more sensitive, and if I got my fingers in the furrow or placed them against the bottom-hole, this was the signal for him at once to shift himself uneasily and babble in his sleep, so after a few attempts I left those dangerous parts alone. I found plenty of interest to my sportive feelings without this, though, and took quite a keen pleasure in keeping Bob's member at high-pitched tension, nurturing it with my hands into stiffness again whenever it showed signs of degenerating. After a considerable spell of this, I wondered whether I might venture to suck it. Bob still appeared to be deep in slumber, so I essayed the attempt, but exhibited the greatest caution. It had no effect on him, however, so I continued; but I found in time that, though I could use my mouth with impunity in an ordinary way, if I drew down the prepuce and let my lips touch the delicately sensitive skin of the lower part of the knob, my patient immediately showed signs of troubled rest. I therefore became prudent in this respect, and otherwise found no hindrance to my crouching over him, and giving his cock as much sucking as I liked. I was so enamoured of my work that time passed quickly, and nearly an hour must have elapsed since I had got out of bed when I heard Jimmy's voice as he sang out, 'Hallo, Charlie! At it already? Are you awake. Blackie? Just look at them!'

I caught a sleepy laugh from de Beaupré, but turned hastily and motioned to them to keep silent, pointing out that Rutherford was asleep. They saw and understood, and I resumed my occupation, but it had only lasted for a few minutes longer when the seven o'clock bell rang. This had the effect of arousing Bob. He opened his eyes and looked down half-dozing, then, conscious of something unusual taking place, put his hands down, bringing them in contact with my head, which he attempted to push away. The resistance he met with served to bring him to his senses, and in a few seconds he was fully awake, and had taken in the situation at a glance.

'What are you doing, Charlie?' he exclaimed, seizing me and dragging me up. 'You have been positively assaulting me in my sleep, I declare! This comes of listening to your yarns, Blackie; you see what mischief you do! But, I say, Charlie! you *have* made me stiff. You will have to finish now!'

'You haven't asked my permission yet,' said de Beaupré, shaking his finger reprovingly. 'Supposing I forbid it?'

'Oh! but you mustn't' replied Bob; 'it wouldn't be fair! This little beggar is to blame altogether. I wonder he didn't make me come before I woke up.'

'Very well!' said Blackie; 'I'll let you have your way this time, but there must be nothing else done this morning, otherwise there would have been no use in our crying off last night.'

'All right!' Bob answered. 'Now, Charlie! We've got plenty of time, if you buck up. Do the best you know how to, as you owe me something, you little villain!'

I smiled, and sat myself down between Bob's legs, taking one of them over my knees, and holding it in position with my left arm, the hand passing under the thigh and grasping his balls, while with my right hand I took his cock and rubbed it up and down with the quick regularity of a piston. It was very hard and hot, and had already been brought near the verge of discharging by my previous attentions. It was not long, therefore, before Bob signified to me that he was coming, and I had scarcely prepared myself to watch the result when a jet of sperm shot out with the force of a projectile and landed right on Bob's mouth, while two or three further clots followed, alighting partly on his nightshirt and partly on his belly, the after-flow emptying itself over my fingers. Bob licked into his mouth the drop which had fallen there, saying with a smile, 'That's the first time I've tasted my own spunk, Charlie.' He then proceeded to remove the traces of moisture from his shirt and body, while I lost no further time in applying my lips to his cock, so as to give it the final touch, without which the full sensuousness of an emission is not experienced.

Blackie's injunction that nothing more was to be done that morning was strictly obeyed, and we confined ourselves to a little jocularity while dressing.

Nothing of particular interest took place that day, but after supper I was talking to little Williams, whom I had had occasion to speak to earlier in the day, and who was not really a bad youngster but had just suffered the misfortune of being placed in Davenport's dormitory. He was telling me of some of the practices of this young gentleman, and I called up my three chums, who were not far away, to listen, requesting Williams to report all he had already told me.

'It is not so much me he bullies, although I've had a taste; but Davenport makes a special mark of that young Elgar, who is a very timid kid. Why, the school has only been open a few days this term, and I'm sure Elgar is beginning to look quite bad already.'

'What does Davenport do?' asked Bob, with growing indignation.

'Well, the first night he and Lawrence – who, of course, always helps him – made up apple-pie beds for Elgar and me, and the other two chaps, Sturgess and Benson. We didn't mind that, as there wasn't much harm in it, only Elgar got very frightened because he tore a hole in the sheet, and started to cry for fear he would get into a row with Mrs Percival, while Davenport made some very nasty remarks, which didn't exactly comfort him. And ever since then Davenport has been down on Elgar, I expect because he is such a weak little chap. The next morning he was asleep when the bell rang, and Davenport tipped up the mattress, chucking him on the floor and giving him an awful fright. I told him he ought to be careful, and Sturgess and Benson spoke up, too, but he threatened to lick us all if we said a word, and Lawrence backed him up, so what could we do? and that little sneak of a Davenport Minor was grinning and jumping about, and doing his best to get his brother to set on us.

'That night, Davenport waited till Elgar was in bed and asleep, as we were too, and as soon as all was quiet he got up and tied a string to the little chap's toe, then, going back to bed, started to haul on it. Of course, Elgar woke up with a scream, and burst out crying, making such a noise that Davenport got out, being afraid that one of the masters would come in, and told Elgar he would give him a bashing if he didn't stop making a row. Elgar did his best, but couldn't seem to keep from crying, so Davenport said, "I'll give you something to cry for, if you don't dry up!" and he and Lawrence held him over the basin and poured a jug of cold water over him, leaving him to dry himself as well as he could, and get into bed again shivering all over. Benson and I told them they were cads, and they started to lam into us with a cane, but we swore we would go and tell Chadwick if they didn't leave us alone, so they went back to bed after that.

'That's how things have been going with us. One morning Davenport poured out the chamber over Elgar, and another time he held him down on the bed and whacked his backside with a watch-chain. And last night, Lawrence kept hold of him while Davenport dropped lighted sealing-wax on his belly and legs. Elgar doesn't like to say anything to Mr Percival or the other masters as he thinks it would be sneaking, but I told him plainly that he was a fool, and the other chaps did so as well, and we all said that if Davenport kept on any more we would go in a body and complain of him.

'And then, Davenport and Lawrence are always playing about with us, pulling out our cocks, and putting ink on them, or something of that sort. Don't you think it's right for us to stick out a bit against him?'

'Certainly!' cried Bob. 'I never knew there was anything so bad as what you say going on, but I'll see that it doesn't continue. As head of the school, I think I can manage it all right, and that will save you from going to the masters. I am afraid it's too late for me to speak to him tonight, but if Davenport starts again you let him know that you won't put up with his treatment any longer.

'Davenport is going too far altogether,' continued Bob to us, after Williams had gone. 'And you owe him something, too, don't you, Charlie? Let him wait a little longer, that's all!'

Our interest in the subject flagged after we had got to our room, and our thoughts turned instinctively to other matters.

'Have you already got a plan for this evening, Blackie?' asked Bob.

'Let me see! Yes!' replied de Beaupré. 'I think I had better engage the services of Jimmy on this occasion, or he will think I am neglecting him. So Charlie can pair off with you, Bob.'

'That's a good arrangement,' said Rutherford. 'If we go on like that, there won't be any cause for jealousy between us, will there? Are you going to give us the details of the campaign, too?'

'I should suggest a "face-fuck", ' Blackie answered, after a moment's thought. 'I will show you what I mean in one second.'

When we notified that we were ready to begin, de Beaupré directed me to lie with my head propped up against the pillows, and then told Bob to kneel over my chest, so as to bring his member opposite my lips, while he supported himself on his hands, and in this position he was to work his cock in my mouth in the most approved style and to the best of his ability. We at once grasped the idea, and proceeded to put it into effect. Bob's organ was already hard, and exhibited every eagerness for the fray; and he launched forward, thrusting it half-way down my throat. The operation was at first slightly discomforting, but I rapidly accustomed myself to it; it soon got into full swing, and was working splendidly. I kept a firm pressure on Bob with my lips, and bestowed little nibbles on him, advancing my tongue also to meet his pushes, increasing his pleasure so much that he voted the performance a first-class one in every way. As he worked his body, I clasped him round the loins and gently stroked his bottom, while in answer his knees closed firmly against my sides. He breathed heavily in his salacious efforts, his pulses quickened, nerving his cock to further excitation, and his fierce emotions communicated themselves to me, the warm friction of his member in my mouth sending a pleasant glow through my frame, and calling up all the dormant eroticism of my nature. I felt as if I could have gone on thus for hours, but for this, as for all things in this world of ours, a period was fixed, and in course of time I could tell by the quick jerkiness that began to actuate Bob's movements that he was fast approaching the goal of his voluptuousness, and about to lose himself in the consummation of its triumph. In another minute the anticipation had become a reality; he gave a final sharp thrust and stopped dead, while his weapon, trembling under the forceful ardour he had infused into it, halted in momentary suspense and then threw off its charge of living essence into my expectant mouth. The short education I had received had yet made me fully appreciative of the sensation, and I imbibed the draught with all the delight of the born epicure, which I have no doubt I was, although I had only just come to a knowledge of the characteristic.

On sitting up, we saw that Jimmy and de Beaupré were deep in the enjoyment of a mutual suck. We did not wish to disturb them, and as I had not so far had the opportunity of soothing the distressful condition under which I was now labouring, I said to Bob, 'Will you let me go in your bottom? I have never tried that yet, and I should like to very much.'

'Certainly!' answered Bob, and he at once placed himself so as to receive my attack.

Getting behind him, I advanced to his rear, and after, on his instructions, applying a little saliva, introduced my cock into his small, round orifice. Although it did not look very large, I found it yield much more readily than I had expected, and I experienced a considerable feeling of satisfaction as my member found its home in this warm sheath offered to it, the walls of which closed upon it with a pleasant tightness, without there being too much constriction. I at once commenced to thrust, and while doing so, put my hands round and took hold of Bob's genitals. His cock was a trifle damp and sticky, and inclined to be limp, having been brought into action so recently, but under the fostering care of my fingers it began to exalt itself once more, and I gently titillated it to bring it up still more. My own efforts, however, prevented me from bestowing more than desultory attention on it in this respect, and as my excitement became greater with every moment I soon almost ceased the action, all my interest being claimed by the circumstances of my own case. I bit my lips and panted with preternatural excitement, and heaved forward with such vigour that it seemed as if I must be piercing into the very centre of Bob's anatomy. He did not appear to suffer any discomfort, however, but evinced a desire to give me every opportunity of wreaking my will upon him, at intervals giving me an additional twinge of pleasure by a well-calculated contraction of his posterior muscles. At length I cried, with a depth of fervour in my voice, 'It's coming, Bob!' and as I gave one last thrust with all my strength, he contracted his bottom-hole again, imprisoning my cock within its hot folds. The action arrested the discharge for a second, but next instant I felt it shoot out and, entirely consumed and eaten up in a supreme attack of lustful joy, I sank down upon him, alive to nothing but the passionate, gnawing rapture that afflicted my generative organ, and flowed thence in flickering, unquenchable flames to even the most remote parts of my body.

I felt quite prostrated afterwards, and made a hurried preparation for bed, anxious to lie down and rest myself after the feverish dissipation, at any rate until I had taken the first keen edge off my fatigue.

The others followed my example, and we were soon all four between the sheets.

'I wonder who had the best time, you or I?' said Bob.

'It would be hard to say,' I replied. 'All I know is that if you came off as well as I did, you were all right. How did you get on, Jimmy?'

'Ripping!' said the duke enthusiastically. 'Of course, it isn't the first time Blackie and I have had a bit of fun, but I think that makes it all the better, as you know what to expect, while it is just as fine at the finish.'

'I don't suppose it's much to Blackie, though, after all he has been through!' I exclaimed.

'Oh! I don't know,' returned de Beaupré, speaking with all the *savoir fair* of a man of the world. 'You mustn't think I despise a little amusement among ourselves. If we could really do as we liked, we could have all the enjoyment in the world; only, of course, circumstances are a good deal against us. Besides, as you know from what I told you, girls can have as much pleasure as they want among themselves without requiring men's services, so why shouldn't we show that we can do without girls if we want to?'

'I've heard someone say just the same before,' said Jimmy.

Bob looked over to me and winked, exclaiming in a stagewhisper, 'Lord Henry!'

'You shut up, Bob!' shouted Jimmy, with a smile. 'I never mentioned any name.'

'Well,' said Rutherford presently; 'I suppose we mustn't expect another yarn from Blackie tonight.'

'No! you needn't,' returned de Beaupré, 'for you won't get one. I'm feeling quite hoarse as it is since last night, and I intend to go to sleep at once. Good-night!'

'The oracle has spoken!' cried Bob. 'There is nothing better to do, therefore, than for us to go to sleep, too.'

Accordingly, we all turned over, and were soon in the arms of Morpheus.

CHAPTER SEVEN

A Reprisal; and A Study in Flagellation

The next day being Saturday and a half-holiday, Bob proposed as we were dressing that we should go as far as the sea, which was only a matter of about two miles and a half from the school. We all greeted the suggestion with warm approval, and I especially looked forward to it, as I had never yet had an opportunity of looking upon the ocean.

During the morning we met Williams and asked him if anything had happened in his dormitory the night before.

'Davenport started on Elgar again,' he replied. 'He tied his hands behind his back, and made him stand up against the fireplace with nothing on until we had all undressed, and then he and Lawrence began to chuck wet sponges at him. I called out to them to leave Elgar alone, and then they turned on me, but I said that if they touched me I would shout till someone came, and that stopped them. They knew that they would get into a bother if anyone did find them out, and, seeing they were a bit funky, I got up and ran to the door. I held this open, and then told Benson to go and loose Elgar and put him to bed. Davenport got into a towering rage and called me frightful names, but I didn't care, only telling him that if he tried on any more nonsense I would be straight to Chadwick and bring him in, as we had made up our minds not to put up with any more of his bullying or let him keep on pitching into Elgar. He got quite white with passion, but Lawrence slunk back to bed and advised him to do the same, so we had our own way, and Elgar got some peace for the rest of the night.'

'You did splendidly,' exclaimed Bob. 'You're a little brick, Williams. If you go on like that you won't have any more trouble with Mr Davenport. But I'm going to have a talk to him myself this evening, and that will settle it once and for all.'

We had arranged to set off directly after lunch, but before leaving I saw Williams again. He had his cap on, and I asked him where he was going.

'Davenport said he and Lawrence were going for a walk,' replied Williams; 'and he told Sturgess and Benson and Elgar and me that he wanted us to come as well. He was very cunning, and mentioned the thing to Mr Chadwick, so we had to say we would go when Chadwick talked to us. However, somehow Davenport seemed much nicer to us all of a sudden, and he actually told Elgar that he hoped he hadn't hurt him with his games. I don't know what has come over him, but perhaps he sees that he has been going it a bit too strong. I hope so, anyhow, as I'm sure we don't want to make any bother, and if he only played ordinary jokes on us we should never say a word.'

'I shall be awfully glad if you are right,' I said; 'although it might be that he has got an inkling of Rutherford's being about to take the matter up. Anyhow, I don't think you ought to have any more trouble, after what you say. You don't know where you are going to, I suppose?'

'I heard Davenport say something about the sea, but I'm not quite sure,' Williams answered.

'Really!' I exclaimed. 'That is where we're going. Perhaps we might see you, then.'

Shortly after this we set out for our walk, striking across the fields and through the woods in a direct course for the sea. It was a beautiful, clear day near the end of May, the air was quite hot, and everything breathed of summer in this favoured part of the land. The trees were in full leaf, the meadows were sheets of wild-flowers, and our ears were filled with the song of birds and the babbling music of the many brooks for which 'fair Devon' is noted. Bright-coloured moths and butterflies flitted and hovered before us, and the multitudinous sights and sounds of the country broke in upon me with such a pleasurable effect that, combined with the happy freedom of the moment, the joy of existence forced itself upon my consciousness more keenly than it had ever done before, and I raised my voice in a merry, lilting song.

'Charlie is in good spirits today, isn't he?' cried Jimmy.

'Yes,' replied Bob with a smile. 'But he had better be careful how he airs his notes, or Mr Percival will be capturing him for the choir.'

On we went, trudging through the long grass and picking our way amid the gnarled and moss-grown trunks of the trees, until our further progress was barred by a rivulet rather too broad for us to leap. We walked slowly along the bank, seeking a convenient place to cross without getting wet.

'There is a lot of fish in here, I am sure!' said Jimmy, climbing out on to a fern-draped boulder that overhung the stream, and peering into the crystal depths below.

We looked, but only caught the reflection of the duke's face mirrored on the placid surface of the water.

'All I can see down there is you, Jimmy!' said Bob. 'I say, you chaps! He looks just like that fellow we were reading about in class the other day – Narcissus you know! who caught sight of his face in a river once, and thought himself so pretty that he couldn't take his eyes away, and then he fell in and got drowned.'

'Shut up, you ass!' replied Jimmy, trying to look annoyed. 'There you are! I told you there were some fish here; I can see lots.'

'Well, it doesn't matter!' exclaimed de Beaupré; 'we haven't got anything to catch them with, so they can stop. And we shan't get very far this afternoon if we are going to hang about like this.'

Not many yards farther on, the stream narrowed, and there were big stones in it which enabled us to step across easily. From here we met with no more interruptions, and Bob told us that we should soon get to the coast. The ground began to rise gradually towards the cliffs which faced the sea, but Bob took us by a path which led through a picturesque, winding gorge, carpeted with short grass and decked with a profusion of creepers and flowering shrubs, down which a tiny river ran in a succession of little waterfalls and rapids on its way to the bosom of the ocean. This turned sharply at the end, and we emerged straight on to the shore.

I could not help uttering an exclamation of delight at the unwonted spectacle. Before us stretched the broad expanse of the sea, its deep-blue surface agitated by a gentle ripple and shining bright beneath the beams of the afternoon sun. Behind rose a tall bulwark of perpendicular cliffs, their scarped and rugged surface ornamented with a drapery of lichens and climbing plants which found foothold in every nook and cranny. The arch of the firmament was above all, and I followed its translucent expanse right out to where on the distant horizon it melted and mingled with the deep amethyst of the sea. I was full of speechless admiration at the glory of the prospect. A wide strip of yellow sand separated the cliffs from the waterline and across this we raced to where the mimic wavelets plashed musically on the smooth firmness of the shore, and drew back only to cast themselves up again with playful sport. I had caught the sea in one of its gayest humours, and as I bathed my hands gleefully in its babbling margin, I found it hard to conceive that it had its terrible moods, too, although I knew that at times this coast was subject to fearful storms, when the great, foam-capped billows rushed in with a force that threatened to lay low the proud rocks themselves.

My comrades laughed good-humouredly at my new-found pleasure, and I followed them slowly along the edge of the water, noting with interest the many varieties of seaweed and shells that strewed the sands, the little crabs that scuttled away at our approach as fast as their tiny legs would carry them, and all the strange marine plants and animals that I now encountered for the first time.

Arriving at length at a miniature bay or inlet, in front of which a line of sunken rocks formed a natural breakwater, Jimmy proposed a bathe. 'It would be just splendid!' he said. 'It's not a bit cold, and it will be the first bathe of the season.'

'But we have no towels or bathing-dresses!' I objected.

'What does that matter?' replied the duke. 'We can easily run about and get dry. And as for bathing-dresses, there is no one else about – and I suppose you don't mind us seeing you?' he added, with a laugh at me.

I smiled in turn, and there being no further opposition, the proposal was carried. We quickly stripped, and were soon splashing to our hearts' content in the briny element, and throwing showers of water over each other in high spirits. Although I had never been in the sea before, I was able to swim, having been used to bathe in the lake at home, and the others were all experienced practitioners of the art. The water did not seem particularly cold, and we came out before we had time to get too chilled. After the bathe, we took to romping and running races on the level sands, and the exertion, united to the effects of the sun, soon dried our bodies. When tired of this, we sat down beneath the shadow of the overhanging rocks to put on our clothes again.

'I think we owe something to Jimmy for his suggestion,' said Bob. 'We should have missed a treat if we had not had that bathe.'

'I'm glad you have recognised my good qualities for once,' returned Jimmy. 'But, I say!' he added; 'doesn't the sea-water shrivel one's cock up? Just look at mine! You can hardly see it.'

'You haven't got much to shrivel up, Jimmy,' retorted Bob. 'But never mind! I dare say it will grow in time. And really! I can't see that it's much smaller than usual.'

'You needn't talk, Bob! I can see yours is just the same. Why, mine is three times as big as this, generally. Just look!'

Jimmy pressed himself forward for Bob's inspection, holding his cock between his finger and thumb, and as Rutherford bent over to make believe that he had to get very close in order to be able to observe it at all, Jimmy sent a stream of warm urine right into his face.

'All right! you little blackguard. I'll pay you out for that,' cried Bob, wiping his streaming features. The duke dashed away with a loud laugh, and Bob bounded after him. After a long chase, the offender was caught and brought back for punishment. Bob pinned him to the ground, holding his wrists with one hand, and then, kneeling over him, used his cock as a sort of hose and sent all the contents of his bladder in a hot, steaming jet over Jimmy's face and neck and shoulders, making him screw up his eyes and turn from side to side in a vain attempt to escape the stream. When Bob had completed his revenge, he let him go, and Jimmy ran down to the sea and washed himself.

This little diversion over, we set about dressing in earnest, and started on our journey again, making for a point not far distant where Bob said there was another gorge leading inland.

'You can get any amount of birds' eggs here,' said Bob, as we went along. 'Thompson and I made quite a fine collection between us; I've got a case full at home now. We had one or two narrow squeaks, too, in climbing about.'

We had nearly got to the point which Bob had indicated, when, on rounding a buttress in the cliffs, we descried a group of boys who were assembled just within the mouth of a rather large cavern.

'Look!' exclaimed Bob, motioning to us to halt. 'Isn't that Davenport there?'

'Yes!' I cried, 'Young Williams told me that Davenport and Lawrence had notified all the chaps in their dormitory that they wished for their company this afternoon, and he said he thought they were going to the beach.'

'That's them right enough!' said Jimmy. 'There is Williams in front, and I can see Sturgess and Benson; and Elgar and Davenport Minor are just behind. I say! can't we give them a little surprise?'

'Here's an opportunity for revenge, Charlie!' said Bob. 'They've fallen right into our hands.'

'What a lark!' exclaimed Jimmy, throwing his cap up into the air, and catching it again. 'What shall we do Bob?'

De Beaupré pulled Bob's arm, and drew from his pocket a box of paints which he was in the habit of using for sketching purposes sometimes, having a little talent in this direction.

'The very thing!' said Bob, pouncing upon it. 'Charlie, you shall have payment with interest of all that Davenport and Lawrence owe you. Won't they be wild! Now, let's get ready for the onslaught!'

'What are they doing?' said Jimmy, watching the group attentively. 'Look! they've got Benson down and are taking his cock out.'

Peering cautiously round the corner, we saw that this was the case.

'This is going to be a bit of fun,' exclaimed Bob. 'We needn't wait here any longer. Let's go straight up to them. Charlie and I will take Davenport, and you two can manage Lawrence. We needn't worry about the others. They won't interfere, and, in fact, they'll be only too pleased to see the tables turned. Now, walk slowly! Don't make a rush; and they'll never suspect anything until we have them nicely. Wait a minute! Have we got anything that we could tie them up with? That would be still better.'

'Yes,' replied Jimmy. 'I've got a couple of little straps in my pocket. They will be just the things for their hands. And your and Blackie's belts, Bob – they're leather; they will do splendidly for their legs. Won't it be glorious!' he added, rubbing his hands gleefully at the prospect; 'they'll be just like a pair of trussed turkeys.'

'Come on, then!' said Bob; and we boldly rounded the corner and made straight for the little crowd.

'Hallo!' shouted Rutherford, as we approached; 'where have you chaps sprung from? Who would have thought of meeting you here! I fancied we had the whole beach to ourselves.'

They roused themselves as we advanced, and Davenport and Lawrence released Benson, who hurriedly buttoned up his breeches.

'We thought we'd like some sea-air this afternoon, the same as you, I suppose!' said Davenport in answer to Rutherford.

'Yes! It's a treat to get to the seaside after having been boxed up in the country for come time, isn't it?' continued Bob, casually sitting down a little to the rear of Davenport. 'Have you been amusing yourselves?' he added, casting a sly glance towards Benson.

Davenport laughed, and Lawrence joined in with his idiotic giggle. 'We were just having a look at Benson's little concern when you came up,' said the elder boy.

'So I could see,' returned Bob. 'I say, Davenport! I don't believe you and Lawrence have ever shown us yours. You seem to have been having a display in that line. Suppose you oblige us now?'

I had placed myself by Davenport's side, awaiting the signal for attack. As Bob spoke, he caught Davenport by the shoulders and pulled him backwards, while at the same instant I seized him round the legs and gripped with all my force. Jimmy and de Beaupré had meanwhile dashed upon Lawrence with equal success. The suddenness of our actions had taken them by surprise, and, having had no chance for resistance, they were helpless in our grasp and sprawling on their backs like two turtles.

Davenport struggled desperately, but Bob had him in a firm hold. 'It's no use!' he said; 'you can't get away. Besides, there's nothing to make a fuss about. We're only going to do what you are very fond of doing to other chaps. There was Benson just now. And then, what about Powerscourt here? You didn't ask his permission when you got hold of him the other day, did you? Chuck over that strap, Jimmy!'

Davenport made one last furious effort, exclaiming, 'Shut up, Rutherford! Don't fool about!' but Bob did not trouble to vouchsafe a reply, and bringing all his superior strength into play, in a few minutes succeeded in securely fastening our captive's wrists together with the strap. This done, it was a work of little trouble to pass his belt round Davenport's ankles and buckle it tightly. This left us free to go to the assistance of Blackie and the duke, who, although they were able to hold Lawrence firmly, had not yet been successful in tying him. With our aid, however, this was short work, and in very quick time the two lay bound hand and foot and completely at our mercy.

The younger boys had stood looking on all this time without saying a word, but evidently not at all displeased at the new turn which affairs had taken.

'These chaps have had a monopoly of this cocking business up to now,' said Bob, with an exasperating smile at the prisoners; 'it is only right that there should be a little variety sometimes. I'm sure you have no objection, Davenport; nor you either, Lawrence, have you?'

'You have taken us at a disadvantage,' cried Davenport, extremely angrily. 'These straps are hurting too!'

'Oh, no!' went on Bob. 'I'm sure that is only your fancy. Well, are you quite ready? If so, we will go on.'

Davenport knitted his brow and bit his lips, but Rutherford still kept the same calm and slightly mocking smile on his lips.

'It's very kind of you, really! to give us this opportunity,' continued Bob. 'However, we won't keep you any longer in suspense. Let's start with you, Davenport!'

He leisurely knelt and proceeded to loosen Davenport's clothing, while that unfortunate individual frowned with vexation. He could do absolutely nothing, however, and had to submit with the best grace he could, while Bob, who was determined to make a thorough job of his undertaking, pulled his captive's trousers down to his knees and turned up his shirt, exposing all the middle part of his body. Davenport went a deep red to the roots of his hair as we all gathered round to have a look at him. He was not a particularly well-made fellow, being rather thin in proportion to his height, and his limbs were loose-jointed and angular. His cock was long and slender, with a disproportionately large and misshapen head, and his balls, which were fairly large, hung flabbily underneath. Neither was their appearance improved by the short, stubbly growth of ginger hair that exhibited itself around these parts.

'There you are, you chaps!' said Bob, glancing round at Elgar and the others. 'You had better have a good look now that you have a chance.'

They pressed forward, doing their best to hide their amused faces, and adding greatly to Davenport's chagrin. Williams boldly took hold of his cock, in order to examine it better, and pressed the skin back sharply, causing its owner to utter a sharp ejaculation.

'Stop it, Williams! or you'll be sorry presently,' he shouted.

'It's all right, Davenport; don't get excited!' exclaimed Bob. 'You'll forgive Williams, I know, afterwards; besides, it's only tit for tat.'

When all the youngsters had satisfied their curiosity, Bob begged them to clear away.

'What are you going to do, now?' asked Davenport, with some misgiving.

'Nothing much!' replied Bob. 'I'm only just going to decorate you a little.'

'Look here!' bellowed Davenport; 'I'm not going to stand any more. Just let me go, and don't fool about.'

'Oh, come, Davenport! you're not going to chuck it up like that, are you?' continued Bob, with an irritating look of entreaty. 'You ought to thank us for trying to improve your appearance; and I'm sure you will when we've finished. Now, please keep quite still. Be sure and don't move, or you will spoil the effect.'

Davenport's face darkened, but he saw there was no alternative but to grin and bear the ordeal.

De Beaupré fetched a little water in a shell in order to mix the paints with, and then Bob proceeded to display his command of the brush on Davenport. The latter lay with hot cheeks, and eyes burning with helpless fury, unable to move. All he could do was to grind his teeth while Rutherford went on to ornament his belly and thighs with rosettes and spots and fanciful designs in vermilion and green and indigo. His task took some little time, but when it was finished he stood up, and we all gathered round to see the result, while Davenport almost collapsed at this humiliation before those whom he had been accustomed to lord it over. He certainly presented a ludicrous spectacle, the various hues standing out in startling relief against his pale skin, while Bob had even circled his cock with bands of different colours.

'My word! Doesn't he look pretty?' cried Rutherford. 'I feel I have been wasting my time hitherto. I ought to have been an artist, and I am certain I should soon get into the Royal Academy.'

There was a sally of laughter at this, which made Davenport go still more scarlet, but he said never a word.

'That will do for him, I think,' said Rutherford. 'We will go and see Lawrence now, or he will be getting annoyed at being left out in the cold.'

We accordingly left Davenport to his reflections, and turned towards Lawrence, who had indeed been all this time a not unamused witness of his comrade's sufferings. He did not display the deep annoyance which Davenport had evinced, as we bestowed similar attentions on him, but treated the affair more or less as a joke, laughing a good deal in his aimless way as Bob engaged himself in drawing little patterns on his body with the paintbrush. In spite of his being a tolerably big chap, and not so very many months younger than Davenport, he had hardly a trace of hair yet, and his cock was short, although thick. The tickling effects of the brush were too much for the latter, and it refused to hang down in a becoming manner, but wobbled about half-stiff against his belly, creating a good deal of merriment among the onlookers, who administered sundry little touches to it when opportunity offered, in a sly attempt to increase its erection, so that when Bob had finished, and we all stood in a semi-circle around Lawrence, his member lay straight along his belly, pointing towards his navel.

After allowing us to enjoy the spectacle a little longer, Bob considered that we had done enough, and gave orders for the prisoners to be released. Lawrence immediately went to a little pool of water not far off, and damping his handkerchief, proceeded to clean himself, exhibiting no trace of annoyance as he did so. But Davenport's pride had suffered a severe blow, and he looked very black-browed and sullen as he went to follow Lawrence's example.

'There is no need to be cross, Davenport!' said Bob presently, after Davenport and Lawrence had cleansed their bodies and were adjusting their clothes. 'I believe you're pretty partial to practising on other people, so you've no right to be upset when the game is played on you. Why, Lawrence here has shown himself ever so much more of a decent chap than you. He's got the good sense to see that neither of you is in the position to make a fuss over the affair. It's all over now, so don't let there be any bad feeling. There's my hand on it.' Davenport took it, though without much appearance of goodwill, and Bob went on, 'There's one more thing, Davenport, that I should like to say. I've been told – it doesn't matter by whom – that there is a little bit too much rough play going on in your dormitory with the younger boys. You know, it's not fair to bully them just because they can't stand up for themselves! and there's nothing particularly grand in it. I don't want to say too much, but we are not used to that kind of thing at Percival's, so I hope there won't be anything more heard about it. You must see for yourself that it's not the right thing! I've never done it, and I don't care to hear about anyone else trying it on.'

Davenport muttered some words of excuse and explanation, but Bob said nothing further, and the matter was not referred to again, all of us starting on our way back in a body and on good terms with each other, even Davenport deeming it best after a time to thaw a little and mix in the conversation.

'I don't think we shall hear any more of Davenport trying to come it over the other chaps,' said Jimmy, after we had returned and were by ourselves. 'He's had a proper setback. My eye! what a figure he did cut – all green and red and blue; and what a sight his ugly, skinny cock was after the way you painted it, Bob! He's had such a take-down, he'll never get over it.'

We laughed at the recollection, and Bob said, 'Yes! it was rather a joke, wasn't it? And it has done some good, too, I think, for it has taught him his proper place.'

We rapidly dismissed the subject from our minds, however, and turned to pleasanter themes.

'Are we to have another yarn tonight, Blackie?' asked Bob, when we had got to bed.

'You chaps are playing me up pretty thick,' said de Beaupré. 'Well, I don't mind obliging you; but I'm not going to make it a long one this time. Let me see! What shall it be about? You know I was telling you of that Russian woman who was so fond of birching! Suppose I relate what I saw when I went to her place?'

'Yes, go on!' I said. 'That will do fine!'

'Well, one day my mother was going out; and I had her permission to call and see Cécile. I felt sure I should find her at home, as I knew that her general habit was not to go out until rather late in the afternoon. To my surprise, however, I found the carriage at the door, and she was fully dressed when I got to her room. "I had no idea you would be here, Gaston!" she said, after giving me a kiss; "I was going to call on Princess Gourkasoff this afternoon. Would you like to come, too?" Of course, I said yes and we started off immediately.

'Princess Gourkasoff lives close to the Champs Elysées and we weren't long in getting there. She's got a very big place, as she is awfully rich, you know, and the hall regularly swarmed with servants in wonderfully showy uniforms. A magnificent footman conducted us upstairs and handed us over to another one, who led us along a corridor and through an ante-room into the presence of the princess. She was a rather short woman, with dark hair, blazing, black eyes, and a nose slightly hooked; altogether, she had a very haughty and fierce appearance, and I could quite believe that she was a terror when she got into a rage. She had on a yellow velvet dress, and wore some splendid jewellery – in fact, she looked exactly like one of those half-civilised queens that you see pictures of sometimes.

'The room was a very large one, and furnished with great display, but what struck me most was the number of people in attendance. As we entered, the curtains of the doorway were held aside by two good-looking girls – Russians, I expect – in very handsome costumes, embroidered with beads and spangles. Two or three others were about the room, doing various things; and, besides these, there were four or five pages, who looked rather pretty in suits of pale-blue velvet worked with pearls and silver thread. One of these was engaged in fanning the princess, for although it was not at all a cold day the room was like a hot-house.

'Cécile introduced me to the princess, who smiled graciously but took no further notice of me for a time, occupying herself in close conversation with Cécile on some political questions, in which she appeared to take a great interest. While she talked, she smoked incessantly, a page doing nothing else beyond attending to her wants in this direction. She begged Cécile to have a cigarette also, but she smilingly refused, whereupon the princess merely gave a little shrug of her shoulders, and said, "Just as you like, my dear! Smoking is such a habit with me that I could not give it up; but I quite understand that it is not the same with everybody." I also noticed a little lapdog of the toy Pomeranian breed which lay in a satin-lined basket, and seemed to be a great pet, as the princess continually put her hand down to fondle it.

'I had little to do beyond eating some bonbons which the princess had caused to be brought for me, and felt rather neglected; but after our stay had lasted about three-quarters of an hour, the princess rose and said, "The usual parade is to take place now. Come, dear Cécile! I know you like to be present at the proceedings." She did not extend her invitation to me, but Cécile motioned to me to follow, and I accompanied them to a large room, thickly carpeted, but devoid of furniture, with the exception of a few chairs. On one of these the princess took her place, and we sat by her side, while all the attendants ranged themselves in regular order at the side of the apartment opposite to us. After a short delay, the princess called forward one of the girls, and said, "Katusha, you were guilty this morning of disobedience and carelessness, and must receive punishment accordingly. Olga and Xenia, will you please assist in preparing her!" Two of the other girls advanced, and the three bowed solemnly, which done, the pair last-named, in a slow and methodical manner, undressed Katusha, denuding her of every article of her attire. She was a splendidly fashioned girl, with full breasts and big limbs, and I felt my cock raise itself up against my thigh as I looked at her. She did not display any concern at being thus exposed before strangers, and gazed straight in front of her without flinching, careless of the fact that my eyes were dwelling with great interest on the white mound of her belly and her scarlet-lipped cunt with its surrounding bush of black hair. "Nadège!" said the princess to another girl; "bring me the rod." This was a long, slender instrument of whalebone, with a gold mount at the end, and Nadège went on one knee as she presented it to her mistress. At a sign from the princess, Katusha now stepped up and, kneeling down, repeated some formally framed sentences in which she expressed great sorrow for her misconduct, beseeching forgiveness and begging her mistress to chastise her for her fault. At the finish the princess held forth the rod, which Katusha kissed, and then, having bent over and touched the floor with her forehead, rose up and placed herself between Olga and Xenia again. They led her to an article of furniture fashioned something like a praying-desk that you find in churches, and supplied with cushions. On this she placed herself in a kneeling attitude, while Olga and Xenia each retained a hold on one of her hands. Having thus arranged themselves, Olga, who was the nearest to us, looked round to signify that all was ready and the princess got up and strode towards them. First taking a brief survey of the culprit's body, she raised the rod on high, and brought it down with a sweeping stroke on Katusha's buttocks, leaving a long, red mark on the whiteness of the skin. After a slight pause, a second blow followed, succeeded by others, a few moments being allowed to elapse between each, so as to increase the impressiveness of the ceremony. Cécile had told me that the princess was not cruel or excessive in her chastisements, but as I watched her I found it hard to believe this, and the criss-cross of livid lines that formed itself on the unfortunate girl's posterior gave me a distinctly uncomfortable feeling as I noted it. Katusha herself, however, made no cry or sign of distress, at which I wondered; her sole evidence of suffering any bodily pangs was a little tremor and twitch at each application of the rod. How many blows were administered I cannot say, but they must have mounted up to a tolerable number, and I was beginning to have quite an uneasy sensation at the length of the punishment, especially on the recipient giving vent to one or two little cries and exclamations, when at last the princess threw down her weapon and returned to her seat with a frown of weariness. Olga and Xenia raised Katusha up, and as she faced us I saw a trickle of liquid on her thighs. I fixed my glance more attentively on this, and the following instant I realised to my astonishment that she had discharged. I cannot tell you how amazed I was! It appeared that the rod was productive of pleasure as well as of pain, then! and the cries which Katusha had uttered had been extracted from her by her sensual feelings in the act of spending, and not by the stinging effects of the rod on her delicate cuticle. After she had risen she picked up the instrument of punishment from where her mistress had thrown it, and brought it to her, and as she came closer to us the traces of her emission were still more apparent to me, her distended slit being wet with spunk, which clung to the hair around it and meandered down her legs, while her eyes glowed with a sombre light as though she had not yet recovered from her voluptuous sensations. She made no gesture, however, which would in any way draw attention to the palpable fact of her condition, and the princess totally ignored it, merely holding out her hand to receive the rod, while Katusha knelt with unconscious grace and kissed the weapon, at the same time thanking her mistress in another set phrase for correcting her; having done which, she retired to the further side of the room, where she unostentatiously wiped herself and took her place among the others, but did not resume her clothes.

'Having been thus reassured as to the character of the punishment, I experienced only a sense of curiosity when the princess called Nadège up for correction on account of some trivial offence – I forget what – which she had been guilty of. She underwent the same treatment as Katusha, and Olga and Xenia again acted their part in assisting while the sentence was carried out. She was also a finely-proportioned girl – as were, indeed, all the maids, no doubt having been specially selected on this account by the princess from among the numerous vassals on her Russian estates. She appeared, however, to be of a more volatile temperament than Katusha, and took her birching with much less composure, writhing and uttering sharp screams, which only aroused the princess to a greater show of energy, so that Nadège's large, rounded bottom presented a mass of pink weals, crossing and re-crossing one another, ere the Gourkasoff had finished. After witnessing the result on Katusha, I was prepared for something similar in the case of this girl, and I was not, therefore, again surprised to find that her orifice had given down its liquor; but I had hardly expected it to be so quite to the extent that it was, for indeed, such a flow had outpoured itself that her thighs were literally bathed, and drops of the thick essence fell on to the carpet as she finally came towards us. This bodily state that she was in forced itself into too much prominence to be overlooked, and even the princess deigned to notice it, commanding the lass sternly to cleanse herself and prepare to receive a further dose of the rod for her importunity. This time, however, the castigation did not take long, the princess quickly tiring, while Nadège, when she advanced for the second time in order to give back the rod to her mistress and take her dismissal, did not on this occasion display the same want of physical control that she had before exhibited.

'The princess now called forward one of the pages, saying, "I am sorry, Ivan, to have to display great severity towards you, but after the warning you have repeatedly had, it cannot be avoided, and you must take the consequences! I trust it will have the good effect of curing your evil habits of laziness and sloth." The words sounded ominous, and I fell to wondering what form the lad's chastisement was to take. Two of the other pages, whom the princess addressed as Vasili and Feodor, were called upon to assist, and between them they quickly stripped Ivan of his bravery of velvet and silver. He was a handsome boy of about thirteen, and his figure was equally well made in its way as those of the girls, for all these Russians seemed to be of exceptionally fine physique. He had a fairly good-sized cock, and the hairs were just commencing to grow round it. It was not stiff, although I expected it would have been after the foregoing scenes, which had exerted a considerable effect on my own, but no doubt custom had used him to these spectacles. He kissed the rod, just as Katusha and Nadège had done, and besought the princess to punish him. Then he was taken to the middle of the room and stood upon a stool. I had noticed there two long chains, with swivel hooks at the end, hanging from the ceiling, and had been at a loss to understand the reason of their presence. The riddle was soon solved, however, for a strap was buckled round each of Ivan's wrists, and the chains were then fastened to these. The stool being removed from under him, he swung in mid-air, suspended by the hands, and in this position awaited the ministrations of the princess. Her previous exertion had in no way impaired her energy, and she wielded her instrument with no light hand, as it seemed to me. The unhappy Ivan cried and groaned, kicking with his legs until he swayed backwards and forwards like a gymnast, while the pliant rod, hurtling through the air, fell on his unprotected buttocks and legs in a smarting shower, his skin glowing crimson under the rapid circulation of the blood thus set up, while his cock swelled and stood out at right angles to his body. Towards the close, the princess shifted her stand, going to the other side, and applying some effective and well-directed blows on his belly and thighs, making him cry out with redoubled force, while his preternaturally-swollen member fairly curled upwards, describing the arc of a circle, in the stress of his anguish. At last the princess's righteous sentiments were satisfied, and he was set free – after he had made his act of submission and dutifully kissed the rod, being allowed to stand back in his place and do his best to calm his ruffled feelings.

'Next on the princess's list came two of the other pages, Vladimir and Dimitri. These were not made to go through the same course as Ivan, their offence being ostensibly more trivial, but, after they had undressed, and the usual preliminaries had been conducted, Vladimir was made to get on Dimitri's back, holding him round the neck, while the other grasped him round the legs, and in this way receive his castigation. This was certainly a much better method, I thought, than that of Ivan's punishment, and there was no doubt some amount of pleasure, it struck me, for Vladimir, as he wriggled against Dimitri's warm back under the princess's strokes; and I fancy the latter were not so severe, either, as in the case of Ivan. Neither did Vladimir let any cries escape him, but only betrayed his perturbation of body by pantings and writhings. Once again, nevertheless, I was not prepared for eventualities, and it was with a corresponding wonder that I observed, when the princess had ceased and Vladimir got down, streaks of moisture on the lower part of Dimitri's back. I at first thought that this was only perspiration, but a closer inspection, on moving a little nearer, showed me that it was semen, and I obtained a further and final proof by a glance at Vladimir's member, which was very much inflamed, while a drop of the white liquid exuded from the top, putting me greatly in mind of a lozenge-shaped pearl. I can tell you that on seeing this I almost envied Vladimir, so much did I crave to satisfy the longings of my own cock.

'It now came to Dimitri's turn, and he next proceeded to mount upon Vladimir's back. His chastisement was even less severe than Vladimir's, but he bore it not nearly so stoically, nor did it have the same effect, for, although his cock was very stiff at the conclusion, he had not spent, which was perhaps due to his being a little younger and less developed than his comrade.

'This finished the series of floggings. All those who had felt the rod were called up and examined by the princess to see that no serious injury had been done to their epidermis, and when she had satisfied herself as to this, she delivered them into the hands of Olga and Xenia, who rubbed them well with soothing ointment. The princess herself superintended the operation, and while it was going on I had a opportunity to speak to Cécile in private. I told her that I had been very much interested in what I had seen, with one exception, and I said that I thought Ivan had been very cruelly treated. "I think so, too!" she agreed; "but it would be useless to say anything to the princess, she is so arrogant – and it appears that he misbehaved himself very much, otherwise the princess would not have used the form of punishment which she did. She only has recourse to it in exceptional cases, I know, and I have only seen an instance once before. It is not an original invention at all: the ancient Romans used to flog their slaves in similar manner – only in their case it was much worse, as a heavy weight, which they called the *centupondium*, was attached to the poor creature's feet. But, as you have seen, there is as much pleasure as anything else in the punishments which take place here."

'The princess now returned to us, and we went back to the *salon*. She regarded me intently, apparently waking up to the fact of my presence for the first time, and more than once she seemed to be on the point of addressing me, but some little time elapsed before at length she beckoned me to her. Taking my hands in hers, she looked at me with a glance of approval, and, turning to Cécile, said, "Gaston is such a nice boy! I quite envy you your intimacy with him. I should love to whip him! Nothing gives me so much pleasure as to practise on a young and tender body like his." I was not at all anxious for the princess to display her prowess in the art of chastisement on me, and cast a warning look at Cécile, who replied, "I am afraid, Vera, that you must forgo your wish. I do not think our young friend is pleased at the idea. And I would not have you hurt him for worlds." "I should not think of hurting him, indeed!" answered the princess; "I had no intention to use anything but my bare hand. Really! I have set my mind on it, and must have my way. It is not much to ask!" I was of a different opinion, however, and as I saw the princess's meshes folding close around me, I felt minded to draw away and hurl defiance at her. The words of point-blank refusal came to my lips, but ere I could speak them the princess had fixed on me her eyes, and their imperiousness and daring shattered my force of will as with a blow. She was one of those individuals whose strength of character enforces obedience and enables them to carry out their desires against any odds. A desperate struggle took place within me to try and give vent to the powerful objections I had to her proposal, but the effort to express them altogether failed, and, conscious of crushing defeat, I was unable to offer the least resistance as the princess drew me closer to her and unloosed my trousers, her face keenly displaying her delight in anticipation of what was to follow. Even Cécile, whom I had hitherto regarded as my ally, failed me in this hour of need, and spoke no word of protest, but remained a silent and

interested spectator of the scene. With an impatience of action, the
princess soon had me over her lap, my shirt turned up, and my bottom
exposed to her enraptured vision. "You cannot imagine, dear Cécile!"
she exclaimed, "what a joy it is to such as I to have a virgin form thus
laid at my mercy." Her happiness was my ignominy, and I felt wroth
indeed with Cécile at not joining forces with me and so preventing the
princess from carrying out her design. But my reflections were cut
short by the shock of my persecutor's flat hand descending heavily on
my buttocks. The blows made me tingle and smart all over, and I cried
out and endeavoured to free myself. But the princess held me firmly,
and even Cécile, traitor that she was! came to her aid, and kept my legs
still. The princess continued her slaps, each one seeming more hurtful
than the last, and I writhed beneath the exquisite pain. At length,
however, a numbness set in, which served to counteract the stinging
sensations I had first experienced at each impact of the Russian
woman's palm; and presently a delicious glow began to make itself felt,
and gradually spread all over me. I don't know whether you have read
the *Confessions* of Jean-Jacques Rousseau, but if so, you will recollect the
pleasure he felt in being birched by his governess. I had read of this,
and thought it childish in the extreme at the time; but I now realised
that there was more truth in it than I had imagined, for my own
emotions were by now decidedly tinged with pleasure. My cock was at
its stiffest and added greatly to the sensuality which had come upon me,
as it rubbed against the princess's leg, while the shock it received at
every stroke of her hand sent a fresh shiver of delight through me. All
notion of painfulness had departed; the spirit of lubricity alone reigned.
I no longer pined for the moment of release, but submitted to my
penance – martyrdom no longer – with a sigh of content. My
lasciviousness knew no bounds when Cécile very slily put her hand
underneath my body, and closed her fist on my overheated cock. My
member worked in this as in a natural sheath, and she aided by sundry
judicious little pressures and well-calculated movements to increase my
joy. All idea of her treachery was dissolved, and I thanked her in my
heart for not allowing me to miss the good fortune I had encountered.
As the princess's arm rose and fell, I rose and fell with it, at each
downward motion striving to force my cock further into the warm nest
offered it by Cécile's shut hand. My breath came and went quickly, and
my jaws tightened under the ardour I felt. At last the human frame
could stand no more; my spirit was moved to its innermost depths and I

emitted an expiring cry as I melted into a delightful ecstasy. My member leaped about like a live thing as it threw off its charge of sperm, while Cécile tightened her grasp on it as the sudden wetness imparted to her the knowledge that I had discharged. My energy was taken away, and I now made no response to the princess's slappings. She no doubt gathered from this that her projects had been accomplished, for after another moment or two she stopped, declaring that she was overcome by fatigue. She and Cécile lifted me up between them, and the latter turned aside to wipe her moistened palm with her handkerchief, while my shirt, falling down as I stood on my feet, concealed the traces of my recent sensual agitation from view. "I thank you so greatly, Gaston, for yielding to me," said the princess, imprinting a kiss on both of my cheeks; "I owe you much for your patience and forbearance." I made some polite rejoinder, and then proceeded to refasten my attire, while the princess turned to Cécile. "This has been too much for me, my dear!" she said; "I must go to seek relief. Will you not come, too?" Cécile expressed her willingness, and immediately rose. "Gaston can amuse himself here while we are away," exclaimed the princess, but my friend took her aside and began to talk in a low voice. She was evidently using her persuasion on my behalf, for the princess finally replied, "Very well, my dear! he can accompany us. I should never have suggested such a thing myself, as it seems scarcely proper, but it cannot matter much, from what you say."

'Accordingly, I went with them to the princess's bedroom, where Cécile and I took our seats on a couch, while our companion started to undress herself. "I get all the pleasure I want in this way from my little Fifine," she said, looking down at the tiny Pomeranian, which I now observed had followed us; "she is a perfect treasure! always ready to oblige me, never sulky nor moping, and does not require to be coaxed into caressing me." "I am sure that she is all that you say, Vera!" replied Cécile; "but I have never had recourse to a similar expedient myself. Still, *chacun à son goût*! If you have a preference for it, I would not dissuade you for the world. Each person has a particular means for gaining pleasure, and 'Unity in Diversity' is an excellent motto." The princess had by this time let her petticoats fall to the ground, and, without betraying any hesitation on account of my presence, lay on the bed, pulling up her chemise as she did so. Fifine was apparently no stranger to the proceedings, for she immediately sprang up and, settling down between her mistress's legs, started licking between her thighs, wagging her tail with a pleased rapidity the while. The princess smiled with the greatest display of complacence, closing her legs on the black, furry body of the little animal as it nestled down to its work with a wonderful zest. "You have no conception of the power that a well-trained creature like Fifine can exert in arousing one's deepest emotions Its tongue has a length and slimness and a capacity of penetration that is unknown to the human member. I can assure you, my dear Cécile! that if you once put my words to the proof, you would readily agree with me. Oh, Fifine! you are too eager, my pet. Oh, oh, Cécile! I declare I am spending already." She twisted and tossed in her access of lust, while Fifine buried her nose still further into the recesses of her mistress's body, licking up with seemingly great enjoyment the emanations that issued therefrom. We advanced to have a closer view, but the princess was oblivious of our proximity, her hands clasped tightly on her breast, and her eyes turned upwards with a rapt look. The sight proved too much for Cécile, and after a brief gaze she dragged me back to the sofa, laying herself thereon with upturned skirts and imploring me with a glance to ease her agitation. I could not refuse such an appeal, and applied my fingers to the burning slit, but this did not suffice, and she besought me by a gesture to put my lips to it. I gave in to her implied entreaty, and brought my mouth to her orifice. She gave a long sigh of satisfaction, and pressed her thighs against my cheeks with deep fervour. It needed very little persuasion by my tongue to draw forth a copious discharge from her impatient fount of love, but this by no means gave her effectual solace, and she would not let me rise until I had assuaged her fierce passions by calling up further supplies from the inexhaustible wells of her being.

'When at length she permitted me to get up, I found the princess sitting on the edge of the bed and watching us intently. "I see you have a most devoted courtier in Gaston!" she said; "I must crave your pardon for extolling the virtues of Fifine before him. I should not have dreamed of doing so, had I known that you were so excellently served already. I begin to take a greater interest than ever in him. Will you not bring him to see me again, one day? It will afford me the highest happiness if you will!" Cécile replied that she would certainly bring me again when an opportunity arose, and I also told the princess on my part that I should be most pleased to take advantage of her kind invitation.

'Our stay was brought to a termination shortly after this, and, having taken leave of the princess, we drove back to the Avenue Hoche.

'There! My tale has taken rather longer than I expected, so you ought to feel correspondingly grateful to me. The meeting now adjourns. Good-night!'

Our attempts to engage de Beaupré in further conversation were unsuccessful, and only elicited exaggerated snores from him, so, as he seemed intent upon keeping to his resolution not to talk any more, we took the broad hint given by him and composed ourselves for slumber.

CHAPTER EIGHT

Glimpses from the Golden Age

I find that I have hitherto conducted my narrative rather in the form of a diary; but it is by no means my intention to continue in this manner, as I do not desire to make too great a call upon the reader's patience.

It may be objected, also, that my memory could not possibly be sufficiently vivid to enable me to pen a truthful journal of what happened a considerable number of years ago. This would be perfectly true, were I to attempt to proceed in portraying the events of my earlier years from day to day; but as regards what I have already written, I am able to vouch for its entire correctness, all the doings and happenings of my first week at school being impressed upon my brain with a remarkable clearness.

With regard to de Beaupré's tales, too, it will probably be thought: How can he retain such precise remembrance of these when they were not experiences of his own? In answer to this charge, I readily admit that no doubt the words and phrases have undergone some changes in the course of transcription by me, but I have endeavoured to retain, as far as my mind will serve me on looking back, the general style of the narrator as he delivered them to us. So far as the facts and incidents are concerned, these are exactly as related; indeed, to make sure of this, I submitted the whole, when written, to my friend de Beaupré, who kindly revised and corrected this portion of my work, so that I have the weight of his authority in giving an assurance of its authentic character. I also take advantage of this opportunity to thank him publicly for his valuable assistance.

At the end of a week I was thoroughly settled down at school, and certainly enjoyed it much better than home, where the surroundings were dreary in the extreme for a boy, particularly when my father's coldness towards me was taken into consideration. I looked forward with no pleasure to the long holidays which would ensue at the close of term, and I sincerely hoped that Jimmy would not forget his promise to get Lord Henry to extend an invitation to me to visit him, for I had little doubt that my parent would consent to let me go, as in general he was only too anxious to have me away from his sight.

In the daytime the varied duties and pastimes of school gave plenty to occupy my attention and interest. I was not lacking in intelligence, and took considerable pleasure in my work, acquitting myself very creditably, and much to the satisfaction of the masters, who made extremely favourable reports on my progress, as I learned later.

The evenings after retiring to the dormitory were taken up as before, alternately with story-telling and more exciting enjoyments, but I shall not weary the reader any further with a minute recital of our doings, and will only stop to give one or two instances which occur more particularly to me.

One night de Beaupré was more at a loss than usual to suggest a scheme for us to pursue. But his inventive mind finally rose to the occasion.

'Have you ever tried the *bâton de sucre*?' he asked.

'No!' we replied. 'What is that?'

'Wait a minute, and I will show you,' he said. 'You remember in that hamper I had sent to me the other day there was a pot of honey, and I brought it up here and put it in my box, so that we could tuck into it whenever we felt inclined. Well, thinking of that put the idea into my head.'

He fetched the pot, and said, 'Now, Bob! you are the eldest, so we will start with you. Lie on the bed!'

Bob did as he was bidden, and de Beaupré then took out some of the honey with a spoon and smeared it on Rutherford's cock.

'There you are! That's the *bâton de sucre*!' exclaimed Blackie. 'Cécile told me how the Parisian *cocottes* do this sometimes; they are very fond of these sugar-sticks. Come along, Charlie! You can have the honour of the first trial.'

I went forward, laughing at the quaint conceit, and applied myself to the task of sucking the sweet morsel. It was a peculiar sensation, altogether, and the novelty of the idea tickled my fancy greatly. I could not help feeling amused as I licked the sugary stuff from off Bob's body, the warmth of which had imparted a strange and indescribable flavour to it. The substance had slowly run down over the column of his member on to his balls, and I released his cock, so as to bestow attention to these lower parts, stopping the flow with my tongue just as it got between his legs and in dangerous closeness to the sheet. When I had saved the situation thus, I returned to his genital organ, which I again took in my mouth, and under the heat so set up, it rapidly increased its already dominant erectness. My lips adhered to the glutinous skin, and seemed to give me redoubled power of suction, and I felt sure that I should soon bring forth an upward flow from the reservoir within. De Beaupré was impatient, however, and presently said, "Haven't you made him come yet, Charlie? Here, hold up a minute! This will do it, I think." I lifted my head and held Bob's member upright, while Blackie dropped a huge clot of honey right on the uncovered knob. I watched it for a moment until it had settled into a smooth and even coat over the distended head, and then once more put my mouth to the latter, rolling my tongue over its surface in the act of removing the stuff that overspread it. The unmistakable aroma pertaining to the human generative parts permeated it, and had an effect on the senses like alcohol on the brain. I appeared to be drinking in the distilled essence of sensuality, so that I might be said to be literally tasting voluptuousness. The effect upon Bob was equally keen, as was attested by his actions, for he squirmed with pleasure under the ardour I was devoting to him, especially as I could not travel with my tongue in the usual ease over his member, the stickiness of the skin preventing me, so that I was constrained to exert more than ordinary force in sucking, and had constantly to apply my natural moisture in order to assist matters. I also set my hands to work on his balls and the base of his cock, which materially aided operations. The anticipated development ensued in good time, and with a rush his sperm emptied itself into my ready mouth. A *soupçon* of the honey was mingled with it as it touched my palate, so that it was a truly nectarous draught that finally found its way down my throat.

Both Bob and I voted the *bâton de sucre* a great success, and a general trial of it was made all round. De Beaupré employed the method on Jimmy, and afterwards the latter devoted himself to making the experiment on me, while Blackie reserved himself until the last for Bob's benefit. In Jimmy's case and in mine, a liberal application of honey was needed before we were taken up into the regions of joy. Indeed, there was barely anything left in the pot when we had finished, but it had well served its purpose, so we did not deem it wasted. Altogether, it had a remarkable effect in increasing one's sensations, as I was well able to testify, and we were unanimously of the opinion that the whole proceedings added yet another sprig of bay to de Beaupré's crown.

We heard of no more trouble in connection with Davenport, and our meting out of ready justice to him had apparently had a salutary effect. He and Lawrence had not only refrained from attempting to ride rough-shod over the juniors, but for quite a considerable time had not even the heart to perpetrate even the mildest form of joking upon them. After a space, a degree of assurance returned to them, but exhibited itself in a very modest way. Williams used to keep us pretty well posted as to what happened in his dormitory, but we never ascertained that anything took place which could not be undergone in a good-tempered spirit. Davenport and his chum would occasionally bring into play their propensity for looking at a youngster's private parts, but they imposed no further terrors than this, and their victims soon recovered themselves after these trifling indignities.

One day I was taking a bath, and had not locked the door of the bathroom. While I was in the midst of my ablutions, Davenport came in. Although I was on speaking terms with him now, our acquaintance was not an intimate one, and, in fact, never gained this status as long as we were together. I therefore felt no particular pleasure at his appearance, but the feeling was not exactly reciprocated, judging by Davenport's actions, for he cast upon me what he no doubt intended to be an engaging smile, and began to undress. Although I did not care for him, and liked his company less in such circumstances, I had to bear with his presence, as I naturally could not order him out, for if I were to do so it was scarcely likely he would go, nor was I capable of turning him out by force – a thing which I certainly should not have tried to do in any case, as it would only have been provocative of an outburst of resentment towards me. My sole plan, then, was to finish as quickly as possible, and with this object I hurried on with my wash. Even in this, however, I was frustrated, for he had only his dressing-gown and slippers on. It did not take him two seconds to divest himself of these, and next moment he had stepped into the bath and stood over me. I rose to get out and give him entire possession, but he did not mean me to do so, and proceeded to show some little playfulness, seizing me by the shoulders and endeavouring to force me back to a sitting position again. I protested that I had finished, but he urged me to remain a little longer. I explained that I was anxious to dress quickly, as I had something I particularly wanted to do, but he continued his persuasions. Finding I was firm, he did not press me again, but put his hand down and took hold of my cock. I pushed him away, but he only laughed and returned to the assault. I covered my thighs with my hand, and made an effort to step out, whereupon he took me by the arm and drew my attention to his own member. I had never seen it since that time which I have already put on record. It was quite stiff now, but looked uglier than ever in its excited condition.

'Let's have a frig, Powerscourt!' he said, trying to pull one of my hands towards his organ; but I repelled his overtures, the suggestion not presenting itself at all favourably to my mind.

'Go on!' he continued. 'I'll do you, if you do me.'

But I declined.

'Yes; do!' he went on. 'Don't be a muff! You've done it before, haven't you?'

'Yes,' I said. 'I know what you mean. But I don't care about it much. I'm in a hurry, too, really!' I got one leg over the side of the bath, and as he saw that it was no use making any further endeavour to engage my services, he exclaimed in an off-hand manner, 'Very well! If you won't, you won't! That settles it. I'll do it myself, then.'

He stood up and began to rub his cock quickly with one hand. I proceeded to dry myself and dress, but took a casual look at him now and then, being unable to resist the inclination. I could never have brought myself to engage in this sort of practice with him, the notion was too distasteful to me, but if he chose to operate upon himself, I saw no reason why I should not take advantage of the opportunity to watch his procedure. He finished before I had completed dressing, and called out to me just before he was about to discharge, 'Here it comes, Powerscourt!' I should not have been human if I had refrained from turning my eyes in his direction. Indeed, I did more than this, for I stepped closer in order to see the denouement. Davenport gave a last quick rub, and then directed his cock straight before him, thrusting out his belly as he did so. A drop of white shot out and fell into the water below, while a little further liquid followed more gently, and slowly dripped off the end of his member.

'That was a good lot, wasn't it?' he cried, turning to me.

I assented, but made no further comment, and he pursued, 'Why don't you let me have a go on you? It won't hurt, and everybody does it.'

'It isn't that!' I replied. 'I know what it is like, but a chap doesn't always feel up to doing it. I'm sure I couldn't manage to make anything come now. And Rutherford is waiting for me, so I must make haste. We'll leave it till another time.'

'All right! just as you like,' he said, and dropped down into the water. I lost no time in completing my preparations for departure, and hurried away as soon as I was ready, glad to escape from his society, for I cherished an unconquerable antipathy to him, which had seemed to arise the first moment we met. Some people have this effect on one. You take a dislike to them, which is never overcome, and yet you cannot give a very definite reason for the feeling. Davenport had never done me any particular harm, and lately had striven to ingratiate himself with me; but it was no use: I could not bring myself to be on really friendly terms with him. It was a case of Dr Fell – 'I do not like thee, Dr Fell; the reason why I cannot tell; but this I know and know full well: I do not like thee, Dr Fell.'

I told Williams of what had passed, and asked him whether he had ever seen Davenport do such a thing before.

'Oh, yes!' he said. 'He and Lawrence have done it once or twice, up in the dormitory. I didn't like to mention it before, as they told us not to, and I never heard you say a word about anything of the sort.'

I ignored this remark, and made no reply, thinking it best not to let him know too much; presently he continued, 'He asked Sturgess to get into bed with him one night, and I could see they were doing something; they had the clothes over them, but I was sure Sturgess was pulling Davenport's cock – in fact, he told me so next day. Davenport wanted me to come in with him another time, but I wouldn't. And one night he and Lawrence got hold of Benson, and made his cock stiff, and then started to rub it up and down. He made no end of a fuss, but I don't think they were able to get anything to come. It's sticky stuff, isn't it? Davenport showed it to me once, and I touched it. It was awfully funny, and something like cream. I tried to make some the other day, when I was in the privy. I got a very rummy sensation, but nothing came, although I did my best to make it, and squeezed the end of my thing until I hurt myself.'

'How is young Elgar now?' I asked. 'I suppose he gets on all right since they have stopped their rough tricks on him?'

'Oh, yes!' replied Williams. 'He's brightened up a lot. He's not really such a bad chap. But he's got an awfully funny cock – all the skin on the top has been cut off. Davenport is always telling him he's a Jew, and he gets frightfully waxy about it – I expect he wishes his people had never had it done. Of course, he isn't a Jew really, but all Jews have the skin cut off like that. Rather them than me! I don't like the look of it much! Very often, if Davenport wants to badger him a little, or if Elgar has been a bit cheeky, he will get hold of him, and say, "Let's have a look at the little Jew!" Elgar flares up, and fights for all he is worth; but he can't do anything against two big chaps like Davenport and Lawrence, and they always put him on his back and get hold of his cock; they generally spit on it, or put some soap on it, or something of that kind.'

Happening to go to the lavatory one day, and finding Elgar in there, I remembered the above conversation, so I said, 'Let's have a look at your cock, Elgar!' He made no bother, but showed it to me at once. It was the first time I had seen a circumcised member, so I was rather interested in examining it. It looked rather peculiar with its bare head, and I cannot say that I was at all agreeably impressed with its appearance. It was too naked altogether, and gave one the feeling that it lacked something. As I got to know in more well-informed days, circumcision is a practice adopted by many different peoples, and is by no means confined to Jews. It is universal among Mohammedans, and numerous savage races in different parts also perform the operation, varying it more or less, according to their own particular customs, while a number of modern medical men approve of it; but such a mutilation would never commend itself to me. It not only detracts from the natural symmetry of the male organ, and therefore offends the artistic sense, but to my mind the absence of the prepuce lessens the sensual effects to be obtained by bringing the member into action, as the movement of the foreskin on the glans is in itself productive of a considerable amount of pleasure, while the deprivation of its natural covering hardens the knob, and takes away a degree of its sensitivity. This may be a mistaken opinion of mine, and I merely give it for what it is worth.

On two or three subsequent occasions, Davenport endeavoured to beguile me into giving him my company for the purpose of mutual indulgence, but I always managed to evade his solicitations by some plausible excuse. I received plenty of evidence, however, at different times, that he was fond of this kind of pleasure. Once I went to the water-closet, and just as I got there he came out, looking rather flushed. He passed me quickly, with a little nod, and when I got inside I could see plainly that he had been amusing himself, for a drop of semen was running down one of the lower panels of the door, while a few other spots glistened on the floor. Another time, when I was out for a walk with my usual chums, Jimmy crawled through a little gap in a tall hedge, in order to see what was on the other side. He was back in a moment, with his finger to his lips, and beckoned to us to come through. We did so very cautiously, and on penetrating the screen of foliage saw Davenport and Lawrence about a dozen yards away, sitting in a little hollow thickly shaded by trees. Both had their cocks out, and Lawrence was giving his companion's a rub. They had no idea that they were overlooked, and seemed to be enjoying themselves greatly. We watched until Lawrence had finished, and saw Davenport start upon him next; but we did not wait any longer, as we did not wish to disturb their privacy, not being desirous of the company of either of them.

There was a boy at the school named Lacy, who was a particular favourite of the assistant-master, Ferguson. The latter, who was rather popular with us, for he was of a very genial disposition and took a great deal of interest in our pastimes, was extremely fond of Lacy, and on whole or half-holidays frequently took him out, while he allowed the lad a free run of his study as well. Rutherford told me once or twice, confidentially, that he was sure there was something between them, and as I kept my eyes open, after this I noticed several little things which all seemed to point to a suspiciously close intimacy between the two. If Lacy were taking a bath, Ferguson would seize an opportunity to look in upon him. When the boy was confined to his bed with a cold, Ferguson was continually visiting his room. And for a whole weekend they were away together, supposed to be on a visit to Ferguson's father, who was a retired naval officer. I knew very little about Lacy, as, although he was an agreeable enough fellow, he did not associate very much with his comrades, most of his recreation time being spent with Ferguson, so I had no facilities for forming an opinion of his character. One evening, Mr Percival sent me with a message to Ferguson. I went to his study, knocking at the door and opening it almost directly. Lacy was seated in an armchair near the fireplace and Ferguson was in another chair near him. As I entered, the master rose to his feet hurriedly, turning towards me and picking up a book from the table as he did so. I delivered my message and left, but while I was in the room I was able to notice that the fly of Lacy's trousers was open.

There was nothing else to be seen but it looked strange for him to be unbuttoned, I thought. I told Rutherford, and he agreed with me that Ferguson must have been doing something with Lacy and I had taken them so much by surprise that Lacy had not had time to fasten his breeches up properly.

A few days after this, I found myself alone after tea, Bob having gone with de Beaupré into the neighbouring village to see about a tennis-racket which had been left there for repairs, while Jimmy had been condemned to do some lines in the schoolroom. Having nothing particular to do, I went into the boys' library, which was a room particularly intended for our use in the winter, or in bad weather when it was impossible to go out. We played bagatelle and other indoor games there, while the shelves which gave the room its name were well supplied with the works of Henty, Fenn, Collingwood and other authors dear to the boyish heart. I picked out a volume from among these, and sat myself down to read in a corner of the old-fashioned, deeply-recessed bay-window. The thick curtains which hung here completely hid me from view, so that anyone coming into the room might have thought it empty, unless they walked right up to the window. I had not been there very long before someone did come in. I did not move, being interested in my book, while I was not expecting any of the fellows would be looking for me. The newcomers, for it sounded to me as if there were two, did not approach where I sat, but took their places on a settee at the other side of the apartment. As soon as they began to talk, I recognised the voices at once as those of Ferguson and Lacy, and on raising my eyes I could see them through a narrow space between the curtain behind me and the wall. They evidently thought themselves to be the sole occupants of the room, and, not wishing to pose in the uncomfortable shape of an eaves-dropper, I made up my mind to declare myself. But I could not resist the temptation to watch for a moment to see what they would do. Ferguson was saying something of a jocular nature to Lacy, while he bent an affectionate smile upon him as he spoke. He held one of Lacy's hands in his, and presently bent forward and touched the boy between the legs. Lacy pushed him away gently, saying, 'Not here, Don!' – Ferguson's Christian name was Donald – 'Wait till we go upstairs to your room.' But Ferguson laughed, and said, 'It's all right! No one will come in here,' and, overcoming Lacy's very mild objections, he unfastened the lad's breeches and took out his cock. It was limp, as I could see, but Ferguson began to caress it, no doubt with the object of making it stand up with more dignity. I felt my position extremely embarrassing now, for I had missed the right moment to make known my presence to them, and to do so after things had gone this length would be a very delicate matter. Not only would it occasion a painful shock to Ferguson, but it could hardly fail to result in his viewing me in the future with no friendly feelings, and I was not at all anxious that this should be so, as I rather liked him. As may be imagined, I was in a quandary. The thought occurred to me to wait until they had gone, without betraying myself; but then, I could not tell how long they would be, and, judging from appearances, they did not intend to hurry, for Ferguson seemed to be quite content with his present task of gently handling and stroking Lacy's member, which was by this time begin-ning to erect itself. Then, again, they might come over to the window when they had finished, and this also would be very awkward for all of us. Thus immersed in doubt, I sat still, watching the pair, whose actions exerted a kind of fascination on me. But finally, affairs were settled in an unexpected way. Something tickled my nostril, so that I felt a sneezing fit coming on. I tried to stifle the inclination, but it was no use, and I had to give vent to a violent noise. I could hear the couple jump up with a start, and in another minute Ferguson advanced to where I was. He looked at me in a peculiar way, and there was just a trace of nervousness on his features as he said, 'I didn't know you were here Powerscourt! You kept very quiet.'

I put on my most innocent expression, and explained that I had been so deeply engrossed in my book that I did not notice anyone entering the room.

'Oh! it's all right!' he said, and there was a note of relief in his voice; 'only I made sure the place was empty, and it gave me quite a start when you sneezed.'

I was very glad that the affair, which gave promise of some unpleasantness, had ended in this manner, but I had made a discovery, and determined to put a leading question to Lacy when I had an opportunity. The chance came one afternoon when I strolled into the bathing-pavilion. There was no one there but Lacy, and after the interchange of a little conversation he asked if I would come on the river with him for a little while. The stream was broad enough to paddle about on, and there were one or two small skiffs and punts kept here for us. We got into a punt, and made our way slowly along with the current. It was a hot day, and we did not go far before drawing up by the bank beneath the grateful shade of a widespreading tree which threw its branches far over the still water, out of which tall flags and bulrushes reared themselves, while water-lilies floated on the surface, the white flowers and broad, green leaves adding not a little to the beauty of the scene. This cosy nook in the stream, with its dense walls of verdure and canopy of over-arching boughs made an ideal place for a *tête-à-tête*, the only intruders on our solitude being the dragonflies as they took their dancing flight across the rivulet, or an occasional bird soaring by above. The time and place were suited admirably to the opportunity I had sought, so, after some general talk, I said, 'How is Mr Ferguson? You seem to be jolly friendly with him. I heard you call him "Don" when you were together in the library the other day.'

He looked rather foolish for an instant, and replied, 'That was a sell, you being there! Ferguson went as white as a sheet when you did that sneeze. I was a bit flurried, too; of course, we both thought we were quite alone.'

'Yes! It must have made you feel rather funny,' I answered, looking him straight in the face. 'You wouldn't have been doing what you were, if you had thought anybody else was there.'

'What do you mean?' he said, shifting his seat and turning his head away.

'Oh, well! I couldn't help seeing what I did,' I went on, determined to stick to my point. 'I wasn't spying on you, you know, as I was there some time before you came in; so you can't blame me.'

'No! It was all Ferguson's fault. I told him what a fool he was, afterwards. He ought to be more careful. It was a good thing that only you saw us. I shall see that we are not caught again.'

'Ferguson seemed to be amusing himself very well. It looked to me as if it wasn't the first time, either, by a long way. Come, Lacy! you needn't be afraid of telling me. I shan't say a word about it; it isn't likely I should want to get you into a row – or Ferguson either, he's a very nice chap. Do you often do anything like that with him?'

'You saw so much, Powerscourt,' replied Lacy, 'that it's no use trying to spin any yarns to you, so I might as well be candid. You all know that I'm very thick with Ferguson. He took a fancy to me when I first came here, about eighteen months ago – I don't know why, exactly; and he's been stuck on me ever since. At first, he only used to give me stamps or coins for my collections, and lend me books, and so on; then he got more friendly still, and took me for walks with him. I didn't mind at all, as he was always awfully nice, and things went on in this way for a good time. He never lost an opportunity of having me with him, and sometimes he would take me to the beach for a swim; also, if he knew when I was having a bath, he would peep in while I was washing. I didn't care very much at first for the way he would look me over when I was undressed, but I got used to that soon, and took no notice of it. Then he gave me a standing invitation to come to his study whenever I liked, to do my prep, and I gradually got into the habit of going there regularly. He used to sit by my side to help me, and was fond of fiddling about with my leg or arm, and that kind of thing. Well, one day we were sitting together like this. I was doing a Greek exercise, and he was leaning over my shoulder, watching me. He had one hand on my leg, and gradually moved it close up against my thigh. I said to him, "Don't! You are tickling me!" and laughed. He laughed too, and dug his fingers into my leg, making me jump. "Are you ticklish like that all over?" he asked, and started to squeeze my leg about again. "Which is the worst part?" he went on, "is it up here?" and he got hold of me right between the legs. I went all of a heap, the way it tickled making me laugh loudly, and I tried to pull his hand away. "Don't make such a noise!" he said; but I couldn't help it, he was tickling me so much. He gripped my hands, and before I knew what he was going to do, he had pulled my cock out. His playing about had made it come on the stand, and as he looked at it, he cried, "How very rude, Archie! Just look at it! You ought to have better manners." He was not holding me now, so I put my hand on the front of his trousers, and said, "I've a good mind to take yours out, to pay you back for doing it to me." Of course, I wasn't really meaning what I said, but he took it up at once, and replied, "All right! you can if you like. It's only a fair return." This quite took my breath away, but when I looked up at him I saw that he was in earnest. I thought it was rather a good joke, so I unbuttoned his breeches and took his thing out. It was a whopper, and no mistake! and it was as stiff as a cricket-stump. He let me pull it about for a minute or two, then he suddenly said that I had better finish my exercise, and we both buttoned up again. I promised him not to tell anybody; but after that, it was the usual thing, when we were alone together, for him to get me to show him my cock, and he used to let me look at his as well.'

'Didn't you ever do anything else?' I asked, being greatly interested by what he had already told me, and eager to know more.

Lacy smiled a little. 'I can tell that you're not a greenhorn, Powerscourt!' he replied. 'It isn't likely we were going to stop at what I have said. Ferguson put me up to a lot of things on the quiet. The next time I had his cock out, he let me play with it and pull it about just as I liked, and I was in the middle of doing this when a lot of stuff came out, shooting on to the carpet and running all over my hands. He told me what this stuff was, and, of course, I wanted to try and see if I could make some, too. We have often done it since then. I dare say you do it also, don't you?'

'Yes!' I said. 'I know all about it; everyone learns about these things sooner or later. Is that all you have done with him?'

'You want to know a lot,' Lacy returned. 'Anyhow, there's no harm in telling you the whole story. We have only had a very few chances – once or twice, when I was supposed to be seedy, and sleeping in a room by myself; and then again, when I went with Ferguson to his home. At these times, Ferguson has got into bed with me, and fucked me between the legs. He wanted to go in my bottom once, but I wouldn't let him. He told me that he had often done it, or had it done to him, when he was a boy at Harrow, but I didn't fancy the idea somehow, so he never asked me any more. But, I say! I've got a cockstand after all this talking; haven't you?'

'I should think I have,' I answered, and showed him. 'Shall we have a rub? There is no one about.'

'I don't mind a bit, if you don't,' he replied, unfastening his trousers. He had a very elegantly shaped cock, not small, though not immoderately large, and with this added attraction, I could well understand Mr Ferguson liking him, for he was a handsome and graceful boy in every way.

I sat down in the bottom of the punt, by his feet, and commenced to finger his member, which was fully as erect as I could have wished it to be. After I had bestowed some gentle friction on it, I said, 'Would you like me to give it a suck?'

'What an idea!' he exclaimed. 'You can, if you wish. I've never heard of that before. Oh, doesn't it feel funny!' he continued, as I brought my lips into play; 'but go on, though! I rather like it.'

'Hasn't Ferguson ever done that to you? I asked, after a pause.

'No, indeed!' he replied, 'He's never suggested such a thing. I've not thought of it before, either. It's a very good notion; I shall tell him about it.'

'Don't you say where you learned it, or who taught you,' I cried, with an admonishing gesture. 'You mustn't tell tales, you know.'

'Certainly not!' answered Lacy; 'you needn't fear about that. But I believe you could teach me a lot – and I used to think you were such an innocent chap. It doesn't do to go by appearances always! Where did you pick up all these things?'

'Oh! I don't know,' I responded, offhandedly. 'I've done this kind of thing before, and you soon get to know a bit. Perhaps I had an extra good training, though.'

'I should think you must have had!' he said. 'You needn't suck any more. Wank me properly, now!'

I obeyed, and soon brought him to a discharge; in fact, a much shorter time than I had anticipated elapsed before the looked-for moisture sprang forth and damped my fingers. After his own affair had been carried to a finish, he turned to me, and by now I was quite ready for his ministrations, in which he showed himself an expert, and he watched the final result with great interest.

'I think there is not much difference between us,' he exclaimed. 'We both made about the same, didn't we? Now we have got to know each other better, Powerscourt, we can pal up to one another more. That is, if you don't object!'

'Not in the least!' I said. 'And my chums, Rutherford and de Beaupré and the duke will only be too pleased, I'm sure, if you join our circle – that is, whenever you can drag yourself away from Ferguson.' I added, with a smile.

'Oh! Shut up!' he answered with a laugh. 'Anyhow, I shan't forget what you have said, as it's ever so much nicer to be chummy together. Well, I suppose we had better be getting back now. It's time!'

After the breaking of the ice between us as I have related, Lacy often joined our company when we were going out for a jaunt together, and we found him a very pleasant associate. In particular, he made a confidant of me, and would inform me of all his adventures with Ferguson. 'I made him very mad the other day,' he said once. 'You know the privy upstairs, don't you? It has some coloured glass in the door, which you can see through if you get close up to it. Well, I was going there, and Ferguson came after me up the stairs. He called me, but I wouldn't stop; and he followed me right up to the closet. I saw him looking through the door as I was letting down my breeches, and, just to annoy him, I pulled up my shirt and began wanking in front of him. I knew it would upset him, and he begged me to open the door, and let him come in. I wasn't going to do that, and I just screwed up my nose at him and went on. He got in a frightful state, and I believe that he would have burst the door open if he hadn't been afraid of attracting somebody's attention. Anyhow, he stayed there with his nose up against the glass, pulling a long face, and drawing in his lips tightly, but I wouldn't have any pity on him and kept at the job until I had finished, calling out to him to watch as I shot. He waited until I came out, and began to blow me up, but I told him not to be silly, and he calmed down after a bit. Still! I got it back in the evening, for he kept on to me to let him wank me again; he wouldn't take no for an answer, and I almost believe he would have done it by force if I hadn't given in, he was so keen on it.'

It will be seen that in one way and another I found plenty of diversion, and I felt very contented with my lot. I could not congratulate myself sufficiently on having the good fortune to make such staunch friends, and both work and play were so congenial that I was as happy as the day was long. There could not be four better comrades than myself and my three special chums, and I do not think we ever had a serious dispute or difference during the whole time we were associated together. I often now go over again in my mind the fun we four had, and, if it were possible to fulfil such a wish, I would be glad to live through that period once more. There is a freshness and vivacity about boyhood that never comes a second time, once it is past; but fortunately, memory remains, and carries the recollection with us to brighten our afteryears. Charles Lamb says, in his *Essays of Elia*, that it is not good or advisable for grown people to associate intimately with the young; but I, for one, refuse to bow to the weight of his authority. I have always found the greatest delight in juvenile society, speaking as a man; and I can regard with some envy those fortunately placed persons, such as schoolmasters, who pass their lives in the midst of a perennial atmosphere of youth, and in so doing, are able themselves to retain a youthfulness of spirit even in advancing age. But I must not stop thus to moralise, only Lamb's words occurred to me as I wrote, and I could not let them pass unrefuted.

❧ ❧

CHAPTER NINE

The First Vacation

The end of school was approaching with quick steps, and as I heard all around me speak with joyful anticipation of how they would spend the holiday weeks, a spirit of gloom, which I could not shake off, would settle upon me.

Jimmy had, indeed, written to Lord Henry Wilmot, as he had said he would do, but only to learn that his uncle was away in the East and would not return for some months. The disappointment was a severe one to me, as I had settled my hopes on this visit which Jimmy had painted in forecast with such glowing colours, and now I saw nothing before me but a wretched vegetation of some seven or eight weeks at home, which would be all the more repelling in its sombre dullness, after my taste of the living fount of life at school. Rutherford, de Beaupré, Jimmy, all were in high spirits, and the more I strove to overcome my despondency, the greater it became. Though I tried to conceal my feelings, the dimmed brightness of my temperament could not but be apparent, and my companions did their best to console me. Bob extracted a confession from me as to the cause, and undertook to try and get me invited to his home, but he was not going thither for the first part of his holidays, as his people were in Scotland, so even in this direction I could not look for immediate relief.

At last the fatal day came when I had to bid farewell to my comrades, and I do not mind confessing that my eyes were rather watery as I found myself alone in the railway carriage on my way home. The word had no affectionate associations for me, and called up no pleasurable feelings as I reflected upon it. There would be no smiles to welcome me, and I might have been going into a weary exile rather than to my father's house for all the joy I experienced at the prospect.

A servant awaited me at the station, but his was a new face, and I only recognised him by the livery he wore; so that even my first impression was not calculated to dispel in any way the dismal forebodings of my mind.

As I expected, my parent's manner towards me displayed no change. Beyond a few curt words, he never spoke to me, and after the dinner-hour he retired to his library and left me to myself. The housekeeper, Mrs Denison, however, was more kind, and made me tell her of my doings while I had been away. I spent the remainder of the evening in her sitting-room, glad of someone to talk to, and she told me that Mr Percival had written a letter to my father, praising me very highly and stating how pleased he was in every way with my progress. Mrs Denison was, of course, perfectly well aware of how my father regarded me, but she had far too much tact to touch upon this subject, her only wish being to make things more comfortable for me as far as she was able, and I shall ever remember her gratefully for this.

The first few days of the vacation I passed in object misery, but then my natural buoyancy of character began to assert itself, and I took more interest in my surroundings, visiting all the well-known haunts of my childish days, swimming and rowing on the lake, or going for long rides. It is due to my father's memory to say that he imposed no restrictions upon me, and allowed all my wants to be provided for, although he held aloof altogether from my society. The smart little bay cob, Crusoe, which Jenkins, the head coachman, had got leave to obtain for me about twelve months before, was still in the stable, looking sleek and well-groomed; and I passed a good many hours on his back, cantering over the level grasslands of the park, or trotting down the leafy lanes, accompanied by Saunders, my especial favourite among the grooms. I was very popular with all the servants, the whole of whom inwardly sympathised with me, and blamed my father greatly for his unnatural disposition in my regard.

I received several letters from Rutherford, but, though I was glad indeed to hear from him, and to know that he was enjoying himself so much at the place in Perthshire where he was staying, haring from him only made me feel more dissatisfied with my own lot. The duke and de Beaupré also wrote to me in the friendliest way possible, and I warmed to them more than ever for their kind remembrance, but all the time I was very unhappy in my desolateness, and the days dragged on with leaden feet.

I think I should have sunk into the worst state of utter dejection, but for one or two incidents which served to enliven me a little, and afford food for interest.

One day, as I was rambling aimlessly about the house, seeking something to occupy myself with, I turned my steps toward the domestic quarters, which was the only part of the place where any signs of life were apparent. As I neared the servants' hall I heard sounds of a scuffle, followed by laughter. Curious to know what was taking place, I walked noiselessly to the door, which was ajar, and through the crack on the hinge side I could see plainly into the interior. The sight which met my eyes was one which I had scarcely looked for, but it was sufficiently interesting to make me remain watching it. Two of the housemaids had got hold of Joe, the boy who helped in doing light work below stairs. As I peered in upon the group, I saw the two maids pick up Joe and lay him on the long table in the middle of the room. He struggled to get away, but they were too strong for him, and held him down in spite of his resistance. Then, with a great deal of giggling, they opened his breeches and laid bare his cock. Walter, the under-footman, was also present, looking on with much amusement. He laughed as the maids unbuttoned Joe's trousers, and, telling them to wait a moment, he went to a shelf and fetched a pot of blacking. Dipping a little brush in this, he daubed it all over Joe's member, while the two girls shrieked with merriment as they kept him fast during the time this was being done. They released him the next minute, and he sat up and regarded his soiled body with a rueful face, casting reproving looks at his late assailants, who only replied with broad grins.

I did not wait to see any more, but the following day I overtook Joe as he was walking down the elm avenue which led to the lodge-gates, and I smilingly told him what I had seen. He coloured up, and seemed to be somewhat nervous, but I assured him that I had no intention of saying anything about the episode, and he soon got communicative.

'Those girls, Nellie and Alice, are always up to something,' he said; 'but I believe Alice is the worst. They won't let me alone, and are always at some games when they get a chance and Mrs Denison or the upper servants are not about.'

'Have they ever done it to you before, Joe?' I asked, wishing to prolong the conversation, and being glad to have found some sort of living interest at last.

'Yes! lots of times,' he replied. 'They are too fond of it. It doesn't do much harm, but I hate being pulled about by a lot of girls. You wouldn't like it, would you, sir?'

I replied in the negative, as he appeared to expect me to do, but I wasn't quite so sure in my own mind. Such a thing might easily be the prelude to greater events, and I flattered myself that if I had been in Joe's place in a case of that sort I would have got something back in return for my own discomfiture. I did not tell him this, however, as I was not lacking in a certain amount of prudence, and it is not well to lay oneself open too much to the observation of one's own servants. I therefore devoted myself to the encouraging of him to further confidences.

'It's nothing to have your cock taken out,' he continued, as I drew him on. 'I couldn't count all the times I've had it done to me. The boys at Warburton' – referring to the little country-town a mile or two away where he came from – 'used to think nothing of it. When we were playing in the fields someone would say, "Let's cock him!" and they would drag you down and have it out before you could say Jack Robinson. It was a regular thing at haymaking time, too, especially in the evening, and dozens of times when I have been going home I've seen chaps pulled down and cocked – and sometimes by girls, for they are just as bad as the fellows. There was a little path between two big walls just near one end of the High Street. We used to call this "Cocking Lane" because it was such a place for it. I remember sometimes two or three big chaps who were fond of playing about would wait for us boys when we came out of school, as a good many of us used to go through there. A couple of big fellows would stand at each end, and get perhaps a dozen of us inside. They would then close up, and take us one by one, and pull out our cocks and spit on them. But we got more careful after a time, and if we saw anybody hanging about there we used to take another way, which was a bit longer, but got us home quicker in the end.

'Alice comes from Warburton, as you know, sir. I was coming down this lane I'm telling you about one night, and came across her talking to two chaps. She was always a saucy girl, and she caught hold of me and said something as I went by. I pulled myself away, telling her to leave me alone, and started to run off home. She shouted out to the fellows with her to catch me, and they came after me and brought me back. "Let's pull his breeches down!" she said. "You'd better let me go, or I'll kick!" I replied. But the two chaps got hold of my arms and legs, and held me out straight. "There you are, Alice!" said one, "he's safe enough now. We'll see that he doesn't kick." With that the hussy clapped her hands, laughing, and took my trousers right down, unbuttoning my jacket as well. She wasn't satisfied with this, but she got the chaps to dip my bottom in a pool of muddy water, and while they did that she put her hand in it and splashed it all over my cock and belly. Then they let me go, and told me to get off as fast as I could. She hadn't forgotten about this when I came up to the manor, and she told the other people about it, for they were always chaffing me at first. I was in the scullery once, helping her to wipe some dishes. Walter was there, and she was telling him all about it. "I wonder if he's got the marks still?" she said. "Shall we have a look?" said Walter. "Yes! we will!" she cried; and they got hold of me and let down my breeches. Walter held me still, while she had a good look at me, and pulled my cock about with her wet hands.

'Walter is rather fond of her. I caught them one day in the pantry; he had his arm round her and was trying to get his hand up her clothes. I gave a shout to frighten them, and then slipped off into the servants' hall. When I next saw Walter he shook his fist at me, and swore he would pay me out. The same afternoon I went up to the stable loft, and found Walter there talking to two of the grooms. As soon as he saw me, he remembered about the affair of the morning, and made a dart for me. I knew what he was after, and ran for the stairs, but before I could get to them I was caught by one of the grooms, who asked Walter if he wanted to get me. Of course, he said yes and it was all over then for me. Walter told the others what I had done, making a lot out of it, so as to get them to side with him. Well, they undressed me, and tied me up to a beam; then Walter got a bucket of flour and water, and pasted me all over with a big brush. While the stuff was wet, they threw a lot of chaff and chopped straw over me, and this stuck to my skin and I dare say made me look funny, although I couldn't see the joke at the time. When they got tired of playing about with me, they made me wash myself; but, I can tell you, sir, I didn't feel comfortable for two or three days afterwards.'

'Does Nellie treat you in the same way as Alice does?' I asked, full of curiosity.

'She's not quite so bad as Alice,' he replied; 'but, I don't think she's very much better. You see, she hadn't seen me until I came to the manor. She's never tried to do anything to me herself, but she's always ready to help Alice. She doesn't carry on with the men, though, like Alice does. Why, one night, rather late, I saw Alice standing talking to one of the under-gardeners behind the stables. They didn't know anyone was near, but I could see them; the gardener had his thing out, and Alice was holding it.'

Joe's information served to excite my interest, and I kept a watch after this on Nellie and Alice. They were both strapping girls about eighteen or nineteen, and had a good deal of pertness about them, especially Alice. Beyond the time when I had seen them in the servants' hall with Joe, however, I never observed them to do anything of a like nature. I took particular care to keep my eyes open, as it gave me something to do, and prevented me from brooding over these depressing holiday times. I learned that both maids slept in a room together, so I made up my mind that it would be an amusing thing to try and have a peep at them when they were going to bed. I had no knowledge whatever from personal experience of girls, and was not a little desirous of having a glimpse of a female form. De Beaupré's tales had served greatly to arouse my inquisitiveness, and I would often lie awake at night, thinking of them and longing to have similar opportunities to those which my fortunate friend had had. The prospect seemed, indeed, a very remote one, but it would be a step in the right direction if I could only carry out my purpose with regard to Alice and Nellie.

Accordingly, I made my plans with this object in view, and taking the first favourable occasion that offered itself, I waited till the household had gone to bed, and then very quietly crept upstairs, with only my nightshirt on. The room which the maids occupied was on the top floor of the servants' wing and at the extreme end of the passage, an ante-room, used as a storing place for boxes and lumber, leading to it. The door of this was open, showing me that it was unlighted, and I stepped silently in, my bare feet making not the faintest noise as I did so. The bedroom door was shut, but I could hear sounds of movement within, while a ray of light came through the keyhole. I bent down, and put my eye to the latter. Nellie was standing before the mirror, looking at herself. Her arms were bare, but she had her chemise on, so I could see nothing of what I wanted. Alice was not within view, but one of the beds was out of my line of vision, so I concluded that she must be there; it never occurred to me as strange that Nellie should not speak, nor turn towards het companion's bed. I was so much interested in watching, and so anxious for Nellie to make some movement that would reveal something of her form to me, that I was deaf to all else, and never heard a soft footfall coming along towards the room. It was Alice, who had probably been to the lavatory or perhaps to speak to one of the other servants, although the former was more likely to be correct, as she was also in her nightgown and bare-footed, like Nellie. She was not aware of my presence until she was close upon me, but as soon as she caught sight of my form she gave a little scream. I was equally startled, and rose upright with a frightened bound. Alice did not faint or go into hysterics or anything of that sort; on the contrary, as soon as she realised that this 'peeping Tom' was only a boy, she seized me and, opening the door, dragged me into the bedroom, while I was too much overcome by the shock of my discovery to say a word.

'Look here, Nellie!' she exclaimed. 'What do you think? This little brat was outside, looking through the keyhole. I just caught him.' Then, as her eyes rested on me, she cried in consternation, 'Good gracious! It's Master Charlie! Why, I thought it was Joe!'

I hung my head abashed, finding no answer, for had I not been caught red-handed?

Alice quickly regained her self-possession, and, turning towards me, said, 'This is nice behaviour, Master Charlie! Aren't you ashamed of yourself to come and spy upon us like that? What will the master say, if we tell him?'

'Oh! we mustn't do that,' interposed Nellie. 'I don't suppose young master meant any harm.'

'That's all very well, Nellie,' continued Alice; 'but if you don't mind being treated in this way, I do! If I don't speak to the master, I shall to Mrs Denison. The idea of a boy like that looking at us just as we were going to bed!' and she tossed her head indignantly.

Nellie laughed, and said, 'No, Alice! don't let us make any unpleasantness. Master Charlie has always been very nice to us, and I shouldn't like to get him into trouble. I'm sure he will promise not to do it again, if we ask him; won't you, Master Charlie?'

With an effort I found my voice, and replied eagerly, 'Yes, really! I'll promise you! indeed, I will!'

'There you are, Alice!' cried Nellie. 'It's all, right. Let him go, and don't say any more about it.'

But Alice was not to be appeased so easily. 'It's not a nice thing,' she said, 'to feel that people may be looking at you through keyholes. I don't like it at all.'

'Don't be a goose!' exclaimed Nellie. 'If it had been one of the men, or even Joe, I should have been as vexed as you are; but I'm quite ready to forgive Master Charlie, as he's never been cross or unkind to us. You must too, Alice – just this once, at any rate. Do, now!' she added, entreatingly.

Alice reflected in doubt for a minute. Then she replied, 'Well! I'll let him off then, this time. But I think we ought to give him a smacking, don't you?'

'Oh, no, Alice!' answered Nellie in alarm. 'What are you talking about? You wouldn't dare to touch Master Charlie, would you?'

'Why not?' said Alice. 'He deserves it, doesn't he?' And she stuck to her guns. 'Don't you think you ought to be slapped, Master Charlie?'

'I don't know. Perhaps I do!' I responded, a faint smile twitching at the corners of my lips.

'That settles it, then! You must let me give you a slapping,' she answered quickly, and it dawned upon me that her indignation had been forced all along in order to lead up to this. However, I was unable to say anything, being glad to get off at any price, so I let her put me across one of the beds, and turn up my nightshirt. Nellie stood by, laughing, and from the way Alice joined in, I saw still more plainly that her anger had been more or less of a pretence. They both spent a few seconds regarding my bottom, and then Alice administered half a dozen light slaps to it.

'There!' she said, when she had done. 'I hope you won't ever do anything like that again, Master Charlie.'

She assisted me to rise, and, whether by accident or design, her hand slipped round my thigh, and rested for a moment on my cock, but I appeared not to notice this, and she did not make any remark about it.

'I shall stop this keyhole up,' said Alice, as I left them. 'We won't have anybody looking at us another time. Just fancy, if Joe were to take it into his head to do such a thing! We should never hear the last of it.'

Thus ended my adventure, in which I had come out very poorly, but although I was sorry then, I did not regret it afterwards, for when I got to a time of greater discretion I saw that I had done a very foolish action, and put myself in a ridiculous position. Still, I was rather sore at the moment that I had not carried out my intention. However, I did not make a further attempt, and determined to wait until a more fitting opportunity occurred for making myself acquainted with the mysteries of the female form.

I used frequently after this to have a talk with Joe, whenever we happened to find ourselves together, and at such times he would invariably favour me with more of his experiences. Before coming to the manor, he had worked a few months for a baker at Warburton, and he had something to relate about this portion of his history, as well.

'Mr Simms' – that was the baker's name – 'was a very dirty chap,' said Joe. 'There was another fellow, much bigger than me, called Billy, who worked for him too. When we were all in the bakery together, Mr Simms would call out to Billy to help him, and they'd get hold of me, lay me on the bench or on the floor, and take my cock out. They never got tired of this, and I believe there was hardly a day when they missed doing it. But once they put me on the bench like that, and undid my trousers. Mr Simms was laughing, as usual, and took hold of my thing. As he did so, I suddenly let fly, and pissed all over him. You should have seen him jump back. He was very careful afterwards, and never gave me a chance to do it again. In the hot weather, we often used to work with nothing on above the waist, and sometimes they would tie my hands behind my back, stand me up against the wall, and let my trousers down; and then they would amuse themselves by throwing little lumps of dough or yeast at me – they called my cock the bull's eye, and used to bet against each other how many times they could hit it. Mrs Simms nearly caught them at this once. She scarcely ever came down to the bakery, but she happened to do so this day. Mr Simms just had time to push me through the door at the other end before she entered, and Billy came out to me afterwards and undid my hands. Old Simms was afraid of his wife; she was a big woman, and often used to row him, but he never said a word back to her.

It wasn't only me Mr Simms used to play about with but he would do the same to any other boys who might chance to look in on us, as very often one would. I remember one time he got hold of a little kid called Johnny Brigson, and rubbed some stove-black on his cock. Little Brigson went away crying, and told his mother. She came to the bakery and went for poor old Simms like anything. She frightened him so much that he was all of a tremble, and in the end, to pacify her, he gave her a big bag of sweet biscuits to take to Johnny. He almost went on his knees to beg her to forget all about what he had done.'

It afforded me a great deal of pleasure to extract all these choice tit-bits of information from Joe, but so far he was the only one I could enjoy this treat with. However, fortune favoured me in another direction later on.

I was out riding one afternoon with Saunders, and our talk turned on horses. He was telling me something about breeding, and I then learned for the first time, that nearly all horses, except those specially kept for stud purposes, were gelded. At my request, Saunders explained to me the operation as he had seen it done, telling me how the animals were thrown on their sides, and their legs secured by chains, while the doctor removed their testicles, either by cutting or by burning away the connecting glands with a red-hot wire. I thought the practice a cruel one, but Saunders did not appear to regard it in the same light, saying that it was done with the best motives, and that stallions – as entire horses are called – were very dangerous brutes to have to deal with. He also informed me that not only horses but other animals, such as oxen, were treated in the same way.

'It doesn't seem very nice, Saunders, all the same,' I said. 'You wouldn't like it, would you?'

'Me sir? No fear! I would just as soon be killed straight away,' he answered.

'Have you ever had anything to do with girls, Saunders?' I asked, thinking it a good opportunity to turn the subject to my own purposes.

'Oh, yes! Of course, sir! Perhaps you haven't yet? But you will before you are many years older, I'll warrant.'

'Tell me something about what you have done,' I continued, anxious to keep up the conversation.

'Tell you something, sir?' replied he. 'I'm not much good at spinning yarns. What do you want me to tell you about?'

'Oh! anything, Saunders,' I answered. 'You see, I don't know much about girls, except from hearsay; and I should like you to tell me a bit of what you've experienced yourself.'

'You're in a lively mood today, sir!' he exclaimed. 'I thought you didn't understand anything about such things yet. If you want me to oblige you, I will; but I'm sure I don't know how to begin.

'I was always fond of the girls, from the earliest time I can remember. When I was a little nipper at school, I used to keep company with one called Lizzie Johnson. She was a merry little maid and we had some rare games in the woods. She used to put her hand in my breeches, and I would shove mine underneath her clothes. Of course, we were too young to do anything properly, but I would put my thing against her little crack, and we would rub our bodies together. We never got any further than that, and I've not been sorry since, as I shouldn't have liked to have worked her any mischief which I might easily have done then without knowing it. She left the village when she was about thirteen, and I've never set eyes on her since. I've often wondered where she is, and how she is getting on, for I was rather fond of her.'

He stopped, but I urged him to go on. 'Tell me of something that happened after you had grown up, Saunders.'

He laughed, saying, 'So many things took place that it's a job to think of any one in particular. When I was about fifteen or sixteen, I was very mad on finding a girl who would let me do what I wanted. But it wasn't so easy then as when I was younger; you see, sir, they were beginning to be afraid of the consequences, as I was a big lad, and very forward for my age, too. There was a Mrs Best came to live in the village. She used to do needlework for a living as she was a widow. I don't suppose she could have earned much at this, but she always used to dress pretty well and look smart, so I began to listen to the rumours that she earned money in other ways, by receiving visits from men. From what I could see, I fancied this must be the case. I determined to make up to her, and by always speaking a word whenever I met her, and so on, I struck up an acquaintance. One afternoon, I was walking along the street, and she stood at the door. I stopped to talk to her, and after a time she invited me in to have a cup of tea. We got very friendly, and she started chucking me under the chin and telling me what a decent-looking chap I was, as women will when they want to get round you. Well, the end of it was that I clapped my arm round her waist and gave her a kiss. She never minded at all so I got bolder, and put my hand under her petticoats. She was waiting for this, and when I had gone so far she made me come into the bedroom with her, where she flung herself on the bed ready for me. I never saw, before or since, such a crack as she had – and I've seen a good many, sir, I can tell you! It was that big I could have got my fist in, and although I was fairly large-made, youngster as I was, I could hardly feel the great thick lips as I slipped in. She enjoyed it all right, but there wasn't so much fun for me, and I made up my mind that I would look round for someone younger after this. She had taken such a fancy to me that several times afterwards she tried to get me to come and see her again, but I never did as she wasn't quite my stamp having had too much use for me. I don't much care about a woman who is always ready to lay herself down to the first man she comes across.'

A few afternoons from the date of the foregoing conversation I was walking by the lake in the park when I saw Joe coming towards me. I stopped to wait for him, and as he approached I noted signs of great excitement in his face.

'What's the matter, Joe?' I asked, seeing that he had something to tell me.

'I've been wanting to let you know what happened the day before yesterday, sir,' he said. 'You remember Florrie Jennings, the head coachman's daughter? Well, I've often had a few words to say to her, and we've got rather friendly. On Tuesday I had leave to go to Warburton, and in coming across the fields on my way back I overtook Florrie. She's very fond of a game and we've often romped together, so we started to play "touch" as we came along. When we got into Bonsor Copse, she came behind me and tripped me up, so that I fell on the grass, and she knelt on my legs and started tickling me. I pushed her off, and as she rolled over, her skirts flew up, showing her drawers. I gave her a smack on the bottom before she recovered herself, and then I held her down and tickled her like she had done to me. In her struggle to get away, she threw her feet up, showing her drawers again. "What fat legs you've got!" I said. "That's nothing to do with you, Master Impudence," she replied, with a saucy smile. Playing about with her had made me feel up to a lark, and I think she did, too; so I said, "Let me have a look at your thing, Florrie!" "Dear me, no!" she cried; but I could see she was laughing so I put my hand up between her legs and tried to get my fingers inside her drawers. She kicked about such a lot that I couldn't get at her, so I took my hand away. "Go on, Florrie!" I said; "show me yours, and I'll show you mine." After a bit, she gave in, undoing her drawers and lying on her back so that I could have a good view. I had never seen a girl properly before so I had a good look while I was about it. It is a funny thing, just like a crack; I don't think it's so nice as a cock, though! Presently, she got up and made me take mine out for her to see. It had got on the stand while I was feeling her, and she seemed to be very pleased with it, as she pulled it about. This made me feel very funny. I had heard about chaps putting their things into girls, and I asked her to let me have a try. She said I could, so I lay over her and put my cock against her crack. It wouldn't seem to go in, though, and when I pushed hard she told me I was hurting her, so at last we gave it up. I mean to have another try, however, as soon as I can get a chance to go out with her again. Anyhow, it's something to have seen a girl's thing, isn't it? And now she has let me once it won't be hard to get her to do it again.'

When we were sauntering back through the fine growth of huge oaks and beeches that clothed the banks of the lake, I said, 'Let me have a look at yours, Joe! I should like to see it.'

He did not display any objection, but immediately took his cock out and exhibited it to me without reserve. It was not very big, but his thoughts, as they dwelt on the events he had been telling of, had acted in such a way on it that it stood up firmly and proudly for all its small size. I took hold of it, and began to rub.

'What will that do?' he asked, as he watched my actions.

He was evidently unacquainted with the operation so I saw an added pleasure in store for me by observing the delighted surprise he would be certain to evince presently. Making him sit down on the turf, I squatted by his side, and set about carrying out the task I had undertaken. He experienced a new species of joy altogether as I went on, and expressed himself to this effect more than once. As the end came, he was carried away entirely, and his eyes sparkled, as he caught my hand.

'Stop, sir, stop! I can't stand it any more, really! What have you done? I can't tell you what I feel like.'

'You would have felt something of that sort if you had done what you wanted to with Florrie Jennings,' I said, endeavouring as I spoke to find out whether any liquid had come forth from his cock; this, however, did not appear to be the case. 'The next time you are out with her, and if you can't do anything else, you get her to do this to you. Don't you like it?'

'Yes, sir! Rather! Thank you ever so much for showing me what to do.'

I was on the point of asking him to perform a similar service for me, but on second thoughts, decided not to and turned my steps towards the house.

CHAPTER TEN

In Lutetia

The days passed slowly by, but as each one went I felt that I was nearer by so much to my liberation – as I viewed the reopening of school. Several weeks had gone by without my having received an invitation from Rutherford to come and stay with him, so I began to lose hope of a respite from this source, and determined not to dwell upon it in anticipation in order to avoid a possible disappointment.

One morning in the fourth week, however, I received a letter from de Beaupré, written from London, to say that in three days from that date he was returning to Paris, and asking if I could get permission to go with him and finish my holidays there. He explained that Jimmy could not accompany him, his mother wishing to have him with her, and as he was most anxious to have a chum to keep him company, he would be very glad if I could come.

It was a long letter, written in a very lively style, and went on to recount some of his doings during the holidays.

'I've had some fine times with my mother's maid, Mignon,' he wrote. 'She's a ripping girl! She helps me to dress, and so on, as my mother won't get a manservant for me yet, thinking the maid can do all I want. I don't mind a bit, as you may suppose. Mignon brings up a cup of coffee in the morning, and we always have a lark together then. She used to start by tickling my feet, but she soon got more daring, and would pull the clothes off and pinch my legs. Then, when I have my bath she comes in to wash me, as she says I am not big enough to do it properly myself yet. Somehow, my cock is always stiff at these times but at first she would never say anything, but just went on soaping and sponging me. She was very fond, however, of touching me between the legs and having a little feel. Naturally, every time she did this it made me laugh. I let her see plainly that I wasn't an innocent, and before long she got into the way of taking hold of my thing and stroking it. Then she boldened, and one day gave it a kiss. This fairly set me off, and I asked her to do it again. She wasn't the least bit bashful, and since then I enjoy myself all right with her, I can assure you. She's got a fine-shaped cunt, just the right size, not too big, and with plenty of hair. She won't let me do too much to her though, as she says she has to be very careful. She has got a lover, who is frightfully jealous, and she told me he would make a fearful row if he thought she had anything to do with another person. So I only use my fingers on her now and again. She wouldn't have me get into her, as she says she doesn't care about it that way much and even a boy like me might do some damage. She has hinted several times that I should give her a suck, but I have never done so; she's a very decent sort, but I don't quite think that I could bring myself to do that with her. I don't mind doing it to Cécile, but she is different. By the way, if you come with me, as I hope you will, I shall find a chance to introduce you to her. I know you will like her immensely.

'Now, be sure and come! And let me know at once. I have got my mother to write to your father, so he can't very well refuse.'

I felt a different being after I had read this letter, and my hopes rose at once to the highest point. I waited eagerly to hear my father's decision, which was the only thing now that stood in my way. At lunch-time, I watched his face narrowly, and I remained in a fever of excitement through the protracted meal. But at its conclusion my father sent for Mrs Denison.

'I've just had a letter,' he said, when she had entered, 'from the Princesse de Beaupré, mother of one of Master Charles's fellow-pupils, asking me to allow him to spend the remainder of the holidays with her son. He is to be in London on Thursday next. Here is the princess's letter! Will you please make all the necessary arrangements?'

I was overjoyed, and began to pour out my thanks, but my father waved me coldly aside and left the room.

The succeeding days I spent in the greatest impatience and I must have proved a considerable source of worry to Mrs Denison; but she, good soul! never murmured and took the greatest pains in making the necessary preparations for my visit.

The eventful morning came at last. Saunders drove me to the station in the dog-cart and I was soon on my way to London. De Beaupré was at the terminus to meet me, and we greeted each other in the heartiest manner possible. A brougham was awaiting us and as soon as my traps had been collected and put on board, we started off to the house in Hill Street which his mother had taken for the season. He had lots to tell me, and rattled away in his best style until we got to the door. His mother was in and he took me straight to her. She was a tall and stately woman, with a very kind manner and at once put me at my ease.

'Gaston has often spoken of you, and I am delighted to make your acquaintance. I am so glad he has made such charming friends. He tells me that you and the little Duke of Surrey and a boy named Rutherford are his principal companions. I know the little duke very well already, and think him a most engaging lad; and I am sure I shall soon be able to say the same of you when we know each other a little more.'

Arrangements had been made for us to leave by the night-mail, and cross the Channel from Dover. It was fine weather, and I stayed on deck most of the time with Gaston, who was eager to relate how he had been passing the holidays up to now.

'I was down in the country with Jimmy for nearly a fortnight,' he said. 'We had an awfully good time. They always put me up in the same room with him when I go there, so you can guess we had some lively games. It wasn't quite so good as the old dormitory for we missed you and Rutherford very much, but we did the best we could. It was beastly rot, Lord Henry being away from England, wasn't it? But I dare say we will have a chance to go there someday. It will be awfully jolly, if we do. I haven't had very much to do with Lord Henry, but I've seen enough of him to know that he's a real good sort. Jimmy and I often used to talk about you. We knew you would not be having much fun, and we would put our heads together to make up some plan for you. We had expected Rutherford would be having you with him, but he seems to be staying longer than he expected up in Scotland. When I heard from him last and found he hadn't been able to send you an invitation, I made up my mind that I would ask you to come with me, and I spoke to my mother, who agreed at once.'

'It was awfully good of you, Blackie!' I exclaimed, gratefully. 'I've been grubbing along in a rotten way at Woodbury, with nobody to talk to, and I can tell you! I was looking forward to going back to school again.'

'Well, you needn't look forward quite so eagerly now,' he continued, 'as I think I can promise you some enjoyment before we do return. As I told you in my letter, I expected Jimmy would be coming as well. But at the last minute his mother was very anxious for him to stay with her, as she was expecting a visit from some very old friends, whom she wished Jimmy to meet, so that meant I had to leave him behind. He was a bit sick, but what can't be cured must be endured, as they say. Anyhow, we had some fun while we were together. I shall have to tell you all about how we carried on. The last night, especially, we had a rare set-to, and I fairly made his bottom sore for him; he was so tired the next morning I had the greatest difficulty inducing him to get up.'

We arrived at Paris in the morning, and a carriage met us at the Gare du Nord. We drove straight to the Beaupré mansion in the Faubourg Saint-Germain, known as the Hôtel Foix, and one of the few grand residences still retained by their ancient owners in that historic locality. Here I made acquaintance with Gaston's father, the Prince de Beaupré, who saluted me cordially. He was a man of about fifty, of prepossessing appearance, his hair tinged with grey. He had a very affable manner, but I gathered the impression that he was quite a second person to his wife in the establishment. In this I was not mistaken. The princess was the ruler of the *ménage*, and the prince filled a more or less decorative position as her husband. He was always present when occasion required, but otherwise he resigned the reins to his better half; on the whole each went their own way and followed their own pursuits. The arrangement worked admirably, insomuch that they were a model pair at the times when they were together.

The French capital pleased me greatly, and de Beaupré diligently took me round to see all the sights. Nôtre Dame, the Jardin des Plantes, the Louvre, the Eiffel Tower, all came in for a share of my admiration; and I was not less interested in the varied sights of the streets, so strange to the country-bred Englishman. Gaston was given full charge of me and I spent almost the whole day in his company. He also took me out at night-time, when the crowds and the animation everywhere apparent on the brilliantly lighted boulevards at such a late hour filled me with astonishment, and led me to conclude that Paris never slept.

Gaston knew his city well, and was able to tell me much about the ways and customs of the people we met. Especially he pointed out to me the *cocottes*, those smartly-dressed women of pleasure, who could be seen parading the thoroughfares with a rustle of silks, and thronging around the fashionable cafés and theatres. He explained to me the system under which they were organised, and told me of the difference which existed between France and England in this respect. This was a subject as to which I had been completely in the dark up till now, but he quickly dissipated my ignorance, so that it was not long ere I was in the possession of as many facts relating to the matter as he himself, and felt quite a man of the world as I endorsed the practical commonsense which had dictated Continental policy. Gaston enlightened me on the subject of venereal disease, and its prevalence in Great Britain, due to the want of control persisted in by an old-womanly statesmanship. He seemed to have quite a fund of information on the question, and quite horrified me by some of the things he acquainted me with. I wondered, indeed, where he had gleaned all his knowledge from, but he said that he had read several works of authority dealing with the topic. One of these he procured and showed me, but a look through it was quite sufficient to disgust me, and after I had seen some of the ghastly plates I had no desire to read the book. It took some little time to shake off the horror I felt, but I finally consoled myself with the reflection that it was largely due to people's own fault if they contracted such terrible aliments; these might easily be prevented by exercising proper care.

Gaston had a good deal to say about the *cocottes*, and also pointed out one or two establishments of the class which had a considerable reputation. He told me that there were some places, besides, where boys were to be procured, as well as girls, and also that some women of fashion even gave such houses secret patronage, and made assignations there with men, while a few went to the length of engaging the services of the girls belonging to the institutions.

Some four or five days after our arrival, de Beaupré announced that he intended to take me that afternoon to see Cécile. I was naturally delighted with the proposal, and impatiently waited for the hour of our visit. At the appointed time, we set out for the Avenue Hoche, which we reached in due course. The concierge evidently knew Gaston, for he gave my companion a friendly salute, and informed us that Madame la Duchesse was at home. We proceeded to her *appartement*, where Marie admitted us, her face lighting up pleasantly as she saw Gaston. She conducted us to the drawing-room, which was large and beautifully furnished in the Louis-Quinze style, and here we found the lady whom we had come to see.

I did not think de Beaupré's eulogies at all far-fetched now that I was brought face to face with their object. The Duchesse de Régnier had a very charming presence altogether, with a pure, clear-tinted face, the paleness of which contrasted well with her dusky hair and eyes; and a figure whose every movement was instinct with grace. I must confess, however, that the serene and innocent expression of her countenance surprised me greatly, and as I looked at her calm and lovely features, I could scarcely force myself to believe that my friend's tales about her were correct.

She rose up as we entered, and, coming forward, kissed Gaston warmly. He then introduced me to her, and I held out my hand; but she disdained such a cold formality, and embraced me with the greatest tenderness, pressing her lips to each of my cheeks in turn, and saying, 'I am so charmed to meet one of dear Gaston's English friends. But your name, Pow–Pow–Powerscourt, is it not? It is much too dreadful for me to speak. You must let me call you Charlie, as Gaston does; will you not?'

I stammered out a polite rejoinder, overcome by the extreme kindness of her reception; but she soon made me lose all sense of bashfulness, and we were quickly talking together in the most animated manner. On Cécile learning that I did not speak French with very great ease, she immediately broke off, and thereafter made use only of English, in which language she could express herself with the greatest fluency. She seemed to devote herself a great deal to me, and I was almost afraid that her attentions would arouse de Beaupré's jealousy, but such an idea never appeared to cross his mind.

'By rights, another of my friends should have come over with us,' he said; 'Jimmy, you know! – I have often told you about him – well, he should have joined us, but at the end he had to stay at home to meet some friends who were coming from abroad. He was very much disappointed, as I promised that I would bring him to see you, Cécile. Anyhow, I've done the next best thing; I've got his portrait with me. There it is!'

He handed it to Cécile. It was an excellent likeness of the young duke, in a neat Eton suit, and Cécile murmured her approval.

'I've got something else, too!' cried de Beaupré. 'Jimmy would be in a wax, if he knew; but I don't care! I shall show you. It's another picture – only you can see more of him in this one. It was a snapshot I took once when we were bathing. He forgot all about it, and I never showed it to him after it was developed.'

It was a fine print, and showed our chum standing on the grassy bank of a lake or river. He had nothing on, a front view of his figure being most effectively displayed. I had a sort of feeling of suspense, as Cécile took the photograph and examined it carefully. It almost seemed a dreadful thing for Gaston to do, but no shadow of annoyance or embarrassment was to be detected on her face, and when she handed it back, she said, 'He must be a very pretty boy, if he is anything like that; but not quite so pretty as Charlie here. You know! I like you English boys very, very much; you are all so fresh and light-hearted, and so, so good-tempered.'

I knew not what to say in reply to these compliments, and I must have looked very foolish as I coloured up and faltered forth a few words in protest against such flattery; but she smiled upon me brightly, and assured me that she meant every word she said. I treasured up the episode, however, to recount to Jimmy when next we met, and I could imagine his indignation at having such a delicate portrait of himself handed round for inspection.

After a time, Cécile said, 'What do you say to a visit to the theatre this evening? There is a very nice thing at the Opéra Comique just now. Shall we go?'

I looked at de Beaupré, referring the matter to him, but he replied, 'Certainly! My mother knew where we were going, so it won't matter in the least if we are late.'

'Very well! Then that settles it,' cried Cécile. 'The thing now is to get the seats. I am so sorry, Gaston, to bother you, but Marie is busy this afternoon, and Julie is not in, so would you mind going to get the tickets. You can take a *fiacre* there and back, so you won't be long. Charlie shall stay here and amuse me while you are away.'

De Beaupré could not well refuse, and in a few minutes departed on his errand. When he had gone, Cécile reclined on a couch, and bade me draw my chair closer to her.

'I was at a ball last night, and feel so very tired today. You must therefore excuse me for lying down,' she said.

Soon her voice grew softer, and her eyes dropped, gradually closing completely. The fan she held fell from her nerveless fingers, and, by her gentle breathing, she appeared to have fallen asleep. In her movements, her dress had been drawn upwards, revealing the lower part of her daintily shaped legs, cased in black silk stockings so thin that the tint of the flesh could be seen plainly through them. How I longed to touch them! I could do so by stretching out my hand, but dare I make the attempt? If only I could be sure that she would not awake, I would go so far. I gazed intently at her face, but to all seeming she had sunk into slumber. I wavered in doubt for a considerable period, but, finding she gave no sign of consciousness, I lightly put my fingers on her ankle. Still she made no movement, and, feeling more assured, I moved my hand to her calf. She stirred, and I drew back in affright, but she did not open her eyes, and the only effect of her motion was to pull her skirts farther up, so that I could see now to her knees. My courage soon returned, and I let my hands wander very gently over her stockinged limbs. Their soft touch thrilled me. What would I not have given to have felt free to pursue my investigations further? But my heart was not bold enough to carry me to such a length. There was an invisible barrier which I found it impossible to break through, though every moment I hung on the very verge of doing so. Cécile's sleep was so quiet and peaceful that I left off watching her face. I did not, therefore, see her eyes open; but as my hand hovered about the bend of her leg, it was suddenly caught in hers. My blood froze at being thus discovered, and I trembled in a mortal terror, bending before the expected blow of her anger. But she only laughed lightly, and exclaimed, 'Oh, you naughty, naughty boy! What have you been doing while I was asleep?'

I hardly dared to look at her, but when I did so I was overwhelmed by the melting passion she displayed in every feature, and my fright evaporated. Though I hardly formed the conclusion at the time, perhaps a dim idea entered my brain, and I felt sure afterwards, that she had feigned sleep for the express purpose of inducing me to some such act as I had committed, and would probably have kept up the comedy longer, had not my backwardness exhausted her patience.

She turned her dark, liquid eyes full on mine, and repeated her question. I could find nothing to reply, and she continued, 'I am afraid, Charlie, that you are a more roguish boy than I took you for. Come, now! what would you have done, had I not awakened?'

I could only stare confusedly at her, mastered by the witchery of her smile; but she would not be content with my silence. 'Proceed!' she insisted. 'Imagine that I am still asleep, and I will forgive you entirely.'

My blood grew hot at this invitation, coupled with the way in which she pressed my hand towards her thighs, hinting to me in the most unmistakable manner to continue. Why should I not take advantage of the occasion? I asked myself. All that Blackie had told me of Cécile came into my mind with a rush, and impelled me to make the resolution. Here at last was the opportunity I had been anxiously waiting for: the chance now offered itself to become acquainted at first hand with womanly charms.

I hesitated no longer, but slowly advanced my hand towards Cécile's middle. I found no obstruction in so doing, and suddenly a tremor passed through me as my fingers touched her warm belly and entangled themselves in the long, soft growth of hair thereon. I groped blindly about, in search of further discoveries, at first without success, but then I remembered what de Beaupré had told me of the position of what I sought, and I moved my hand lower down. Next instant, I almost gave a cry, as I encountered the warm slit that formed the entrance to the regions of love, and as my fingers trembled timidly upon the lintel, Cécile pressed her legs together, imprisoning my hand between her burning thighs.

All reserve vanished, driven away by the intense excitement I felt, and I pushed her dress high up, so that I might gratify the sense of sight as well as of feeling. Cécile made no effort to deter me, and I feasted my eyes upon the novel spectacle without let or hindrance from her. De Beaupré's descriptions had been so vivid, however, that what I saw only coincided with the ideas I had already formed. Still, this did not prevent me from revelling in the freshness, and I was lost to all else but the wondrous interest of the moment as I viewed and felt her glowing, dark-fringed cunt, rounded belly, and the funny little clitoris, which latter was quite stiff as I touched it.

I was possessed with a desire to see her discharge, and with this object I tickled and rubbed her private parts in a way that I calculated would have this effect. She did not try to stop me, but opened her legs to give me better play. I was a little afraid of putting my fingers far into her sheath, which I was not yet sufficiently acquainted with to understand properly. She seemed to note this, and, taking my wrist, forced my hand so far in that I wondered where it was going to, and marvelled at the capacity of the regions I was invading. As she appeared to like it, however, I did not mind, and titillated her with such a display of energy that in a very few minutes her sperm ran out in a hot flow. Fascinated, I watched the phenomenon, while she crossed and uncrossed her legs in her lascivious joy. I had taken my hand away, so as not to impair the view; but she excitedly seized it, and pressed it to her quivering vagina, forcing me once more to caress it, and thrust my fingers into its dripping depths. I was not loth to continue, delighted at

the resignation of herself to me, and fully satisfied with this, my initial
experience of femininity. I dived and delved into all the recesses of her
body, while she tossed and turned in her wild enthusiasm. I had gained
no proper conception of a woman in her lust, when the fit was upon
her in its entire fierceness; and the frenzied intensity which overspread
Cécile's every feature made her look very different from the chaste-
souled being she would have been taken for when I first spoke to her.
She throbbed and flamed throughout in her ardour, raging in a fever of
lubricity; and this finally culminated when, with a cry almost of despair,
her semen once again burst forth in an abounding volume.

After allowing herself a moment or two to recover, she rose and said,
'You are a dear child, Charlie! I was ready at once to take you into my
friendship as a comrade of Gaston; but you would have won your way
there without his aid. Never fear for him! my heart is large enough to
hold you both – and your other friend, too, if he had been here as well.
Now, it is my turn, and you shall let me regale myself on your body. I
am dying to do so – for one with so lovable a face must, I am sure, have
an equally enchanting form.'

'But will not Gaston be back in a few minutes?' I asked.

'It does not matter! We will prepare a little surprise for him. But, tell
me! has my young friend ever mentioned me to you?' she went on.

'Oh, yes! He has often told me about you, and what a good friend
you have been to him,' I replied, equivocally.

'You little rogue!' she cried. 'I mean, has he ever given you a
particular account of visits to me? But I am not fair in asking you. I do
not wish you to betray your friend's confidences. It is quite sufficient
that I know you, and have you with me now. Come with me! and we
shall see what we shall see when Gaston returns.'

She took me to her bedroom, where she helped me to undress, and
laid me on the bed.

'Beautiful! Charming!' she exclaimed rapturously, as with burning
eyes she proceeded to devour my body. 'You are a little angel, and I
shall feel under an eternal debt of gratitude to Gaston for giving me the
privilege of your acquaintance. My only sorrow is that I will so soon
have to say farewell to you, but I shall hope to see you again, when you
come to stay with your friend another time.'

She kissed me fervently on the belly and between the thighs, and
took my cock in her fingers, murmuring, 'What a ravishing love-jewel!'
It was hot and stiff, and its erection did not diminish under her

caressing touch, especially as she artfully tickled my balls with a magnetic effect, sending deep vibrations of voluptuousness through my frame. At length she took it in her mouth and sucked it with an ardour that caused me to remember how fond she was of this amusement, according to de Beaupré.

She was in the middle of doing this, when we heard Gaston's voice, calling to know where we were.

'Stay here!' said Cécile to me. 'I will bring him in.'

She left the room, but almost immediately returned, followed by de Beaupré. He gave a look of momentary surprise on seeing me lying naked on the bed, but it quickly changed to a smile, as he glanced from me to Cécile.

'I say!' he cried; 'you have been getting on very well together while I have been away. I never thought Charlie would know so well how to pass the time.'

'I don't fancy Charlie is much in need of your assistance, monsieur,' said Cécile. 'And I think I ought to be severe with you, for I am afraid you have been telling tales out of school. But never mind! I will pardon you, if only because you brought such a dear boy to see me. Suppose you undress, too! I should love to see you both together like that.'

'All right, I'm ready!' he replied; 'it will be a nice prelude to the theatre. But you must join us in the same way, Cécile.'

'Indeed, monsieur! but you are very overbearing in your demands. However, if it will please you, I will do so; but it is rather for Charlie's sake than for yours.'

They both divested themselves of their clothes, and when they had reduced themselves to utter nudity they took their places beside me, Cécile being in the middle. The situation enthralled me, and I was transported into the seventh heaven. I could not take my eyes from Cécile, and I greedily drank in every detail of her lovely form, stroking her white belly, squeezing her plump thighs, and pressing her firm, globular breasts; while she in turn repeatedly kissed me on the lips and bosom, now and again turning to bestow a corresponding caress on Gaston, while her hands were occupied in devoting soft embraces and titillations to our respective members.

We spent quite a long time in these idyllic proceedings, and I was overwhelmed with delight; but finally Cécile began to hunger for more powerful sensations, our wanton play being insufficient to satisfy her passionate cravings.

'Let us get closer,' she said. 'Come towards me, Charlie!' and she turned on her side, facing me. 'You, as the guest of the occasion, shall have the post of honour accorded to you. I will deliver over my back to Gaston. No doubt, he will find satisfaction there.'

She drew me against her, and as my warm flesh touched hers I thrilled again. I took no initiative, but let her do as she listed. Finding I did not move, she put her hand down, and taking my cock, placed it against the hungry mouth of her orifice of joy. This done, she threw her arms round me, and squeezed me tightly towards her. As I felt myself sinking into this haven of happiness, a smile of rapture broke over my face, seeing which, she pressed her lips to mine in a long, sweet kiss. I had now penetrated into the arena of love; and my instinct told me what to do. Gaston, on his part, had not suffered himself to be neglected, but had forced an entrance into Cécile's bottom-hole. His lustful movements coincided with mine, so that Cécile was thus between two fires, being assailed both at back and front. The dual embrace filled her with the greatest excess of pleasure, and she gave herself up to us with uncontrollable abandon. Her emotions were raised to such a pitch that I quickly experienced another new sensation as my cock was drenched in her hot emission, but this only served to add fuel to her salaciousness, and she held me tightly, lest I should seek to disengage myself. On my side, the heating struggle, the rasping of her sheath on my member as it gaped and shut in its alternations of excitement, and the strong suction it seemed to be exercising on my very veins, were rapidly bringing me to a violent condition of amorous fury. I could tell, also, by Gaston's heavy breathing, that he was tottering on the brink, preparatory to plunging into the sea of consummated lasciviousness. Another downpour from Cécile's bursting cunt shed itself in torrid streams over me; in her madness, she seized upon my mouth, almost choking me with hot caresses; and this acted as the last incentive to my already overstrained body – I gave a desperate lunge, and then I felt myself eaten up as with tongues of living fire, pangs of exquisite delightfulness filled my entire form, taking away all power of volition, and I sank in limp exhaustion on Cécile's breast. She held me close, and while I lay thus, only half-awake to my surroundings, I heard Gaston cry – and his voice sounded to me as if it came from afar – 'Ah! At last! It is coming. Oh! don't squeeze like that, Cécile. I am overpowered!' and he, too, fell upon her nervelessly. But she only laughed at our inanition, and chided us mirthfully for being overcome.

In a little while, we regained our energies, and sat up, but our cocks presented a bedraggled and shrunken appearance, causing Cécile to seize them with a little gesture of derision. We could not, however, aspire to such heights of excess as she, and Gaston told her so in as many words. She dropped her raillery at once, and said, 'You must not take notice of me. You have both been very good boys, and I have not enjoyed myself so much for months. What a delightful afternoon this has been! I shall not forget it for a long time. You cannot imagine how glorious it was to have your darling little members in me at the same time – the sensation was too lovely to be explained in speech.'

We wiped ourselves, and then Cécile insisted upon sucking me. I was for postponing this, having scarcely yet recovered from my commerce with her; but she pointed out that she would not have a further chance, as it would be necessary to get ready for the theatre before long, so I had perforce to give way to her. It made my cock ache a good deal at first, but this feeling wore off with returning voluptuousness, and she kept at her task until she had made it come erect again; but the sensation was too intolerable, every stiffening tremor of the organ sending a deep, shooting spasm through me, and at last I had to beg her to stop.

'Very well!' she said. 'I must not overtax you. And you have afforded me such great pleasure that I cannot deny you something in return. I will go to poor Gaston now. See how patiently he has been waiting! He is a little saint, is he not? never to make a murmur.'

Possibly Gaston was possessed of more stamina than I was, but at any rate he seemed to bear himself better, and submitted to Cécile's endearing caresses for quite a long time. At length, however, even she deemed it advisable to cease, and we all three proceeded to dress again.

Cécile ordered dinner to be prepared rather earlier than usual, and while we were partaking of it, she said. 'Do you remember, Gaston, that place I once took you to, where we met Hélène and the others? It was a society, as I told you. I dare say Charlie knows all about it, too, but I will not embarrass you by asking whether he does. Well, there is a special meeting a week from today, and, if you like, I will take you both. No, Gaston! you will not need to pose again as my little cousin, Elise. The meeting I speak of is one of a particular kind, and is not of frequent occurrence; on such occasions, though men are excluded, boys are not forbidden; and, in fact, it is usual for a member to

156 THE MEMOIRS OF A VOLUPTUARY

introduce one, if she can manage to do so, but the conditions for the eligibility of these young guests are so stringent that it is rather a distinction to be able to bring one. You, however, are both qualified in every respect, so I shall be doubly honoured in having an escort of two. You see! it is necessary that they be well-born and attractive, and also discreet. Now, I can vouch for you as all three, so the rest is easy. Our rendezvous is not the place that you know, Gaston, on this occasion, but a villa in the environs. The boys always present themselves in costume, but I will make all arrangements of that sort. You shall come and see me tomorrow, and I will take you to my dressmaker; she will see to everything that you want.'

We spent a pleasant evening at the theatre, where the singing and scenery charmed me very much, although I could not follow the words to any great extent. On coming out, Cécile took us to supper at a restaurant not far away, and then drove us home, and bidding us goodbye, requested that we would come to see her at noon the next day.

CHAPTER ELEVEN

The Rites of Flora

In the morning, we were awakened by Mignon, who brought us coffee. Owing to my presence, she preserved a modest and respectful attitude, which extracted sundry whimsical remarks from Gaston, who tried to give her a kiss. But she drew back, exclaiming, 'No, no! You must not, monsieur. Monsieur Charles is looking at us.'

Gaston laughed loudly, crying, 'What of that, Mignon? You must not take him for a simpleton. You wait till you know a little more about him.'

He sprang out of bed and, rushing at me as I lay, seized my hands, saying, 'Here he is, Mignon! Come and have a look at him.'

Mignon frowned a reproof, but was unable to repress a smile, and at last obeyed de Beaupré's injunctions, and came towards me.

'What is the matter with you?' continued Gaston; 'why don't you pull the clothes down?'

'Oh! but monsieur, I could not,' she replied. 'Perhaps Monsieur Charles would not like it?'

'Oh! wouldn't he? You try, and see!' persisted Gaston, and, thus urged, Mignon did as she was bidden. The sight of my legs, as she uncovered them, further prevailed upon her, and she no longer exhibited any hesitation, but turned up my shirt with a little laugh, and placed her hand on my private parts. I curled myself up as she did so, but made no protest, and she played lingeringly with my member, finally giving it a kiss; but she then concluded that this was enough for the present, and threw the coverings over me again. However, it was a beginning, and spoke of more eventualities in the future.

By midday, we presented ourselves at Cécile's, and found her ready for us.

'We have not much time,' said Gaston, 'as we must be back for luncheon.'

She took us to the *couturière* she patronised, who made the necessary measurements, while Cécile supplied her with all the particulars she required. The confabulation was such a long one, that we got a trifle impatient, but it was over at last, and we made all haste back to the Faubourg St Germain.

A day or two later, Cécile called on the princess, and told her of the invitation she had given us, merely saying, of course, that she would like us to spend the evening with her.

On the day in question, we repaired to the Avenue Hoche rather late in the afternoon, and found Cécile impatiently awaiting us. After a pleasant hour or two, she took us to the dressing-room to be attired for our parts. Marie figured largely in this scene, being assisted by Julie, whom I regarded with considerable interest, recollecting de Beaupré's account of what took place on her engagement by madame. She was a decidedly pretty young girl, but was scarcely calculated now to give one the impression of strict convent breeding, for she tripped about in the liveliest manner, and displayed very much less reserve in her demeanour than Marie.

Cécile had made the most elaborate preparations for adorning our persons. Our costumes were of the eighteenth-century period, and I felt myself quite imposing when I had attired myself in a pair of white satin breeches, white silk stockings, shoes with diamond buckles, a white brocaded waistcoat, and a full-skirted coat of white satin glittering with embroidery of brilliants. My full cravat and ruffles were of the finest lace. My own hair was concealed by a curled and powdered wig, to the queue of which a broad ribbon was attached and brought over on to my breast. A brooch of diamonds fastened my neckband, and a collar, with pendant cross, of the same stones encircled my throat, while a large star blazed and sparkled on the left side of my coat. A light sword with jewelled hilt hung at my side, while Marie added the finishing touch by slipping some of Cécile's magnificent rings on my fingers.

Gaston displayed equal splendour in a suite of lemon-coloured satin, which suited admirably his dark complexion and jet-black hair and eyes. The coat was richly worked with pearls and brilliants, which also profusely ornamented his long, flowered waistcoat His peruke was tied with a black ribbon, and Cécile's store of jewellery was again overhauled to deck him out in as lavish a fashion as myself. As we sat down to dinner, we looked like two young exquisites of the *ancien régime*, and quite put into the shade Cécile, in the classical simplicity of her plain, cream-coloured silk robe, which hung in straight folds about her, and was only relieved by her splendid ruby ornaments.

I was unaccustomed to such finery, and it took me a little while to get used to it, but by the time dinner was concluded I felt more at my ease. Cécile took another survey of us afterwards, and stuck a little black patch on my right cheek, declaring, after she had contemplated the effect, that this had been the one thing wanting to make me absolutely perfect. And really, when I surveyed myself in the mirror which she handed to me, I was fain to admit that the 'beauty-spot' added a wonderful piquancy to the general expression of my features. It was only natural, too, that my comrade should want to have a like addition made to his armoury of attractions, so Cécile put one also on his face, but lower down than mine, and just near the dimple that made itself shown when he laughed.

We were now ready to start, and as soon as we were notified that the carriage was at the door, we descended to the porch.

The drive was a long one, taking us right away into the furthest suburbs; but we finally passed through a gate and along a short private road, drawing up before the portico of a large stone villa. The doors were shut, but on knocking we were admitted into the hall, where our cloaks and Cécile's wrap were taken from us by a servant. We were then led along a wide passage, and passed through a pair of big folding-doors into a great hall or winter-garden with a glass roof. This presented a truly brilliant spectacle, with its countless lights, its richly decorated walls, its tessellated pavement spread with soft carpets, its multitude of silk-covered couches and its huge, branching palms.

We were late arrivals, and the rest of the company was already assembled. Gaston pointed out to me Hélène, Isabelle, Yvonne and others whom he recognised, and we were soon in the midst of them, as they trooped around us. None of them, however, gave any sign of remembering having seen him before as Cécile introduced us. Their costumes were all marked by the same simplicity as Cécile's, this seeming to be *de rigueur* for the occasion. There were some dozen other boys present, all in eighteenth-century dress, but I do not think it too much to say that Gaston and I quite outshone the rest in plumage.

In addition to the members and their guests, there was quite a number of attendants in evidence – both boys and girls. The boys wore rose-coloured silk stockings with black satin garters tied in a bow at the side, and elegant satin shoes, together with a very short, open jacket, in shape not unlike that of a Spanish matador, brocaded and sewn with spangles and coloured stones, and finished of with a border of black velvet. This constituted their sole attire, leaving the whole front of their bodies and their posteriors perfectly open to view. The girls had a broad scarf of purple silk bound round them just below the breasts, and little shoes with long purple silk ribbons crossed round the leg, trellis-fashion, to the knee – their apparel being thus even more primitive than that of the boys.

'Now that you have come, Cécile,' said Hélène, 'we will go and have a little refreshment. Then the entertainment can commence.'

We repaired to a room laid out with a long table, where various light and stimulating dishes were served to us, accompanied by copious libations of champagne and liqueurs, well calculated to arouse the senses. At the finish, wine of a peculiarly exhilarating kind was brought round in glasses fashioned to represent the male organ of generation, the vessels themselves seeming to impart a flavour of lasciviousness to the beverage. This was undoubtedly the idea, and it will be remembered that Juvenal (*Satires*, II, 96) mentions that drinking-cups of the same kind were used at similar gatherings in his time.

I was seated between Cécile and Hélène, and was all eyes and ears amid the strangeness of the situation. The conversation which took place was tinged with considerable freedom, but there were no liberties of action so far, such being reserved till a late moment.

I was rather amused by Hélène enquiring of Cécile how her cousin, Elise, was.

'Oh, poor child!' replied Cécile; 'she has gone back to the country again. Our frivolity in Paris unnerved her altogether, but she will be quite happy at home in her own quiet way; I do not think she would ever have accustomed herself to our manners, and it really seemed a sin to disturb her peace of mind by insisting upon her remaining with me.'

Hélène gave the signal to rise, and we made our way back to the great saloon again.

A hidden orchestra began to discourse voluptuous music, and when we had all taken our places where the fancy led us, two boys and two girls entered and advanced to the middle of the hall. They wore sandal-shoes and loose, short tunics of the thinnest white gauze and carried each a tambourine. The unseen musicians struck up a fresh air, and the quartet kept time to the measure in a graceful dance, leaping and pirouetting with agile cleverness, shaking their tambourines as they did so and accompanying their steps with every sort of wanton gesture. It was a performance such as Nero loved to watch, or Petronius to write of, and the inciting effects were plainly visible on the faces of the women, at they looked on. The last shreds of reserve were disappearing fast, and when the dancers paused for a space, a general sigh went up at the breaking of the suspense. After a short breathing-time, the dance started again, and waxed more furious. The boys' members stood violently upright, vibrating with their every movement, while the swollen clitoris and distended vagina of each girl spoke of equal excitement. They carried out their terpsichorean revolutions to the utmost limit of their capacity, but at last, responding to the nimble touches which the boys administered to them, the girls collapsed and sank into their partners' arms, while streams of white semen ran down their thighs.

At this conclusion, the ladies of the audience rose as of one accord, with ardently shining eyes and panting breasts. With a common consent, they cast their robes from them, revealing themselves in complete nakedness, their shoes and stockings being also removed by the deft attendants. On a marble pedestal at one end of the hall, a beautiful little boy, with body all nude, was stood, and the women thronged around him, as before an altar, kissing his feet and body, and casting votive offerings of roses – white and red and yellow – before this living personification of the god of love, until the floor around him was heaped with perfumed blossoms in loveliest profusion. Then they joined hands and circled about him in a bacchanal dance, shrieking a wild chorus of licentious abandon. I stood lost in amaze at the scene, to match which one would have had to go back to the days when the Roman women celebrated at midnight, with closed doors, the mysteries of the Bona Dea. It was just such a sight as this that doubtless met the eyes of Publius Clodius when, disguised as a singing-girl, he penetrated into the most sacred precincts of Caesar's house in order to witness for himself the rites partaken in by Pompeia. Never could the maenads of those archaic times have exhibited greater frenzy than these, their latter-day imitators. Breaking apart from each other, they screamed for the attendants to come to them, and each claimed the services of a boy and a girl – the boy to soothe and at the same time aggravate their lust by swiftly working their fingers on clitoris and vagina, while the girl stood ready with a goblet in which to catch the outpour that was to follow. One after another, in quick succession, each salacious female, trembling in a madness of lubricity, with deep sighings and half-groans, stooped down and gave forth of her overflowing abundance of spermatic fluid into the receptacle held for her. The contents of these were all emptied into one gleaming, sculptured chalice. This Hélène, as high-priestess, took in her hands, and held aloft for a moment, like a pontiff offering sacrifice, uttering a loud cry as she did so. Then she advanced towards the naked boy on the pedestal, and bent the knee before him, her fellow-worshippers also prostrating themselves. Rising, Hélène poured the whole of the warm, thick liquor over the shoulders of the boy, thrusting the chalice into the arms of a ready attendant when she had done so. The dense volume of these commingled essences ran in a pearly flood over Cupid's body in this baptism of lasciviousness, and at the sight the women, drunk with passion, flocked about him fiercely, like souls possessed, striving with one another in a desperate effort to smother him with their embraces, smearing the coagulated semen over his form with their hands, and lapping up the moisture with their tongues in demonic fanaticism. I have only to close my eyes, to bring the vision before me again, and see those wild-eyed creatures indulge once more in that riot of sensuality.

I almost expected to witness the hapless lad torn to pieces in the frenzy of his devotees, but by some providence he escaped unhurt, or perhaps his adorers were less violent in their caresses than they seemed. Anyhow, Hélène at last gave the signal for cessation, and her colleagues drew back and forced themselves into comparative calmness. Warm water and sponges were brought, and they cleansed themselves, just as the Baptae, the priests of Cotys at Athens, were wont to wash after their nights of debauchery. Hélène reserved to herself and Cécile the coveted distinction of bathing and wiping the body of the deified boy.

When the purification was over, attention was directed to the next event. A girl, blindfolded and muffled in thick wrappings, was brought in and placed in the centre of the hall. The bandage was taken from her eyes, and she looked about her with a startled glance. She was very young – not more than fourteen – and seemed to be very much disturbed by her surroundings. She had little time for reflection, however, as in another minute three sturdy and muscular-looking youths of about sixteen came in at a run. They were quite naked, and their well-developed members, fringed around with dark hair, were at fullest erection, beating against their bellies as they moved, while their big testicles swayed prominently from side to side. Rushing upon the girl, they seized her in their clutches, while she screamed wildly, and struggled to get away. But with strong hands they rent her garments from her, until not a stitch remained to hide her nudity. She shrieked and writhed in vain attempts to free herself, but they paid no attention to her remonstrances, and one of the lads supported her body and held her wrists from behind, while the second, kneeling down, gripped her ankles, also from behind. The remaining one then approached and, forcing open her thighs, inserted his virile weapon into her undefended sheath. She shrieked again, and strove once more to obtain liberation, but the effort was useless. Her ravisher drove his member with violent force into her secret regions; she cried aloud under the pain inflicted upon her, then fell to trembling and whimpering in utter despair as her outrage was completed and the seducer thrust his organ into her vital parts with tremendous lustiness of energy. As he did so, he clasped her head and shoulders with his arms, and pressed his face against hers, and before many minutes had elapsed, she succumbed to a conquest of the senses, her cries ceased, and her struggles resolved themselves into a series of excited responses to her assailant's movements. She found voice again, however, as her maiden essence began to flow, and gave vent to several agonised shouts when finally the youth came to a finish and, pushing for the last time with all his might, closed tightly up against her as he discharged his sperm into her quivering body.

When he had concluded, he moved from his position and gave place to one of his companions, who, worked up by the sight of the preceding operations, was eager for the contest, and roused the girl to renewed agitation with the zest of his embraces. She made no more cries, however, but met his attack with soothed resignation, and, as nearly as I could judge by her features, appeared to be spending again. This youth, too, was not long in coming to a head; and, in his turn, he gave way to the third. By this time the girl was prostrated, and it was the work of the two non-combatants to support her failing form rather than to hold her, as she was assailed by the last of their number in his pristine vigour. She had no strength wherewith to reply to his actions, and she trembled and sighed as he pursued his purpose. She was overcome altogether, and at the end fell back with a groan against those who held her. Stricken nature had given way, and she seemed to have become insensible. However, she had served her part, and the three youths carried her away between them.

I pointed out her condition to Cécile, but she replied, 'That is nothing! You must not think she has been hurt. Her tribulation was brought about more by nervousness than by terror. She knew beforehand what was to be done to her, and only the pleasure will remain in her mind when she recovers.'

The little drama had wrought its effect on the spectators, and now that it was over they seized the opportunity to indulge in indiscriminate tonguings and ticklings among themselves; Hélène and Cécile laid themselves side by side, kissing and at the same time eagerly fingering one another. As I looked about me, I saw that the remainder were all engaged similarly, and my own blood began to mount hotly within me, causing me to pluck at my itching cock.

Close by my side, Isabelle and Yvonne were deep in the delights of *soixante-neuf*, and I fell to gazing at them intently, as they squeezed each other's bottoms with their hands, and feverishly dipped and twirled their long tongues in one another's apertures. One discharge only was the rule, however, and by the time the pair I looked at had, with many a pant and wriggle, given off a deluge of warm cream each, the others had all arrived at the same terminus.

Again they performed their ablutions, and then composed themselves for a further spectacle. The actors consisted of an Arab boy and girl, a little, dusky-coloured pair, not numbering more than a score of years between them, but these children of the tropics come to maturity, genitally speaking, at a far earlier age than those of colder climes, and the young boy's sexual furniture was of a kind that many a grown European youth could not have shown, while the girl was very little behind in the same respect. On the signal being given to start, they went through a regular series of lewd enactments, displaying extraordinary powers of sustentation. To begin with, the girl stretched herself out, and the boy mounted her in the orthodox fashion. When he had entered into her, she clasped him round the shoulders and twined up her legs round his, squeezing and pressing him, thrusting her belly to meet his pushes, and doing all she could to increase their mutual delight. This soon brought the consummation of their energies, but, after only a moment's rest, the boy lay down, and the girl knelt above him, taking his member, still wet with his recent emission, in her mouth, while the boy replied by burying his face in her thighs, and penetrating into her moist and dripping vagina with his tongue. It would be impossible to conceive a greater exhibition of wantonness than that given by the little couple, as they locked themselves in each other's embrace, and writhed and twisted in the greatness of their ardour. Even when they had finished this bout, they had not exhausted themselves entirely, and, after the girl had worked her partner's member up again to the requisite degree of stiffness, she sat over him and, bringing the top against her wide-open orifice, sank slowly down until she had swallowed it up to the hilt, and then rose and fell with measured movements, humming a monotonous but weird chant, until once again she bathed the boy's organ with her precocious abundance of life-fluid, and followed it up in good time by extracting a further draught from the living tap she played upon. This marked the close of the show, and the two then made a deep salutation, and took their way out.

All this had excited the women to an insupportable height, and Hélène called out with a loud voice, 'Bring forth the weapons of delight, and let all make themselves ready!'

In response to her command, a number of dildos was brought, sufficient to furnish half the company of members with them, and the attendants assisted in the fixing on of these instruments. As such things had already been described to me by Gaston, I was not astonished by them; but the presentment of the women, as they stood fitted with the curious artifices, was sufficiently startling to excite my deepest interest. Cécile and Hélène each had one on, and apparently it was the older and more experienced of the sisterhood that were so equipped. As the females present belonging to the society numbered exactly thirty, there were fifteen on each side. The two divisions drew up in line, facing each other, at a distance of several yards. All were then blindfolded, and at a signal made by the striking of a gong they advanced towards each other, spreading out their hands in front of them. As soon as one of the artificially accoutred members had laid hold of a girl from the other company, each removed the bandage from her eyes, and both made their way together to a couch. It was thus left to chance to decide the arrangement of the couples. It so happened that Cécile picked out Yvonne, the very girl whose virginity she had taken on the occasion when she had introduced de Beaupré into their circle, and it was a strange but not unhappy fortune that again put Yvonne into her arms. Cécile gave a quick look round to see where I was, and finding I had not shifted from my station, led her companion to the divan against which I was sitting, with the intention

of affording me the fullest scope for observation. Yvonne laid herself
out to receive Cécile, and the latter, full of heat, quickly got into
position over her. It needed no force to effect the entry of the dildo,
which slipped with ease into Yvonne's impatient vagina, already well
oiled by her previous emissions, and the girl gave a cry of delight at the
ingress of the hard, stiff weapon. Cécile performed the man's part with
fullest proficiency, and it amused me vastly so see the perfect way in
which she could imitate every masculine movement. Her posteriors
were turned towards me, and her own gaping aperture yawned redly,
with protruding lips. I could not withstand the temptation to touch it.
I approached my hand, and inserted two fingers in the palpitating slit.
She uttered a startled exclamation, but her surprised look developed
into a smile of grateful pleasure as she turned her head and noted the
cause of the unlooked-for sensation, and I understood that she wished
me to continue. In a very short time, Yvonne gave evidence of being
about to reply to the calls upon her body, and next moment her sperm
began to flow.

'Squeeze the balls, Charlie!' cried Cécile, and in obedience I took
one and gave it a violent pressure, which fairly electrified Yvonne into
renewed activity as the charge shot swiftly and powerfully into her. I
was about to send the contents of the second ball into her as well, but
Cécile stopped me with quick gestures. Meanwhile, I had not relin-
quished my operations upon Cécile, and on the succeeding instant her
love-juice rained out in a voluminous flow, covering my hand and
running on to Yvonne's legs. My proceedings were apparently of an
unusual character, and I do not think the example was followed in any
other case, but, whether unrecognised or not, in the universal excitement of amorousness no notice was taken of it, and my by-play had
very possibly escaped detection. Anyhow, Cécile had no cause to be
dissatisfied, and pressed my hand with mute thanks as she arose.

After general purification, another interval ensued, to be enlivened
by a further exhibition of an inflammatory nature. This took a new and
extraordinary form. A fine she-goat, milk-white, carefully combed and
washed, and decked with coloured ribbons, was led in by two boys. A
majestic-looking he-goat, with a long beard, was also conducted into
the middle of the hall from the opposite end by two girls. The male
animal snorted, threw up its head and pawed the ground, on nearing its
natural mate, to which it would have rushed, but for the hands that
held it back. The two boys then placed themselves on either side of the

female beast, so as to keep her still, and a strong mulatto youth, with an enormous genital organ, approached and took up a position in its rear. The creature moved its head and shifted uneasily, making a peculiar noise as it did so, but the boys quietened it with their confining hands, and when its equanimity was restored, the mulatto took advantage of the opportunity to invade its anterior fecunditive passage with his stiffened member. The brute started forward, and would have got away, had it not been restrained, and it showed signs of anxiety as the youth penetrated it. It was compelled, however, to retain its position, and the services of two more boys were called into requisition to hold its hind legs. The mulatto's part was now easy, and he bestowed his zealous embraces on the animal with seemingly great enjoyment. I was fascinated as I gazed at the strangely-matched pair, and could not take my eyes away until the youth's zestful efforts had been crowned with triumph, and he drew forth his dripping member from the beast's orifice, which brimmed over with exuding moisture.

The he-goat was now to be brought into action, and the scent of the late copulation had aroused him to such an extent that it took half a dozen pairs of hands to hold him and keep him in check. A huge black woman was to be his spouse for the occasion, and, crouching upon the floor on all-fours, she presented her massive posteriors before the excited animal. He was led forward and sniffed with his nose at the woman's thighs. The odour still further worked up his sensuality, and he threw his head high into the air. His fore legs were lifted up and placed around the woman's body, while one of the girls inserted his heated penis into the wide-open sheath which awaited it. There was no need to do anything further to urge him on or incite him. He knew perfectly well what was expected of him, and went to work with a lustiness that astonished me. The negress seemed to take matters very coolly as she bent beneath her brute-lover's embraces. The goat's mouth opened, and the hot breath steamed from its nostrils under the ardour it displayed, but such energy could not last long, and the woman was thrown backwards and forwards under its last vigorous strokes until it stopped abruptly and trembled from head to foot in the act of discharging its burden of cerebro-spinal fluid into her capacious interior. Its passion now quelled, it suffered itself to be lifted from its position, and the members of the group took their departure, both animals looking much less fiery now than when they had entered.

Following upon this interlude, wine was brought round to us in the same priapic vessels as before, and a truce was called while the beverage was being consumed. The orchestra was playing the Venusberg music from *Tannhauser*, and under the influence of the moving strains, Hélène turned to me and with impatient fingers loosened the front of my breeches. Diving her hand in, she brought to light my cock, which reared itself aloft in pleasure at its liberty.

'What a delightful little object!' she exclaimed, regarding it joyously and toying with it with her hand.

Cécile cast a look coloured, perhaps, with a little envy, at Hélène, but the expression vanished in a moment, and she cried, 'Here is my other cavalier!' proceeding to expose Gaston's member, which raised its head just as obtrusively as did mine. On the other side of Hélène sat her own invited gallant, a handsome lad with a poetically pensive face, attired in a suit of pale-blue satin, heavily laced with silver, whom she addressed as Henriot. Leaving me for a second or two, she laid him open to view also, and then both she and Cécile fell to a comparison of our respective merits.

'It is a male edition of the Three Graces, is it not?' said Hélène enthusiastically, as her glance wandered from one to another of us in this modern and reversed Judgment of Paris, while Isabelle presently came up and joined in the inspection. 'I am less bold than Paris, however,' continued Hélène, 'and fear to give the palm to any. One trembles to choose, when confronted with such a galaxy of perfection.'

I fancy Henriot had the advantage of size, as his weapon of virility was of fairly big proportions, but, indeed, he appeared to be a trifle older than Gaston and myself.

'I think we ought to set forth our devotion in some way,' said Hélène presently. 'Let us signify it by bestowing upon our admired ones the salutation of Eros!'

Thus speaking, she went on her knees before me and took my throbbing cock in her mouth, sucking it with the most delicious effect. Cécile followed her example with Gaston, while Isabelle, taking the cue from them, lavished her warm caresses upon Henriot of the dreamy countenance. The soothing touch of Hélène's lips and tongue over-joyed me, and I doubt not that my two fellows experienced equal delight; but the happiness was too soon over, for they ceased when they had wellnigh brought us to the verge of bliss, and left us shivering in an agony of suspense.

'Poor darlings! It is cruel of us, I know,' said Hélène; but the rules do no permit of more, and as president, I dare not set a precedent by breaking them. Please forgive us, and try to remain content.'

They would not even permit us to gain relief by our own manual exercises, but themselves refastened our nether garments, so that we had to control ourselves as best we could.

The next proceeding of the women was to pair off again, and give exit to their feelings once more by mutual tongue and hand play, their hungry apertures being still further excited by applications of pungent and aromatic liquids, which they squirted in with their mouths, and also with little syringes into their bottom-holes. The effect was tremendous, and sent them almost mad with erotic fervour, so that little screams and groans resounded on all sides as their essence streamed out in unabated force and volume, while their bodies shook with violent tremors.

At the ensuing pause, two well-grown girls introduced themselves, together with a pair of huge, dun-coloured hounds. The girls knelt down, just as the negro woman had done, and it needed little inducement to get the dogs to mount them. The animals, growing hot and lusty at the prospect of the encounter before they had well started, exerted every muscle in their ferocious embraces, and with lolling tongues went furiously at their business until the object of the union was accomplished; and when they had spent they remained within the unaccustomed precincts until they were removed by those in charge of them.

Nude maidens, crowned with flowers, next performed the graceful Ionian dance with classic pose and rhythm, while a quartet sat themselves down, singing and playing upon harps of antique pattern.

The dance over, several naked boys, with wreaths of myrtle on their heads, ran about amid the women spectators, striking them with light thongs on the thighs and body, in imitation of the custom at the festival of the Lupercalia in Ancient Rome. This was supposed to increase sexual arousal, and in this case the objective was achieved, for a general uprising took place. The dildos were caused to be brought again, this time being bound upon those who had before played the submissive part. The couples, however, arranged themselves as on the first occasion, there being no fresh choosing, so that Cécile prepared herself for the onset of Yvonne. I was moved to practise upon the latter as I had done the first time upon Cécile; seeing which, Gaston performed a similar function in the case of Isabelle. Not to be behindhand, Henriot devoted himself in like manner to Hélène, while the remainder of the boyish guests, observing our actions, each exerted themselves upon one of the fair. Cécile was one of the first to respond to the assault, and she did it right generously. I did not need to be told what to do, but as soon as I perceived the signs of ecstasy on her face, I lost no time in pressing both rubber balls, one after the other, causing Cécile to wellnigh expire in rapturous intensity under the strength and prodigious quantity of warm milk, mixed with isinglass, that I pumped into her.

When all had finished, Hélène said to me, 'You deserve our united thanks, Monsieur Charles, for your happy thought, and the wonderful way by which our pleasure was increased in consequence. As a token of the gratitude which all the members must feel for your delightful inspiration, I ask you to accept this as an expression of our united feelings, and she took off a superb diamond and emerald bracelet that she wore, and slipped it on my wrist. I was overwhelmed with confusion, and blushed crimson at being thus made the cynosure of all eyes, but Hélène would not listen to my nervous protests, and said I well merited the guerdon, and should be regarded ever afterwards as a benefactor to them by reason of my inventive genius.

I understood from Cécile that the meeting was shortly to be brought to a close, and I thought it spoke a great deal for the powers of endurance of them all that it had gone on for so long already. As a finale, all the boy and girl attendants were marshalled to the front, and went through a course of not unpleasing evolutions, half-dancing, half-posturing. They were all in a heated condition, as a glance at their members told, and at last a signal was given, and each boy flung himself into the arms of the girl nearest to him. Now that their hitherto controlled sensibilities found an outlet, they let their glowing desires have full play: and our eyes roved over a mass of seething, struggling young humanity, engaged in amorous encounters with all their powers, wrestling and striving with one another with unbridled lustfulness in a chaos of tossing arms and twisting legs and writhing bodies, while the air grew heavy with their deep breathing and the peculiar smell arising from their perspiring bodies.

This proved at last too much for the onlookers, and they fell to embracing each other again with all the remaining frenzied force of their wellnigh used-up strength, letting themselves loose in a perfect madness of caressing and incitements in an effort to drain from each other the very last drop of seminal essence that their taxed natures could produce. It was a triumph of nymphomania, and my flesh crept with amaze as I contemplated the orgy. Nothing was to be heard but their straining pants, followed by sobs and gasps as their sap drained out, and the indescribable odour of all this prodigal expenditure of sperm percolated densely through the atmosphere and hung in the nostrils at every inspiration. Not only myself but Gaston and all the other boy-guests remained silent and spellbound, unable to move or speak in presence of such an illimitable display of passion, and I forgot even my own warmth of feelings as I turned my head from side to side in an endeavour to assimilate into ordered comprehension all the varied aspects of concentrated eroticism that met my astonished gaze.

There was still a further act to be performed, however, and in preparation for this, the attendants were ordered out, and the doors closed, leaving only the members and their guests within. A curtain at one end was drawn aside, revealing the statue of a nude female, life-size, in an alcove. Offerings of flowers were made to this, and while the sacrifice was in progress, I questioned Cécile as to its purpose.

'That is the image of the goddess Flora, who is the presiding genius of our revels,' she replied. 'We throw flowers before her now, but a further and more important offering is to follow, as you will see. Look! here it comes now.'

She pointed, and I saw Hélène coming forward with a large salver, on which were what appeared to be some portions of animal flesh.

'In the constitution of our society,' continued Cécile in explanation, 'we followed upon the lines instituted by the old Roman votaries of the Bona Dea, substituting, however, the goddess Flora for the deified wife of Faunus. It was the custom in classic ages to offer to the latter the womb and udders of a sow, and these are what you now see borne by Hélène.'

In front of the statue was placed a brazier of live coals, and while the rest of the females gathered round attentively, Hélène performed various ceremonial rites, and then cast her burden into the fire. At the same instant the lights went out, so that there was dense gloom everywhere, except by the brazier, and as the portions of flesh rested upon the red-hot embers, they sizzled and burst into flame, the flickering flare lighting up the surrounding group of worshippers with the most weird and uncanny effect, which the smell of burning meat, as it smote upon the olfactory nerves, did not lessen.

After a time, the lights went on again, and the women rose. From behind the image, the little boy who had before figured as Cupid made his appearance. He had a bow in his hand, and a quiver was slung over his shoulder. Taking the light darts, he fitted them one by one to the bow, and sent them aloft into the air, continuing until his stock was exhausted. Each time one fell upon a woman, she seized it, and, imprinting a kiss upon the tiny weapon, pressed it to her bosom. Two touched me, one entangling itself in the folds of my cravat, and when I pointed this out to Hélène, she congratulated me warmly, saying that it boded well for my future happiness and success in affairs of the heart.

This concluded the proceedings; the attendants were recalled and the females put on their attire again. Leaving the hall, we went to the supper-room, where a substantial meal awaited us. A different tone altogether now pervaded the whole gathering as the women sat themselves down 'clothed, and in their right mind'. It did not seem possible that they could be the same people, I thought, as I listened to the commonplace topics being discussed on all sides, and I could hardly believe that all I had seen was more than a dream.

A general breaking-up followed after supper, and very shortly afterwards Cécile, Gaston and myself were ensconced in our carriage, and being swiftly taken back to the city.

As we were on the way, Gaston fumbled at his breeches, and took out his member, holding it with his hand.

'I cannot help it, really!' he cried. 'I must do something to it, or I shall go mad. Look at what we have had to go through, Cécile! and with never so much as a little amusement for ourselves.'

Cécile smiled. 'I admit,' she said, 'that it must have been very provoking for you. But you must remember that you were there as spectators, and nothing else. It is a little cruel that we should exercise our vanity to such a length as to take you there, and be unable to give you any satisfaction; but those are the rules laid down, and it could not be helped.'

'Well! I am going to have some satisfaction now,' continued Gaston, starting to rub himself.

'Oh, no! You must not!' exclaimed Cécile. 'Look here! I promise that you shall have a soothing balm when we return, if you will refrain for the present;' and in obedience to her entreaties, Gaston at last reluctantly buttoned up again.

It was growing light when we arrived at the Avenue Hoche, and as we made our way upstairs, Cécile said, 'It is quite impossible for you to go home now. You must stay here, and return before lunch.'

I did not like the idea, myself, of going back to the Hôtel Foix at such an hour, and thought Gaston very wise to agree to her proposal.

The maids were there to help us to undress, but Marie left directly afterwards, so that only Julie remained.

'I have not overlooked my promise, Gaston,' said Cécile. 'Julie, you have not forgotten Monsieur le Comte, have you? Will you oblige him and Monsieur Charles with a little diversion?'

Julie smiled acquiescence, and Cécile bade her remove her clothes. She then made me lie on the bed with my back against the pillows, and when Julie was ready, she knelt between my legs and began to suck me. On Cécile's suggestion, Gaston mounted behind her, and, bringing his belly against her posteriors, thrust his member into her conveniently placed sheath. Both of us were thus able to receive satisfaction at once, while Julie enjoyed not less pleasure in her doubly well-placed situation, as she experienced the same happiness in her own body that she was giving to me. Speaking for myself, I was filled with the most complete gratification in, at long last, finding assuagement to the deep emotionalism I had been suffering from all the night without being able to get relief. All the pent-up sensuality of my nature worked tempestuously in me as Julie fanned the flames of voluptuousness with skilful art. I heaved wildly in excess of feeling, while my cock was the fulcrum around which all the boiling currents of my sensibilities surged and foamed. Gaston was in equal plight, and as I looked in his face, noting its passionate workings, I saw a reflection of my own. We had held ourselves in reserve for so long, however, that we were not a great length of time in labour. Gaston was the first to give way, and, with a few final agonised convulsions, he fell forward, clasping Julie with his arms. I was not far behind, nevertheless, and before many more moments were over, I felt my inmost being disturbed, an excessive glow of rapture rose up and swirled through me, purling riotously into every corner, and I pressed my genital weapon further between Julie's lips with a last effort, and then subsided, as the dams that held back my sperm found an outlet in the girl's willing mouth.

The tension of our bodies dissipated, both Gaston and I felt lassitude creeping upon us, and were anxious for sleep. Cécile put us to bed in the room next to hers, and almost before she had left the apartment we had closed our eyes.

CHAPTER TWELVE

Lord Henry

My stay in France soon came to an end, and I cannot recall to mind anything else particularly worthy of note.

A few days before leaving, we went down to the family's country seat in Languedoc. Here I met Gaston's grandfather on the paternal side, the old Prince de Foix, Duc de Beaupré. He was verging upon eighty, and had seen many vicissitudes in his time, but was still erect of bearing, and a picturesque figure, with his long white moustache and hoary locks. A glance at the *Almanach de Gotha* showed him to be a very important personage, being a Knight of St John of Jerusalem and Malta, and a Chevalier of the Order of Christ. He was an ardent Royalist and Catholic, and in his declining years devoted himself entirely to these interests, taking no part in social life; but he was very gracious in his manner towards me, and nourished a particular affection for Gaston, hoping that he would prove a worthier successor to his dignities than the prince, of whose abilities and tastes he had rather a poor opinion, judging from one or two remarks of a slightly sarcastic nature which I heard him utter.

I must also mention that the princess gave an entertainment before I left Paris, and among the guests were Hélène and Isabelle, as well as Cécile. They smiled at me in a friendly way when I was introduced, but let fall no hint with reference to our previous encounter. They comported themselves now with as much regard for propriety as any of their fellow guests; and I gathered that they both filled positions in the front rank of society, when I heard them spoken of, and was informed of their full titles – Hélène was the Marquise de St Pol and Isabelle, the Comtesse de Charente – which in both cases evidenced their alliance with great houses.

I again begged Hélène to let me return her bracelet, as I was at a loss to know what to do with it, but she would not hear of such a thing, saying that I must keep it in remembrance of her; so I was compelled to be satisfied with this.

My visit came to an end at last, and I took farewell of my newly found friends with genuine regret. The princess travelled with us to London, but from there I left for Woodbury, to spend the last two days of the vacation at home. The reaction from the liveliness of the past weeks was great, but I had not, happily, to suffer it long, and the morning of my departure for school soon dawned.

I had a letter from Rutherford requesting me to look out for him at Bristol, where I had to change. As my train drew up, I saw him on the platform, and I jumped out and ran towards him. His face lighted up with the greatest pleasure as he greeted me, but he stopped my flow of words, and suggested that we should secure our seats before starting to talk, so we despatched a porter to look after our respective belongings, and, after choosing a compartment, settled ourselves down to chat. I had such a lot to tell my friend that it occupied a considerable portion of the journey, and he complimented me upon the good use I had made of the last part of the holidays.

'I am awfully sorry,' he said, 'that I could not have you with me; but I had no idea that we should stay such a long time with the Campbells. We only got back to Everton a fortnight ago. I had a very good time, indeed; but I think you have beaten me.'

All was excitement at the school, and everyone was eager to relate the adventures he had gone through during the vacation. The house resounded with our chatter, but the masters only smiled at the exuberance we displayed. Jimmy looked in fine form, and fatter than ever, and he kept both Gaston and me busy in recounting the incidents of our sojourn in Paris. When I told him about the affair of the photograph, he shook his fist at de Beaupré, but suffered himself to be mollified on being told Cécile's comments on his appearance.

When we gained the dormitory, we showed considerable interest in surveying one another's appearance after our long separation. The intervening weeks since we had parted had added a modicum of development to our persons; indeed, Bob's member seemed to me to be a good deal larger than before, while Jimmy's had also perceptibly grown. On their part, they pronounced a similar opinion upon Gaston and myself.

'I've got some hairs coming; nearly as many as Blackie!' cried Jimmy, with much pride, as he offered himself to view.

We looked, and laughed at the gross exaggeration; but certainly there were some faint traces of an incipient papillary growth on his middle regions. He affected to be annoyed as we smilingly refused to recognise his claims, but he could not keep up the pretence for long, and said, 'Well, of course, Blackie has more than me, I know; but still, you can see for yourselves that mine are growing all right.'

'Come here, Charlie!' said Bob, presently. 'I'm dying to feel your hand on me again. It seems ages since we were last together like this.'

I had no objection, and advanced to where he lay on the bed. Taking his cock in my fist, I drew down the skin, and moistened the top with my tongue, lingering over the operation, which came with a pleasing freshness to me, not having seen and touched Rutherford's member for so long. At length I started to rub it sharply.

'Oh!' cried Bob, making a sudden gesture; 'look out! I'm sorry, Charlie, but you were pulling my hair, and it hurt rather. That's all right now. Go on!'

As I continued, I watched as keenly as ever the sight of the swelling purple head, as it was covered and uncovered by the movements of my hand and it fascinated me just as much as it had done on the very first occasion when I had devoted myself to a similar task with Rutherford. He was enjoying it, too, and gazed at me with a smile as I went on with the work.

'You haven't forgotten how to do it since you have been away,' he said; 'but I dare say you have been practising with Blackie pretty often, haven't you?'

I laughed, and replied, 'Well, of course, we had to keep ourselves up to the mark, you know.'

He was soon taken up too much by his feelings to indulge in any further conversation, and had no thought for anything but the delight I was giving him. In a few minutes he signified that he was about to discharge, and I quickly covered his cock with my mouth, just in time to receive an abundant flow of warm, creamy juice.

'Now it is your turn,' he said, and I took the place which he vacated, gladly suffering him to allay my voluptuous desires. Blackie and the duke were similarly engaged, and we did not get into our beds until all had received a taste of blissful joy.

I do not intend to say much about the events of this term, and can only state that it was not less pleasant to me than the one preceding it.

There were not many changes among the pupils. Two new juniors had come in, but with these we had no concern. Davenport had left, and there were few regrets expressed at that. Lacy still remained, and we kept up our friendliness with him.

Jimmy and I were taking a bath together one day, and while we were doing so, Lacy joined us. 'Keep your eyes open, you chaps!' he said to us; 'Mr Ferguson will be having a peep in a minute – he saw me come in,' and he winked at us. Sure enough, a little later the door opened and Ferguson's head appeared in the opening. When he saw that Lacy was not alone, however, he merely said a few words and retired. We had the best of him on that occasion, for the three of us had a jolly time, following it up until we had spent all round.

Before the close of term, Jimmy wrote to Lord Henry Wilmot, and received in reply an invitation for the whole four of us to spend the Christmas vacation with him at his place in Northumberland, Hebworth Castle. I obtained the desired permission from my father, and it was arranged that, as soon as the term was over, I should proceed to Lord Henry's. At the last moment, however, both Bob and the duke were asked by their people to spend Christmas Day and Boxing Day at home, while Jimmy's mother also particularly wished de Beaupré to come to her, too. I found myself rather awkwardly placed, as I did not want to go home. Rutherford said I could come with him, and sent a telegram to Lord Henry, explaining the situation. He wired back, asking if I could not come by myself, as he should like some one of us to go to him, he being quite alone.

'Why don't you go, Charlie?' said Bob; 'that would settle everything nicely. You won't have long to wait for us, and I know my cousin will make you feel at home. It seems a shame that he should be kept all by himself waiting for us.'

Thus urged, I agreed to the proposal, and acquainted Lord Henry of my decision. He sent a further telegram, asking me to let him know the train I should come by, which I did; so, to cut matters short, I may say that I started alone on the long journey to the North, having impressed upon my friends that they must join me as soon as possible.

It was late and quite dark when I reached the little station where I was to alight, and I did not feel in very good spirits after the prolonged and chilly journey. A tall man, muffled up in a thick overcoat and with a tweed cap pulled well down on his head, stood on the platform, and as I got out he came towards me, saying, 'Master Powerscourt, I presume?'

I replied in the affirmative, and he held out his hand, exclaiming, 'How do you do? I am very pleased to meet you. Although we have not seen each other before, I seem to know you quite well, after all that my cousin Bob and that young scamp Jimmy have told me about you. But I mustn't keep you waiting here in the cold. Come along!'

A closed carriage stood ready for us, and we set out on a long drive. The darkness did not permit me to see much of where we were going, but I noticed that we passed between hedgerows and across open moorlands, the country all about seeming to be quite uninhabited. My companion did his best to enliven the way with genial talk, but I was cold, and, moreover, felt a little bashful in his presence, so that I am afraid my society did not afford him very much satisfaction.

At length we stopped at a battlemented gateway, with tall and ponderous doors, which were presently opened for us and closed and barred after we had gone through. Our way then led along a drive, between tall, overhanging trees, and we finally pulled up at a deeply recessed Norman porch. As the carriage stopped, the door was flung open, letting a flood of light upon the scene. We stepped out and made our way to the door, the tall towers and buttresses of the castle looming hugely before us in the uncertain dimness of the night. As soon as we had entered, a gigantic negro carefully closed the door after us, and we proceeded up a steep, stone staircase, lighted by tiny, grated windows, which led to a lofty and spacious vestibule with groined roof and pavement of stone flags, all in good repair, but quite bare of furniture. However, when we had gone through a pair of double doors, the scene changed, and I found myself in a tall-ceilinged corridor, wainscotted and floored with oak, thickly carpeted, and lighted by foliated casements of painted glass, with antique benches and armoires, horns and skins, and stands of armour and weapons here and there.

Passing along this, the negro went on ahead, and drew aside a curtain at the further end, which gave us access to a large and brilliantly lighted saloon or hall, where the walls were hung with exquisite productions of Eastern looms, and the floor was spread with splendid specimens of tiger and other skins, while on every hand were to be seen masterpieces of art from the far Orient, in the shape of wonderful carved and lacquered cabinets, sculptured and inlaid tables and chairs, marvellous porcelains and bronzes, and countless other similar objects.

'Welcome to Hebworth!' exclaimed Lord Henry, flinging of his cap and coat; and now that he had removed these and was in the light, I was able to take stock of him.

He was, as I have already said, tall, and had an Apollo-like figure, broad-shouldered and slim-waisted. He was under thirty, I fancied, and the absence of a moustache gave him a still more youthful appearance. His face was a handsome one, with clear-cut features, hair of the deepest brown, almost black, and eyes that had a peculiar intensity of expression in them. The sensuous lines round the lips betokened the aesthete and the voluptuary; but withal, there was a nobleness about the forehead, and a look of kindly sympathy in the long-lashed hazel eyes, that showed his nature to be altogether foreign to the cruel callousness of the genuine *roué*.

'You must be tired and hungry after your long journey, Charlie,' he said presently. 'Go and have a wash. That will refresh you, and in the meantime I will have something got ready for you to eat. Peter will show you the way.'

The negro conducted me to a dressing-room, where I freed myself from the stains of travel, and when I had done so I returned to the saloon. Lord Henry was awaiting my appearance, and at once conducted me to a room nearby. Eastern tapestries and carpets, furs, carved furniture and quaint ornaments also entered into the appointments of this chamber, and a table near the hearth was laid with an appetising meal. Lord Henry bade me sit down to this, and I was able to do full justice to it, but all the while I was conscious that my host was regarding me with a very intent gaze.

When I had finished, the table was cleared by Peter, assisted by another negro, equally as gigantic. Lord Henry saw me observing them, and when they had gone out and closed the door, he said, 'They are two very good fellows indeed, and devoted to me. I picked them up in South Africa a year or two ago, and they have been with me ever since. I have christened them Peter and Paul, as their native names are too cumbersome for ordinary use.'

We were left to ourselves now, and my companion bent his shining eyes in a strange way upon me. The effect was half-hypnotic, and made me feel just a little uncomfortable, so that I was only able to answer in monosyllables, or in the shortest possible sentences, the questions that were put to me.

A little while passed in silence, and then Lord Henry, who had been gazing for a brief space into the fire, which glowed brightly in the broad, low grate, turned and beckoned me to him.

'You are very friendly with my two young relatives, Charlie, are you not? Both of them mentioned you in the warmest way in their letters, so I know the intimacy must be an exceedingly close one. They have doubtless often spoken to you of me, and have, I am sure, told you that I am extremely fond of boys, and like to see them in the utmost freedom possible. Now! would it be too much to ask of you to reveal yourself to me in beauty unadorned?'

I flushed at the words, as their import dawned upon me, but under the commanding fire of his eyes I felt unable to refuse. As I did not speak, he took my dumbness for consent, and said, 'It is quite warm here. You can undress with perfect comfort.'

I took the hint, and mechanically acted upon it, slowly unfastening my garments, while he sat with his chin on his hand, watching me with a steady glance. I did not especially like the idea, as, after all, he was an absolute stranger to me, but I was impelled by the subtle influence he exercised upon me to carry out his wish. With mute imperiousness he made me go on until I stood in utter nakedness before him. The crimson blood mantled my cheeks again, and my eyes dropped downcast, as Lord Henry, without moving from his seat, surveyed me critically and with a look of unfeigned admiration, while I seemed to feel the actual contact of his sight, as his eyes roved over my body and limbs from head to foot in a minute and protracted examination. When he had sufficiently feasted his gaze upon my front, he bade me turn round, so that he might wander with his burning vision over my back, keeping me thus, in perturbation of spirit, for several more minutes.

When he had finally satisfied himself with this, he rose, apologising for having troubled me, and thanking me in the most gracious terms. Drawing up a large, broad couch near to the fireplace, he directed me to lie on this at full length, and, bending down, gave me a warm, wine-laced kiss, full on the lips.

He then went to a Japanese cabinet, from a cupboard in which he took out a book, and, giving it to me, bade me read it aloud to him. The singular request, combined with the peculiarity of my condition, created a feeling of reserve in my mind, but I could not well decline to do as I was asked, and, taking the book, I opened it at the beginning and began to read, while Lord Henry took his place on a low stool by the foot of the couch. The volume proved to be an erotic romance of the most lurid description, and ere I had got through the first few paragraphs, the whole situation so affected me that my face burned anew, and a shiver almost of compunction ran through me. A deep nervousness, hardly less than a terror, seized upon me, and the final touch to my distress and abasement was to follow, when my companion put out his hand and gently began to toy with my private parts, so that I stopped reading, closed the book and glanced with open-eyed dismay at him.

'Do, please, go on!' he said, with a winning smile, and a whole world of uncombatable persuasiveness in his dark eyes.

I felt thoroughly subdued, and continued with the reading of the book, while Lord Henry went on with the utmost nonchalance with the fingering of my genitals. This tried me sorely, the printed words seemed to swim before my eyes, and it was only by a deeply concentrated effort that I was able to proceed. When I recovered possession of myself somewhat I was conscious of another sensation, and a momentary glimpse showed me that Lord Henry was stooping over me, and had taken my cock in his mouth. Had it been Rutherford, or any other of my intimate friends, I should have experienced nothing but pleasure; but my acquaintance with my present host was hardly to be counted in more than minutes, so that my horrified wonder at his procedure was indescribable, and a shudder passed through my frame; but Lord Henry was either unconscious of this, or took no notice of it, for he went on with his self-imposed task with much apparent zest, drawing the foreskin back to its fullest extent, and sucking and rolling his tongue round the knob with voluptuous relish, varying this now and then by taking the whole member between his lips, or by licking my balls and thighs. My cock had up to the present been in its limpest state, but by degrees the shock wore off, the lubricity of the book began to interest me, a feeling of curiosity to know more of its contents grew upon me, infecting my body with the undefinable sensibilities of passionalism, while the blood grew warmer in my veins. This revivification communicated itself to my member, and it began to stiffen, at which sign Lord Henry coaxed it with his hands with the utmost persistence, until it enlarged and erected itself with more than usual firmness. As soon as this consummation had been attained, my companion again began caressing it with lips and tongue with greater avidity than ever, kissing and sucking and licking the distended knob with the utmost fervency, while with his hands he tickled and titillated my balls and thighs, and, pressing open my legs, pushed one finger into my bottom-hole. I was in a fever of mingled discomfort and excitement. My voice grew husky, the finger penetrated so far up my bottom, and worked about so much in those interior regions as to hurt me, while an occasional pressure of Lord Henry's teeth on the head of my cock, and the force with which he every now and then pressed back the prepuce, also caused me some little pain. Once more I stopped reading, but once again the gentle but inexorable voice and eyes bade me resume. The voluptuousness of the descriptions of the book, with their unbounded salaciousness, began to fascinate me, unbidden little thrills ran through my body, and my limbs twitched spasmodically, while my belly and posteriors wriggled and squirmed in spontaneous lasciviousness. This scene continued for some time, until my awakening lust conquered all other sensations. At length, a sudden glow of irresistible delight surged through me, giving promise of something yet more pleasurable to follow. My member throbbed and grew more stiff, sensible of which, my host applied himself to sucking it with still greater insistence, while his hands worked on my balls and in my bottom-hole with feverish quickness. The fires of voluptuousness flamed still fiercer in my veins, and my body writhed under the influence of this current of libidinousness. My voice faltered, it seemed as if I could bear no more, and then the resistance within was forced aside. I felt a series of throbs and thrills of inconceivable yet almost agonising pleasure shoot through me, while my cock leaped with uncontrollable vehemence, and discharged its liquid in gushes from the end into the mouth of Lord Henry, who sucked with all his force, causing me an excruciating though exquisite rapture, so that it was beyond endurance; I could see no more to read, my head fell back nervelessly, I gasped and groaned, and my fingers clutched the book convulsively, almost tearing it. I strove to rise and free myself, but my companion with firm hands stayed my struggles, and did not cease from his labial operations, which threw me into a frenzy of emotional madness, until at last I could stand no more, and, bending down, dropping the book I held, I clutched wildly at Lord Henry's head. He looked up with an insinuating glance, and requested me to go on reading; so, feeling compelled to obey, I picked up the book again, and, forced to ignore the deep agitation which shook my frame, began again in as calm a tone as I could manage, all the time filled with a raging bodily irritation, which was all the more aggravated by my having to remain passive under it, while my cock ached and smarted and tingled beneath Lord Henry's tongue and lips, the flesh round the root palpitated, my balls hung down poignantly sensitive, and my intestines twisted in an interior travail. My soul seemed verily to shrink within me beneath all these symptoms, and I read on half in a dream. It was not until I had finished another two chapters that Lord Henry desisted from his attentions, at last got up, took away the book, which he replaced in the cabinet, and brought a warm dressing-gown, which he directed me to don.

When I had put this on, my host said it was time to retire, and conducted me to a very large bedroom, wainscotted with oak, and equipped with splendid specimens of massive, antique furniture, with an enormous, old-fashioned bed at one side. A huge fire blazed merrily in the capacious fireplace, and diffused a pleasant warmth throughout the apartment.

I looked about for my night attire, but Lord Henry said I should not need it, and made me get into the large and luxurious bed quite nude. I was not likely to be cold, however, as above the embroidered silk counterpane there was a thick down quilt, and a great coverlet of soft, warm fur over that.

It was evident that my host intended to sleep with me, for he began to disrobe, and when he had divested himself of everything, he, too, got into bed. Turning back the bedclothes, so that I was fully exposed, he next started to osculate me all over, kissing repeatedly and with the utmost fervency my breast, thighs, shoulders, neck, cheeks, arms and legs, sucking my toes, tickling my back, groin and belly with his tongue, licking my feet, hands and face, imprinting labial caresses all over me, and finding out all the most sensitive parts – under the arms, the nostrils, the ears, the soles of the feet, the palms of the hands, the throat and the inner part of the thighs – and lavishing unbounded philanderings on the smooth rotundity of my buttocks, kissing and mumbling them all over, licking the furrow; finally, pressing the cheeks apart so as to obtain better scope, he stretched open the bottom-hole with his fingers and inserted therein the tip of his tongue, making me squirm with the peculiar sensation thus created. When at last he had satisfied himself with all this, he put me flat on the bed and knelt over me the opposite way, so that his thighs came above my face. Directing me to follow his example, he began to suck my cock again. I hesitated to do likewise, as this was the first time I had ever been engaged with a man in lewd practices, and I felt rather backward. However, he repeated his wishes, so I somewhat gingerly took hold of his fiercely erect member and applied my lips to it. It seemed impossible that I could get it in my mouth, it was so large, but, after the first moment's repulsion, I quickly warmed to the work, and sucked and tickled it with my tongue as well as I knew how. Lord Henry, meanwhile, was doing his best to arouse my cock, which had lapsed into inertness, into new vigour, rubbing it with his hand, sucking the top, and working one finger smartly in and out of my bottom-hole; I, in return, caressed his balls and posteriors with my hands. My companion was raised to a considerable pitch of excitement, and the crisis was not long in approaching. I was a little apprehensive of this, but when it came he pressed his thighs and belly closer to my face, so as to prevent me from moving my head away, and in another minute my mouth was filled with a tremendous discharge of hot, thick cream, which shot down over my tongue and palate and throat, almost choking me, and which, of course, being in the position I was, I was forced to swallow. But this only added to my own emotions. My member was beginning to rise to the occasion, but in a somewhat half-hearted way; when the last drop from Lord Henry's weapon had found its way into my mouth, my companion changed his position, and, kneeling down by the side of me, worked my cock up and down with his hand in a rapid manner, at the same time tickling my balls and bottom with his disengaged hand. The process proved rather protracted, but Lord Henry's energy was tireless, and at last attained its fruition. My member was sore and inflamed from its first effusion, and pained and smarted somewhat, particularly when now and then my companion gave it a little suck, while the continual pulling down of the skin as far as it would go hurt me a trifle, but I thought it useless to expostulate, and bore the operation in silence. Presently, the same glow of voluptuousness as before spread over me, the thrills of vital electricity once more went shooting through my frame, I heaved and writhed and clenched my hands together, my breath came in short gasps, and, as Lord Henry bent down and commenced to suck my cock with all his force, my whole consciousness was drowned in a flood of sensuality, my head fell back with upturned eyes, and I sank into a swoon brought on by the intolerable keenness of my physical sensations, prefacing this lapse of consciousness by a smothered groan and cry.

When I came to, I found that Lord Henry had risen, and was regarding me with anxiety, but, on seeing that my senses had returned, he lay down beside me and drew the bedclothes over us both. Then he clasped me tightly to him, my breast against his, and fastening his mouth to mine, kissed me with all a lover's ardour, forcing my mouth open with his tongue, which he thrust inside against mine, making it stay there while our saliva mixed. He held me thus for a considerable time, and then he caused me to turn round; anon, lying close to me, he put his cock between my legs and commenced to work gently in a backwards and forwards movement, while with one hand he took hold of my member and softly moved it up and down, an action which caused me some unpleasantness, as it ached and was sore after its recent experiences, but I said nothing and schooled myself to bear it, being a little curious to ascertain how my companion would continue. This went on for a period, and then Lord Henry's movements became rather more brisk, until at last he emitted a copious outflow, which bathed my thighs in a warm fluid which he rubbed with his hand over my balls and cock and belly.

After this, I was permitted to compose myself for slumber, which I was not sorry for. Lord Henry did not seem greatly inclined for conversation, and, after a few sentences had passed between us, he recommended me to try and go to sleep. He did not attempt to prevent me, but, until the time I lost myself in oblivion, I felt my companion's hands caressing me unceasingly all over, but more particularly between the thighs, while ever and anon he imprinted kisses on my back and shoulders and the nape of my neck.

CHAPTER THIRTEEN

Hebworth Castle

I slept soundly, and did not awake until the following morning, but when I did so it was to find that Lord Henry held one of my hands fondly in his, while with his remaining one he was playing with my cock.

As soon as he saw me open my eyes, he gave me an affectionate morning greeting, and asked if I had slept well. I replied that I had – very well indeed. With the new day, I began to feel a warm friendship for my host, and the experiences of the preceding night softened themselves in my recollection, so that I upbraided myself, in thought, that I should have ever been nervous or frightened. There had been no occasion for it, as Lord Henry had uniformly exhibited the greatest kindness towards me, while, when I came to review the whole circumstances calmly, I saw that I need not have felt surprise, considering what Rutherford and the duke had told me about their relative, and the hints they had let fall concerning him. I determined, therefore, to take full advantage, from this time onward, of all that my present visit might have to offer me.

The fire still burned brightly, having evidently been tended during the hours that we slept. Shortly after I awakened, the door of the room opened, and two good-looking Japanese boys of about thirteen years of age, clad in richly embroidered kimonos, entered, bearing on silver trays a morning repast of rolls and cakes and hot-house fruit, with jugs of warm milk. These trays they placed on little tables either side of the bed, and then stood at attention, waiting until we might finish.

'These are my two hostages from the Land of the Chrysanthemum,' said Lord Henry. 'They are a nice pair, are they not? Their names are Yakuri and Ko-San.'

They smiled when their master spoke to them, and appeared to be on excellent terms with him. When we had done, they went away with the trays, and after this Lord Henry rose. I followed his example, and looked round for my clothes, but my host, divining my glance, directed me to put on the dressing-gown again, donning a similar garment himself. Before robing, however, I went to get the chamber-pot, but on seeing this, Lord Henry made me lie back, with head and body on the bed and feet on the floor; then, pressing my legs apart, he knelt down between them and, bidding me pass water, took my cock in his mouth. The doings of the previous night had wellnigh taken away my capacity for amazement, and, anxious to relieve myself, I took him at his word, and poured forth a hot stream of urine. He swallowed the whole, and did not remove his lips until he had sucked off the last few drops that clung to the end of my member, taking a draught of milk afterwards to clear his palate.

After this, my host took me to the bathroom, which was a large apartment, furnished and decorated with considerable luxury. Here we found the two Japanese lads and also an English boy, rather younger, and very handsome, with clear, blue eyes and curling, golden hair. He wore slippers, and a kind of loose tunic of figured stuff, with flowing sleeves. Lord Henry patted him on the cheek, and said, 'This is my little friend Jack. He has been with me quite a long time now, and is altogether devoted to my interests. I have taken care of him ever since his parents died.'

It was no doubt owing to the lateness of the hour, that I had not see these boys the evening before. It was thus I mused as I looked at them, and I was waiting for them to leave the room, so that I might bathe; but apparently they were in no hurry to go. Then it occurred to me that my host was about to ask me to bare myself before them all. The idea was not altogether pleasing, and the carmine entered my cheeks again.

'I think we might bathe now, Charlie,' said Lord Henry. 'Then we can go and sit in the hall.'

I turned a last look at the three boys, and then glanced questioningly at my host, but he averted his eyes and directed his gaze at the trio, who, as if understanding the unspoken command, threw off their robes. The two Japanese boys advanced to me, unfastened my dressing-gown and drew it off. I neither offered resistance nor made protest, only experiencing a degree of injured modesty at being thus exposed before them. However, the proceedings went on without regard to my feelings.

Jack fetched a large pot of soap, a dish of hot water, and a big brush, like an overgrown shaving-brush, and went on to cover my body with thick layers of soapy lather, which Ko-San and Yakuri rubbed in with their hands. I stood on a perforated slab or kind of large, shallow basin, while this was going on, to allow the water which was poured over me to run away – as there was more than one application of the lather, each time it being washed off with hot water. At first I felt some humiliation at being manipulated in this way, for Yakuri and Ko-San held no part of my body sacred from their touch, and pulled about my arms and legs in all ways to suit their convenience, while Jack seemed to take an impish delight in paying particular attention with his soap-brush to my thighs and belly and posteriors, thrusting his instrument right into the furrow of my bottom, lifting up my cock while he lathered my balls, and generally acting in an abandoned way, laughing gleefully the while; but I could not help finally entering into the spirit of the thing, and joining in his mirth myself.

When I had been thoroughly washed and dried, Lord Henry, who had in the meantime performed his own ablutions, brought me a superb kimono of Japanese embroidered silk, lined with fur. Slippers edged with fur were placed on my feet. My host then begged me to accompany him to the hall. I rose to do so, but was rather startled to find that my robe had no fastenings. Apparently, I was not to be allowed even now effectually to hide my nakedness, but as I followed Lord Henry, I drew the voluminous folds of the garment around me, and held them together as best I could with my hands. We stood in the hall for a brief space, where we were joined by the three boys, who had resumed their clothing. Lord Henry said something to the young Japanese, which I did not catch, and they placed themselves casually one at each side of me. Presently the negroes entered, clad only in loose, closed tunics. They made a deep obeisance to their master who acknowledged it and addressed a few words to them in their native tongue, pointing to me as he did so. They turned to me and repeated their salute; at the same moment, Ko-San and Yakuri each seized one of my hands and led me forward a pace, whereupon my robe, being released, fell open, so that my nude body was exposed to the gaze of these black-skinned menials, causing a further trial to my sense of modesty.

Lord Henry conducted me to a seat, and gave me a richly illustrated volume of travels to look at, while he also took up a book. We stayed here until the servants came to announce that the midday meal was ready. This was plentiful and of excellent character, the negroes serving, while the boys also waited in attendance. Afterwards, when the utensils had been taken away, but before the cloth was removed, Lord Henry said, 'We must have a final course of sweets!' and he directed me to take off my robe. When I had done so, I was laid at full length on the table, my legs slightly raised, and my knees bent as far apart as possible. My host told me to remain in this position, and then, with a spoon, he smeared my cock and balls and the adjacent parts of my thighs and belly with a plentiful coating of a rich, thick, Oriental conserve. This he applied himself to lick off with the greatest relish, not stopping until he had cleared away every particle with his tongue, and, indeed, keeping on after all had gone. Not content even then, he uncovered the head of my member, and put another large spoonful on this and all around the sides under the knob, also licking this off. And when this was over, and I expected to be at last released, more of the conserve was put on, and each of the three boys took a turn in sucking it off. I was then, however, allowed to resume my robe, and, as I did so, I said, 'I have known that before. It is what is called the *bâton de sucre*, is it not?'

Lord Henry smiled and replied, 'That is certainly a very appropriate name, although I do not remember having heard it before. How did you get acquainted with it?'

I told him, and he listened with much interest, saying that he should get me to relate more of my adventures to him.

He gave me a volume from a bookshelf, and I ensconced myself in an easy-chair by the fire, while he himself sat down at a desk and began to write. My anticipations of a quiet time were not to be realised, however, for Jack placed himself on a huge cushion at my feet, and, throwing my gown wide open, commenced to play with my cock and balls. I softly thrust him away, and pulled the edges of my robe together, but Lord Henry was observant and, shaking his finger at me, smilingly commanded me to occupy myself with my book and leave Jack to do as he liked; so I resigned myself to the inevitable, and let the boy handle my private parts as he listed, pulling and bending my cock this way and that, covering and uncovering the head, squeezing it with his hand, tickling my balls and stroking and caressing my thighs and belly and bottom. Once he started an up-and-down movement on my member, which was beginning to swell under his manual exercises, but Lord Henry saw this and frowned disapproval, so Jack contented himself with less exciting caresses, varying his programme by rubbing and chafing my legs and feet, kissing and sucking my toes, insteps, soles, calves, thighs, genitals and belly, and otherwise putting into action all he could devise in the way of blandishments.

Lord Henry wrote for a considerable time, then, rising from the desk, he took a chair on the opposite side of the hearth to me. As he could see, my member was by this time standing up in a condition of excitation. Calling Jack to him, he made him kneel on a hassock in front of his chair, and, opening his garment, presented his cock to him to suck, which Jack did with much gusto. When the moment came for him to discharge, he held Jack's head between his hands, and told him not to swallow the liquid, but to keep it in his mouth. Jack did so, and Lord Henry brought him over to me, ordering me to hold my head back, and open my mouth. I obeyed instinctively, and Lord Henry directed Jack to give me a kiss. This the boy did, and, putting his mouth against mine, he let Lord Henry's sperm, mingled with his own saliva, roll down my throat, assisting the operation with his tongue, and glueing his lips to mine, so that not a drop might escape.

'There!' said my host, with a laugh; 'that is an equal distribution of pleasure, is it not? It reminds one of the old proverb about killing two birds with one stone.'

Lord Henry then composed himself to smoke a Turkish narghile, which occupied a fair period, during which Jack again amused himself in toying with my private parts.

Having finished smoking, Lord Henry opened his robe again, and asked me to come to him. Bidding me remove my garment, he made me sit on his lap with his cock between my legs, while he held my hands with one of his, and with the other stroked and smoothed my breast and belly. Then he caused Jack to kneel down in front, and take my cock between his lips, but would not allow him to suck it too strongly, making him remove his mouth at short intervals, and change the order of things by licking my balls and thighs, tickling my belly and bottom, and so on, as he was desirous not to make me come to a crisis, the arrival of which he feared from the way in which my cock stiffened, while, indeed, I was praying for the event, so greatly had my passions been aroused. This went on until it was plainly advisable, from the spontaneous contortions of my body, that a cessation should take place, so our mutual conjunction was broken.

A light repast of tea, cakes, fruit and honey was now brought by the Japanese boys. Before we commenced, Lord Henry said, 'I know you like the *bâton de sucre*, Charlie. Try it now; it will serve to remind you of your friends.' Making Jack lie down, and covering his private parts with honey, he instructed me to lick it off, insisting upon my doing it thoroughly; and when I had finished, Lord Henry caused Jack to lie the reverse way, with his buttocks well thrust out, and applied another plentiful coating of honey to his bottom, smearing it thickly in the furrow and all round the fundament. This also I was requested to lick off. My task ended, there yet proved to be one more preliminary before eating. Lord Henry made me sit on a stool, and taking hold of my cock, which was still half-erect, he pressed back the prepuce and coated the knob and column with honey; then he presented the *entremet* to Jack to enjoy. The lad found the sweet so appetising, and sucked to such purpose, that Lord Henry had to pull away his head, lest he should bring about the result my host did not seem to wish for.

After tea, we repaired to the saloon, where the rest of the household also assembled. The first thing which happened was the fetching of a large bowl of rose-water by the negro, Paul, which he offered to us to dip our fingers in.

The two black men then stripped, and performed a little series of feats of strength and agility, displaying a tremendous power of muscle, finishing by catching up Jack, who had put off his garb, and throwing him from one to the other, balancing him on their hands and shoulders, and so on.

All this time, I was seated on a luxurious divan between Ko-San and Yakuri, who each held a hand of mine on one of theirs, and with the disengaged ones stroked and patted my body and played with my cock and balls.

When Jack had concluded his acrobatic performances, he made the negroes stand close together near me, facing each other, and taking their members in his hands, squeezed them and pulled them until they rose to the occasion in the full majesty of their tremendous proportions, when he deftly and briskly rubbed them up and down, till white jets of sperm spouted out, splashing over each the other's breast and belly, and bathing the youthful operator's hands, at which Jack seemed hugely delighted. When he had finished, he lifted his wet hands and the negroes licked them dry.

Ko-San and Yakuri now, doffing their kimonos, gave a very spirited exhibition of wrestling, in which both proved themselves lithe and active, and neither had much advantage over the other. After a long bout, Ko-San lay underneath, with Yakuri over him in the opposite direction. Ko-San seized his opponent round the loins, but, instead of continuing the combat, Yakuri took hold of the others's cock and began to work it about. Ko-San thereupon did the same. Presently they rose and performed a lascivious Eastern dance, swaying their bodies, arms and limbs in a variety of voluptuous movements, making a sort of lewd pantomime, and touching, patting, titillating and pulling each other's private parts until their members were as stiff as bars. When they had wrought themselves up to a frenzy of excitement, they gave a cry, and Jack bounded forward. Ko-San stretched himself flat on the floor, and Jack knelt over him the reverse way, taking his cock in his mouth, tickling his balls with one hand, while with the other he pinched and fingered the Japanese lad's bottom, and thrust one finger into the hole, working it in and out with great energy. Ko-San clasped him round the body, and kissed and licked his belly, while Yakuri came up behind, and, pressing open the cheeks of Jack's posterior, licked the furrow and thoroughly lubricated the aperture with saliva, and then thrust in his cock and pushed forward until it was completely engulfed, and his belly rested against Jack's buttocks, when he commenced a vigorous backwards and forwards motion. All three wriggled and writhed for a time with voluptuous delight, in expectation of the coming joy. Ko-San was the first to reach the haven of bliss; his belly heaved heavily as he strove to thrust his cock further into Jack's mouth, his legs twisted together, his toes contracted, and then his limbs collapsed as he shot a discharge, which Jack swallowed as he felt it spurt into his mouth; but Jack did not relinquish the hold of his lips. Soon after, Yakuri's movements became shorter and more rapid, one or two slow, heavy lunges succeeded, and then he stopped, as his genital organ, which was as far in Jack's bottom as he could get it, delivered itself of its essence with throbbing pulsations. Yakuri let his cock soak for some moments in Jack's warm and now moist bottom-hole, and then withdrew it, whereupon Jack turned and took it between his lips, sucking all the moisture off it. Ko-San now began to suck Jack's cock, which was very stiff by this time, and was an extremely fascinating member, although of modest proportions as yet, and quite innocent of hirsute adornment. Yakuri changed his position slightly, brought his face against Jack's bottom, held open the dividing furrow, and stretching apart the pink orifice, thrust in his tongue as far as possible, working it about in the interior with all his might, as it seemed to me, and making Jack throb and tingle, as I could see, under the tickling and licking of the hot, moist, dart-like member, and the sucking and mumbling of the mobile lips.

When this had been going on for some time, Lord Henry clapped his hands as a signal for them to cease, and called Jack to him. Lifting the boy up, he sat him on my lap. Jack immediately put his arm round my neck, and, drawing my face towards his, kissed me warmly on the mouth and cheek. I was rather taken with this bright-faced lad, and I returned the embrace, supporting him with my left arm. Jack then took hold of my right hand and directed it to his stiff little cock, which he placed between my thumb and first finger, and moved my hand up and down, telling me to go on. I had no objection, feeling thoroughly in the mood for any kind of sensuality, and soon completely succumbed to the fascination of the task; while Jack's belly began to heave and his bottom to wriggle, and he stiffened his legs, crossing and uncrossing them in his erotic emotion; and when the finality arrived, he twisted his body about snake-like, almost unseating himself, and broke into low, hysterical laughing as the transports of voluptuousness seized upon him; but after the first paroxysm was over, he climbed to his feet on the divan, facing me, and guiding his member with his fingers, thrust it between my lips, holding it there for me to suck off the few drops of embryonic sperm that suffused the top.

Lord Henry now came to sit beside me, and said, 'I am afraid, Charlie, that you will spend a dull Christmas here. It was perhaps hardly kind of me to wish you to come, when all the society I had to offer you was my own.'

'Not at all, Harry,' I replied – he had begged me to call him by this name – 'I have been looking forward to my visit here for ever so long. I did certainly feel a little shy about coming by myself, but now that I am here, I am pleased, and I thank you very much for your kindness. You know, I was hoping to come in the last holidays.'

'Ah! I remember,' he answered; 'but unfortunately I was away. And that reminds me; I want you to tell me all about your adventures. I heard of your visit to Paris with de Beaupré.'

I gave him a detailed account of my stay with Gaston, and he listened with the greatest interest. When I told him about the meeting in honour of Flora, he went on to give me a lot of information on the subject, and was evidently extremely learned and well-versed in the classics and history, telling me a great many curious and interesting facts which were quite new to me.

'If you would like to read of such matters,' he said; 'I have a number of books which you can amuse yourself with while here. I have made quite a large collection of rare volumes during my time, and you cannot come across such everywhere.'

All the time we had been talking, Lord Henry regarded me intently, and fondled my hands and feet, but did not make use of any exciting caresses. His conversation, however, roused me greatly, and at last, taking hold of my cock, I began to titillate it in a very determined way. But he stopped me, saying with a smile, 'I forbid it positively, Charley. Self-indulgence is entirely contrary to the laws in force at Hebworth. Please wait, and in due time you shall be rewarded.'

When my host had finished a cigarette which he had lighted, he requested me to accompany him to the bathroom. Thither the Japanese boys and Jack also came, and I was told to seat myself in a large round bowl or tub. The three lads then gathered round and deluged me with their urine, the jets from the living fountains splashing over my face and neck and body, and running down me in hot streams. After this I was douched with warm water, and went through a bath as in the morning.

On getting back to the saloon, we found that the evening repast was ready, and repaired to the dining-room. The negroes served, as at lunch, and Ko-San and Yakuri also waited upon us. Jack was there as well, but the part he took was to crouch by the side of me, or underneath the table at my feet, and finger and handle my cock and balls throughout the meal, keeping me in a perpetual fidget of irritation, which was not, however, altogether disagreeable.

Afterwards, we went into the hall again, where Lord Henry made me sit on a sofa and finish reading aloud the erotic book which I had begun the night before; and while I did so, Ko-San and Yakuri, who had placed themselves by my side, played with my member, squeezing it and pulling it about until it got erect, and keeping it stiff by their pertinacious handling, the flagitious chapters of the book, as I read them, also serving to excite my organ. In the middle of this, Jack brought a book-rest to put the volume on, and stood by to turn the pages over for me; my hands now being at liberty, the Japanese lads each took one and held it against his private parts, squeezing his thighs together to keep my fingers in place; but they soon ceased to do this, when they found that I was quite ready to hold their cocks and tickle their balls of my own accord. My member naturally grew so very stiff that finally Lord Henry got me to stretch myself out on the sofa. He then took hold of my upright genital instrument, pulled back the skin and dropped a large spoonful of condensed milk over the swelling head, the thick substance running down the short column and on to my thighs and balls. He himself sucked me, licking it off, and Ko-San, Yakuri and Jack were given a similar treat, Lord Henry watching carefully to see that they did not do their work too well and cause me to discharge. Jack was then laid down, and a good quantity of the sweet, coagulated cream put on his cock and testicles. I removed this with my lips and tongue, and a second lot was placed on his bottom where it joined the legs, and this I also licked off.

By this time it was getting late, and Lord Henry proposed that we should retire. I was devoutly looking forward to the promised easing of my inflamed feelings, which were now troubling me considerably, and I had hopes that the sought-for relief would now come. I was prepared for anything which would lead to this end, and I was perfectly ready to obey, therefore, when, after we were undressed, Lord Henry directed me to lie with my back on the bed and put my legs over his shoulders. I was not quite sure what he was about to do, but I soon grasped the fact that it was his intention to penetrate into my bottom. This made me feel nervous, seeing that he was a large-made man and up to the present I had only received the members of boys. He, however, re-assured me, telling me I need have no fear; and he put some ointment on my fundament. He then brought his great member, raging with lust, to the attack, and I shuddered a little as he put the head against the orifice of my posterior and pressed forward with all his might. I gave a cry as the big knob found its way inside, but Lord Henry soothed me, and continued his pushing until his organ of offence had effected a complete entrance. I found it a very different matter to taking in even Rutherford's tolerably large cock, and was on the point of protesting against the painful sense of distension, but my assailant spoke comfortingly to me, and I clenched my teeth and made up my mind to endure his advances as long as I could. I felt, however, as if something dreadful must happen soon, but fortunately the pent-up fervour of my companion was quick in finding an outlet, and within a brief space he shot a plentiful emission into me; this served to counteract all the unpleasantness, oiling the passage and setting up a warm and delightful emotion within my body.

He then made me lie flat on the bed, and, kneeling at my feet, commenced to suck me. I cannot describe the wonderful relief this was, after the sensual provocation I had been suffering all day. I stretched every muscle in my efforts to respond to his attentions, and in a remarkably rapid time, as it seemed, Lord Henry succeeded in drawing forth my vital essence. I had grown wild with voluptuous pleasure under the persuasive influence of his lips and tongue, and I lay inert for several minutes, prostrated with exhaustion, after he had taken himself away from me.

We then got into bed, but my companion insisted upon holding me in a wanton embrace. During the night, I woke up to find him sucking my cock, and indeed, I verily believe that all through the hours of rest he was doing something of this kind.

It was fine and mild next day, so I had an opportunity to go out and have a look at my new quarters. The place seemed remote from the world altogether, while, further to seclude it, the whole demesne was surrounded by a high stone wall. The place had come into the possession of Lord Henry from his father, Jimmy's grandparent, and was then in a sadly neglected condition, not having been dwelt in for many years; but he had exerted himself to put it into repair and make it thoroughly habitable, its position making it in every way suitable as a retreat where he could come to stay without fear of being intruded upon; and the doors of Hebworth were never opened, save to his especial and intimate friends.

The structure was of fair size, enough not remarkably extensive, but a number of the rooms, especially in the upper part, were bare and never used. A caretaker and his wife, with another servant, lived here, but their quarters were quite apart and shut off from the portion of the building made use of by its owner. As he was not here regularly, and did not have much company when he was in residence, there was no necessity for a large establishment, and the people at the lodge helped in the household work if occasion required.

Beyond saying that as the days went on, my enjoyment of the stay increased, I shall not further particularise my doings. Lord Henry proved a model entertainer, and his brilliant and discursive conversation was always full of interest, while he gave me, as promised, a selection of highly pleasing and instructive hooks to read.

Soon after Christmas, my friends arrived, all in excellent spirits and eager to avail themselves of the delights of Lord Henry's hospitality. Our host was thoroughly in his element, and averred that the walls of Hebworth had not resounded with so much merriment for many a long day.

As both his relatives were now with him at the same time, they could not any longer put their tongues in their cheeks, like the augurs, when speaking of him before one another. Each, however, knew Lord Henry well, and therefore made no pretence, but were well content to take things as they found them. He would not let the duke call him 'Uncle', but insisted upon us all addressing him by his Christian name, saying that it sounded more familiar, and put us all on a friendlier footing.

'How well Jimmy seems, doesn't he?' he exclaimed, when we met the party at the station. 'I'm sure from his looks he's a bigger scamp than ever, too!'

He had a previous acquaintance with de Beaupré, also, so it can be imagined that we made a very happy and vivacious party.

'It is not very nice weather today,' he said, on the afternoon following their arrival. 'We will go to the Turret Room.'

This was a square room, not too large, in the south tower of the castle, hung with tapestries and thickly carpeted. The apartment had evidently been prepared for us, and an immense fire burned on the hearth. On the opposite side, and directly facing the blaze, was a very large daïs or divan, spread with innumerable rugs and cushions. We had only our dressing-gowns on, and ere we lay ourselves down, Lord Henry asked us to take these garments off, so that he might enjoy the sight of our nude bodies. The room was so warm that we readily complied, and did not suffer in the least from cold as we nestled amid the pillows, but, on the contrary, rejoiced at the sense of freedom thus given us. Jack and the Japanese brought us pleasant drinks and sweetmeats, and we felt quite at ease and jolly as Lord Henry rattled on with his sparkling talk.

Presently he called Jack and said something to him. The boy left the room, soon afterwards returning, followed by the negroes. Lord Henry spoke to the latter and they took off their tunics. Peter lay at full length on the ground, and Ko-San worked at his member until it was erect; Yakuri did the same to Paul. At a signal shortly from Ko-San, Paul squatted over Peter, bringing his buttocks over the latter's thighs, while Ko-San guided Peter's stiffened weapon into the aperture of Paul's posterior, first well moistening both this and Peter's organ with saliva. Paul now proceeded to rise and fall like a man on horseback, causing Peter's cock to work in and out of his bottom, while Yakuri continued to rub Paul's member up and down, and Ko-San tickled Peter's balls and chafed his thighs smartly. The denouement was not long in arriving: first of all Paul shot out strong jets of sperm on to Peter's neck and face and breast; very soon after, Peter made a sign that he was about to discharge, and when Paul felt the liquid injected into him he rose up, leaving Peter's cock reeking with its owner's emission.

The parts which they had taken had greatly excited Ko-San and Yakuri, and each began to pluck at his stiff cock as if it irritated him, seeing which Jack ran forward. They fell upon him, and knelt down, Yakuri in front and Ko-San at his back, the first-named sucking and licking Jack's cock and balls, while the other caressed his buttocks with lips and tongue. When they tired of this, they rose to their feet, and Ko-San made Jack bend over while he inserted his cock in Jack's bottom-hole, whereupon Jack straightened himself again. Then Yakuri put his member between Jack's thighs, just under his testicles, and made him close his legs together as tightly as possible. When they had got into position, Ko-San and Yakuri began working backwards and forwards energetically, twining their arms round Jack, who was immensely pleased with the sensation of being sandwiched thus between their warm bodies, the movements of their thighs and the wrigglings of their legs and trunks, pressed closely against him, sending a delightful tickling all through his frame, as he told us afterwards, while he kissed Yakuri all the time, and Ko-San, not to be backward, exerted all the exciting force of his tongue on the nape of Jack's neck. All three panted and grew hot as their passion increased, and at last Ko-San stopped his motions, while at the same time Jack called out to us that he felt a moist warmth in his bottom, and we knew that his rear assailant had discharged into him. Quickly afterwards, Yakuri gave one or two short, hard pushes, and then also ceased, the hot essence he gave forth trickling down Jack's legs. The three then disengaged, and Yakuri knelt and licked off the liquid from Jack's limbs, Ko-San following his example behind, Jack stooping and opening his legs so as to give him better play.

Jack's cock was by this time standing up in a particularly impudent manner, energised by having been agitated between his own and Yakuri's bellies. Lord Henry, who watched everything narrowly, turned to me with a smile and made me lie on my face on the daïs, with my knees drawn up, so as to place my bottom in the most convenient posture obtainable, and he then called to Jack, who rushed forward and sprang towards me. First kissing and licking my posteriors, and well lubricating the hole with saliva, he brought his cock to the attack, and pushed it in. I felt it enter, but he was a very different case to Lord Henry, and I experienced little unpleasantness. Indeed, after a short time I began to feel a sensuous emotion, as Jack worked his member in and out of the tight passage; and this was added to by my young ravisher, who clasped his arms round my waist and fingered my testicles and genital organ, which latter rapidly expanded and grew harder as Jack held it. He was in a salacious mood, and worked fast, his lunges growing shorter and quicker, and he breathed heavily with sensual excitement. At length, he gave a final plunge forward, forcing his cock to its furthest extent into me, and then collapsed on my back, while I felt his little weapon jump and throb inside my bottom, and was conscious of a sudden hot and wet sensation therein.

Presently Jack got off, and, lying down, pulled my head over his thighs, motioning me to take his cock in my mouth. Seeing that it had but just emerged from my rear entrance, I at first recoiled from the idea, but Jack laughed and urged me again; so, summoning up my resolution, I next moment closed my lips on his member. I did not find it by any means so dreadful as I had anticipated, and I was to a great extent kept up to my task by Jack, who patted my cheeks, and took my cock between his feet, pushing it from one side to the other, and working the skin back with his toes.

After a prolonged bout of this, Jack got up and, directing me to lie down, started to suck my member, while Ko-San and Yakuri began to tickle and caress me, the lustful enjoyment of all this creeping throughout my body, and entirely taking possession of all my faculties. Jack was a past master in his wondrous use of mouth and hands, while the Japanese boys were equally dexterous in their methods of excitation. I completely succumbed to the voluptuousness of the moment, while Jack employed all his arts to intensify and draw out the pleasure – now taking my cock in his mouth as far as possible, then just touching the tip with his tongue, anon sucking the head strongly, and afterwards tolling his tongue round beneath the base of the knob; then he would leave my cock alone and suck or tickle my balls or thighs or belly, or thrust his lingual organ between my legs underneath the testicles; and, again, he varied all this by stroking my member with his hands, rubbing it smartly for a second or two, following this up by agitating it with the lightest touch of his deft fingers, pulling up the prepuce till it made a sort of funnel down which he darted his tongue, covering and uncovering the head with the slowest deliberation, tickling my balls and rubbing quickly underneath them between the legs, scratching and chafing the lower part of my bottom, and putting a finger in the hole and working it about therein, running his fingers over my bare pubes in an apparent search for symptoms of the hair which had not yet put in an appearance, and passing his hand over my abdomen with a gentle smoothness. My body writhed lasciviously, and my senses reeled in lustful frenzy; my cock was hot as fire, and quivered and throbbed intermittently. My teeth shut tightly as I felt the ecstasy approach; my belly heaved and contracted; my whole frame shuddered, and then the delirium seized upon me; I gasped and half shrieked with the exquisite joy, the glorious, intolerable anguish of the boiling tempest of unbounded pleasure that overwhelmed my being; and a mist grew before my eyes. Meanwhile my cock was chattering against Jack's teeth, and discharging a quite copious flow of warm vital fluid into his mouth; and when he had extracted every drop of this elixir from its source, he quickly raised himself, and putting his mouth against mine, which seemed to open of its own volition, he opened his lips and let my own essence run down my throat. In the passion of the moment, I swallowed it greedily, appreciating the odour and taste, and I licked Jack's lips and thrust my tongue into his mouth, in an anxious attempt to obtain more.

While this was going on, Ko-San fastened upon my member with his lips, sending fresh currents of smarting rapture through me; and Yakuri, lifting up one of my legs and holding it so with his arm, pressed his face against my bottom, pushing his nose between the cheeks, and sucking in the furrow, tickling it with his tongue, and thrusting that member as far as he could into the sensitive orifice.

Jack and I continued our mutual kissing and tonguing, caressing each other with our hands at the same time. After some period, Jack lifted his head from me, and, propping me up with cushions, knelt with his thighs against my face, and inserted his cock between my lips. I sucked it with avidity, and found much pleasure in prolonging the operation, until, to my great surprise, some hot fluid exuded into my mouth. For a moment, I thought that Jack had discharged his essence again; but a salt taste as the liquor rolled down my throat proclaimed that it was urine. I did not refrain from sucking, nevertheless, and presently Jack, with a light laugh of merriment, let some more of the warm juice escape from his cock; but I still did not turn from my task. A little while before, I should never have deemed such a thing as I was doing possible; but now I appeared quite to enjoy the sensation as Jack, at short intervals, squirted little jets of greater or less quantity into my mouth, and I actually smiled at the caprice of lubricity which prompted him, as the hot liquid splashed over my tongue and against my palate prior to being swallowed.

While this had been going on, I had been so engrossed in my own affairs that I had not troubled to observe the doings of the remainder of the company. But I now saw that they were all amusing themselves in some way or other. Bob had procured the ministrations of Ko-San, while Yakuri lent his services to Jimmy. Lord Henry had devoted himself to de Beaupré, and had him across his lap, so that he had every opportunity to indulge in a luxury of hand-play, and Blackie, in return, held Lord Henry's member, and bestowed soft rubs to it. Being now unemployed, I could lie at my leisure and watch the lot of them; and the sight was so exhilarating that I could almost feel the deeply pleasurable emotions which all gave the fullest evidence of experiencing. The scene was over too soon for me, for before very long Rutherford and the duke gave way under the young Japanese lads' caresses. De Beaupré had been kept artfully in suspense by our host, but at last he too succumbed, after which Lord Henry, who had held himself back by making Blackie stop his caresses whenever they promised to be too seductive, let himself go, and in a few seconds discharged his sperm vigorously, causing Gaston to hold his member straight upwards, so that the emission leaped high into the air and fell back in white patches, partly on him and partly on de Beaupré.

We then settled ourselves down quietly, and resumed conversation.

'You have a pretty good time at school,' said Lord Henry. 'You enjoy yourselves very well, from what I can hear. You are very lucky to be so well placed. Of course, there is general scope for pleasure at schools, but they do not always offer such good opportunities as you have found, nor is there invariably such a jolly lot of fellows gathered together. Very often there are two or three prigs present, who spoil a good lot of the fun. I used to get on all right myself, I thought; but I must confess that I was far behind you. You see, I was at Eton, which makes a great difference; there is a certain amount of disadvantage in one of the very large public schools, on account of the many different classes of boys there. Still, I had the luck to get in one of the best houses, and there were several awfully decent chaps with me. I was further favoured, in addition, for in my fagging days I was "taken up" by a charming fellow named Everest. We kept up our friendship long after we grew up; but the poor fellow joined the Lancers and was drafted out to India, where he was so badly mauled by a tiger that he died.

'But all boarding-schools and colleges are very much alike, and always have been. There is ever the chance for enjoyment, if one looks for it.'

He went on to tell us a number of highly-spiced anecdotes, and as I listened to them my emotions began to arise again. Jack found this out, as he set himself down to play with my cock, which commenced to enlarge itself and turn up its nose until it was quite erect, when he amused himself by continually pulling it down and letting it rebound with a thump against my abdomen.

At length, Lord Henry, noting my distress, which was even greater than that displayed by my companions, gave some rapid instructions to the negroes, who came and lay upon the divan. Peter placed himself behind me, and forced his member between my legs. Paul lay in front, taking my cock between his thighs, his own stiff weapon being squeezed between our two bellies. The negroes then began to work vigorously, almost smothering me with their lustful embraces as they pressed against me, making me gasp for breath beneath the hold of their strong arms. But I could not help myself, if I had wished to, and the lewd blacks laboured on, a complacent smile expanding over Paul's charcoal-coloured visage, which was the only one I could see. Soon, Peter discharged, drowning my thighs with his hot emission, while, almost immediately after, I felt a torrent of warm sperm from Paul's member gush over my belly.

'That is what might be called, in sporting phraseology, a "double event", Charlie,' said Lord Henry, when we had finished, looking at me with a smile into which a considerable amount of fondness entered, for he appeared to have developed a strong regard for me since our acquaintance.

'It might have been a "treble event", if Charlie had come too!' said Jimmy, with a saucy laugh, in which we all had to join.

Jimmy was quite right when he said that I had not discharged that time, which was hardly to be expected as I had done so not long before; and though matters went on in a very lively and agreeable way for the remainder of the afternoon, none of us seriously attempted to bring on a crisis again, Lord Henry being in no way an advocate of too great excess.

CHAPTER FOURTEEN

L'Envoi

At length the time of departure came, and Lord Henry travelled down with us to London, where he intended to spend a day or two.

Another parting of a more dismal kind, however, had to take place, for Rutherford was not returning to the school any more but going under an army coach, in preparation for Sandhurst. We felt that the loss of his society would make a great difference to us at Mr Percival's, and none of us cared to view in anticipation the rift in the circle of our comradeship. We could only put on brave faces, and, as we wished him good luck, try to hide the sorrow we felt.

It was a great grief to me to think that I should not again be cheered by Bob's habitual good humour and never-failing support under all circumstances. I had not forgotten that he had been my first mentor in opening up the paths of pleasure to me, and I regarded him with affection accordingly. I was only too confident in my own mind how greatly I should miss him. But our life in this world is made up of meetings and partings.

Bob came to the station to see me off, as he was remaining in town. We shook hands warmly, and as the train started on its journey with puffs and snorts, I put my head out of the window to catch one more glimpse of his smiling face, wondering how long it would be before I should see him again.

Wordsworth Classic Erotica

❧ ⅋ ❧